PAGES

Book Two of the Stanley Cooper Chronicles

Scott A. Johnson

ISBN-10: 0692165266
ISBN-13: 978-0692165263

Edited by Lily K. Coy-Johnson

Printed in the USA

Second Edition

This book is dedicated to the person who gave me back my life and made me feel like me again. Thank you, Katie. Without you, this book wouldn't exist.

The author would like to thank:

There is a long list of people without whom this book would never have been written. Therefore, it is from the bottom of my heart that I offer thanks: First and foremost, to my wife and children, my parents, my brother and the rest of my family for your support and love. To my friends at Evergreen, the people of Monroeville, and the Lifeless, a big heartfelt thank-you is also in order. To Gary Braunbeck, Tim Waggoner and Mike Arnzen for all their wisdom, wit and friendship. To Dr. Pus, Kody Boye, and Heather McCrocklin, for putting this book together, and to all my friends, students, colleagues, and fans, without whom I wouldn't have a job. To the faculty, students, and alumni of Seton Hill University's WPF program. Also to Steve, Debi, Nomad, Buzz, and the rest of the Dread Central staff. And finally, to the great state of Pennsylvania, and more specifically, Pittsburgh, for making such a lasting impression on this Texas boy.

Addendum: It's so funny the path that life sometimes takes. In 2013, my life was over. I fell apart. I didn't want to write anymore, didn't want to really do anything anymore, and all I wanted to do was just slip quietly away and not feel for a while. My friends loved and supported me, brought me out of the funk a bit. And so, to Nikki, Ward, Wes, Jake, Kristin, Paul, and Jarred, I can never thank you enough. To Professor Emcee-Square, Pointy, Hellga, Stiffy, the Mummy Girl, and the rest of the *It's Alive* crew, thank you also. And to my daughters, who never let me feel like they didn't need me, thank you. And, most of all, to my Katie. Thank you so much for making me whole again.

The tiny brass key fit in the lock and I held my breath. I could tell by how difficult it was to turn that what lay behind the door was bad, very bad. Images snapped through my mind of what could be inside, and although I knew snakes and rats wouldn't be hiding in my mailbox, somehow I found them preferable to the avalanche of mail that greeted me as I swung the door open. Half the pile fell to the floor while the other half remained wedged in the tiny rectangular compartment. With a groan, I stooped and gathered what fell, then went through the arduous task of freeing my letters from their aluminum prison.

I hadn't spent too much time at my apartment recently. There were too many memories of horrible things that still plagued me like phantoms, and too many faces that stared at me as I walked down the halls. Only a few of those faces belonged to living people. The rest died a little over a year ago, but I still saw them. It took me a while to convince myself it wasn't my fault, that the monsters that tore them apart weren't my doing. But in the back of my mind, a little voice kept telling me if I hadn't poked my nose where it didn't belong, those people would still be alive. I gathered the awkward pile and headed down the hall.

The old elevator rumbled and creaked as I rode up, like

the building was breathing again. It made me smile. When I reached my floor, I kept my eyes down at the pile of mail, read the names on all the envelopes. Most of them were addressed to "Current Resident" or "Our Good Neighbor At..." But a few carried "Stanley Cooper" on their faces, and most of those appeared to be bills.

Keeping my eyes down wasn't just a way to catalogue what the postman delivered, and it wasn't because I was unfriendly. I had to keep my eyes down. That's what people do when they see ghosts everywhere they go, or at least, that's what I imagine they would do. And while my building wasn't the most haunted spot in Pittsburgh, it did have more than its fair share of disgruntled spirits. Most of them crossed over a week or two after their bodies died, but a few of them just couldn't let go. And at least two of them still blamed me for getting them killed. Lucky for me, they didn't have the power to do more than just stare at me as I walked down the hall, so I kept my head down and pretended not to notice.

When I reached my door, I juggled the key and my mail until I managed to get the door unlocked. The air inside smelled stale, musty, like old laundry. I looked around at my belongings and realized just how much I missed this place, and just how long I'd been away this time.

My apartment wasn't much to look at, but it did have its advantages. Sure, the bedrooms were tiny and the galley-kitchen was barely large enough to accommodate a single butt, there was only one bathroom and the laundry facilities were deep in the bowels of the building, but my apartment was one of the safest places I knew for someone like me. I don't mean it was burglar-proof, though it did have a steel fire-door and there were cameras set up in the hall. Along every wall, every opening, and across the ceiling and under the carpets were Latin words and strange symbols inscribed by me with a silver paint-pen. The same was true around all the electrical outlets, phone jacks, and even the faucets. They all said the same thing, more or less. "Keep Out." Nothing negative could enter my apartment because of the wards. Ghosts couldn't just walk in and surprise me in the shower either. Of course, that didn't mean they couldn't stand on the other side of the wall and whisper, which they did sometimes, though not so much as they used to. As time passed, and repairs in the building were made, they started crossing over, moving on, whatever. A year after every tenant in the building had been wiped out in a brutal massacre, families were starting to move back in, and the whispers weren't so bad anymore.

I closed the door, sat down on the couch, and sorted through my mail. Junk, bills, junk, bills. Sale flyers and coupons. The same things I always got. Until I came across a large padded manila envelope. When I touched it, my skin tingled, as if there were batteries attached to the inside of whatever was in it. The tattoo on my wrist itched like it wanted to crawl away from the parcel.

Crawly skin art on the average person might not be something to write home about, but for me it was reason enough to take notice. My tattoo isn't just a random picture. It's a sigil, a shield with enough energy forced into its knotty lines to protect me from all things nasty. It comes in handy from time to time. When it itches, there's evil nearby.

I turned the package over in my hands. On the front, written in thick black ink, was my name, Stanley Cooper. But there was no address, no stamp, no sign whatsoever that it had ever been through the postal service. How it got into my mailbox, I couldn't begin to guess.

To most people, unsolicited parcels in the mail might seem odd. In this day and age, most people would probably panic and call the police for fear of getting an anthrax Valentine or an exploding love note. Me, I can't say I'm used to getting strange things slipped magically into my mailbox, but it has been known to happen. It's part and parcel of being what I am.

I pulled the tear-strip off the top of the envelope and reached inside. Whatever it was, the person who'd sent it wrapped the contents in plastic. The anthrax theory was starting to seem not so far-fetched. When I pulled the plastic out, I just stared.

What I held looked like pages torn from a very old book. The words were in a language I didn't recognize and the ink was faded to a dull brown, but they weren't what drew my attention. On the top page was a graphic depiction of a human body, cut open and splayed with every vital organ tagged and labeled. I didn't bother unwrapping the pages, but tucked them back into the envelope and left them on the couch while I went to shower and change.

There are lots of names for people like me, and most of them aren't very nice. I've been called crazy, psychotic, out of touch, and spooky. I've been called clairvoyant and psychic. My best friend calls me a necromancer, whatever that means. I tend to think of myself as cursed, depending on the day. Whatever people call me, their meaning is always the same. I see dead people. See them, talk to them. Sometimes I can't get away from them. I can also see the energy that surrounds all living things. Auras, some people call them. It's not something I was born with, or even wanted, but something that just sort of happened after I died.

Yeah, that's right. I died. I fell from a building and took the great last step toward oblivion. Then, for whatever reason, I got better. I don't know why or how, but here I am, and my life has been weird ever since.

As I drove down Carson Street, I marveled at all the construction going on. It wasn't all that long ago that most of the buildings were gutted and many of the shop owners were injured or killed. Where the buildings used to glow with the love and life that their tenants poured into them, they were empty husks, holes in the scenery. But the people on Carson Street were a special kind. More than any of Pittsburgh's natives, the Carson Street vendors were hearty. The quirky shops on the street were more than their livelihoods, they were their lives. Just over a year later the shops already had healthy, vibrant energies to them that told me that, whatever the denizens of Carson Street were, they weren't   quitters. After so much destruction, seeing the area not just come back to life but thrive made me smile.

I turned a corner and pulled around back of one of the buildings until I came to a large red sign that said *"Employees and Brooms Only! Violators Will Be Toad!"* Over the pun was huge cartoon toad in a witch hat. I pulled my Chrysler up in front of the sign and parked. As I picked up my bag, in which sat the envelope, I shuddered.

The block was bustling by the time I rounded the corner and made my way to the front of the building. Across the street, large signs proclaimed the purpose of the shops and wide windows displayed their wares. Rock Rags, which sold pre-torn jeans and concert t-shirts, along with bongs and jewelry, stood just down the street next to a second-hand bookstore and a deli, from which the luxurious scent of soup wafted. Next door was a three-story shop that sold nothing but vintage toys, some from before I was born. But the shop I headed to had no sign. The windows in front were so dark that most people didn't realize they were there. The only thing that marked its door was a symbol: two crescent moons with a full moon between them.

"Stan?" Maggie called as I opened the door. "Is that you?"

"Nope," I called back. "It's the boogeyman, come to steal your virtue!"

"You're a little late for that," she said as she came through the back curtain. "But I'll give you whatever I've got left."

She was dressed in black yoga pants that hugged her legs and a t-shirt that didn't hug anything. Her long red hair was tied up with a purple scarf that hung loose over her shoulders. She was barefoot, as she usually was inside the shop, and for some reason it made her all the more beautiful to me. Maggie had curves and was not afraid to show them off. She was proud of her body, and refused to be shamed by unrealistic expectations. Her confidence radiated off her so that, despite her stature, no one doubted that she was a woman of considerable strength.

Not to mention the fact that she was a practicing, honest to goodness, spell-slinging witch.

She crossed the floor and put her arms around me, and gave me a quick smooch.

"Glad you're here," she said as she turned toward the back of the shop. "Some of these boxes are heavy."

Maggie's shop was hit hard when the shit hit the fan last year. She'd lost everything, and wasn't sure how she would, or even if she could, rebuild. But I stuck around and helped her out as best I could. It started off with me just helping her clean up the debris and scrubbing the walls, but it evolved into my being her partner. Somewhere along the way, I decided to stop being pig-headed and just admitted that I loved her. She took the news well. I didn't go back to my apartment for more than a week.

"I stopped off at my place to get my mail," I said.

"I don't know why you don't just sell it and move in here with me."

The thought of waking up beside Maggie every morning was wonderful, but there were still a few aspects of her life I couldn't quite reconcile. I decided that now wasn't the time to have the argument again.

"*Anyways*, I got something weird in my mailbox. I don't know what it is, but I thought maybe you should take a look at it."

"Sure thing," she said, as she plopped down on a stool behind the counter.

I reached into my bag, pulled out the envelope and handed it to her. She frowned.

"How'd this get in your mailbox?"

"Don't know."

She bent the tabs on the envelope and stuck her hand inside.

The color drained from her face and her eyes went wide, her jaw slacked and she began to breathe deeply.

"What... the hell... is this?" she panted as she drew the plastic-covered pages out.

"Don't know," I said. "I was hoping you could tell me."

"There's so much power here," she gasped. "Raw... dark... I can feel it on my skin."

She placed the package on the counter and unwrapped it as if she were handling a rare painting. There were nine pages in all, stiff and crinkled, decorated with the same strange writing in the same rust-colored ink, all bore diagrams of people in various stages of dismemberment. On the last page, there was a drawing of a pair of eyes next to a disfigured man.

"This was in your *mailbox*?"

I nodded. "You ever hear of anything like this?"

"No," she said. "I don't know what language it's in, but man... someone put some serious hoodoo into these pages. And they don't feel like regular paper, either. Why don't you..?"

I closed my eyes. One of the first things Maggie taught me when I met her six years ago was how *not* to see the things I could. When I met her, I couldn't turn it off or on, it just came and went. It was like spending half my days on a bad acid trip, the other half trying to convince myself that what I saw wasn't real. She taught me how to control my sight through will power. I willed the doors in my mind to open, the walls to lower, and when I opened my eyes again...

"Holy shit!" I cried, staggering backward. The pages of the book held power, that was a fact. But when Maggie said it was dark power, she couldn't have known just how dark or how much energy there was. In the nine pages before us, I saw energy, a thin corona of blue surrounded by a swollen mass of black flame. It was almost as if the book were possessed. More alarming, when I looked at Maggie, her hands seemed to be stained where she'd touched them. Her normally white and pink and yellow aura had smudges of black in it.

"Let 'em go!" I said, slapping them down to the counter-top. Maggie looked hurt for a moment, but then her face changed to one of curiosity. "It was black. So black. The energy radiating off these pages, it was marking you wherever you touched them."

She stared at the pages for a moment.

"So what do we do with them?" She turned her eyes toward me, but continued to cast wary glances at the pages.

"I don't know. But I'd sure like to know why someone sent them to me."

"Me too. Maybe Evergreen could help."

Evergreen. The strange and mystical society of coffee-drinking, book-store-meeting, demon-trapping mystery men and women. They were made up of people from all different religions, the knowledge of which they used to try to keep balance in the world. Or at least in Pittsburgh. If there was something metaphysical going on in Steel City, chances were good that they already knew about it. If they didn't, they would want to.

"Give Bill a call," I nodded. "Tell him I've got something to show him."

Maggie nodded and hustled to the back of the shop.

I stood there and stared at the grotesque images and rusty writing as I tried to puzzle out who would possibly send me something so strange and dangerous. The envelope contained no letter, no instructions, not even a postcard or a hastily scrawled note.

The bell over the door sounded. A mop of curly dark hair peeked inside, followed by a pair of enormous green eyes and pale skin.

"I... I'm sorry," he said as he peered around the room. "I think I'm in the right place. Is this the...."

He cast a nervous look over his shoulder.

"Witchcraft shop?"

"Yup," I said. "C'mon in. You're in the right place."

What followed his head was dressed in black down to his canvas Chuck Taylors. He was skinny and tall, two things I'd never been, and looked nervous as a cat. Most people who visited Maggie's shop knew what it was, and knew what they were looking for. For the most part, only serious practitioners of the Craft visited. The "fad-crafters" could go down the street to a half-dozen other shops for their bumper stickers and love potions. People that came here were looking for herbs that only Maggie could find, hand-made grimoires, or energy-charged oils and candles.

The lanky kid couldn't have been more than sixteen years old, and he seemed scared out of his mind, like he was sure that at any moment, a cage would drop from the ceiling and I'd drag him into the back and use his boiled carcass to make flying ointment. Apart from how ridiculous such a thing was, it would also be bad for business. I didn't tell him that. In fact, I stayed very quiet while he looked from shelf to shelf, skirting around the outside of the store, casting nervous glances toward me every so often.

"I left a message for Bill," said Maggie as she came back through the curtain. "He'll call me as soon as he gets... Oh! Hi!"

The boy went rigid the moment he saw her, all the nervousness replaced by abject terror. I'd seen the same look on other boys' faces the first time they saw Maggie. Hell, I'd worn it myself when we'd first met. I wasn't afraid she'd eat me or turn me into a toad. I was petrified she'd actually *talk* to me. The more beautiful the woman, the more intimidated lots of guys become. And Maggie was not only beautiful, she had the confidence to stare down the Sphinx.

She made her way around the counter and over to him, her most winning smile on her face and her hand outstretched. I knew she meant to be warm and welcoming, but to a terrified male being greeted by someone like Maggie, it was like coming face to face with a Playboy playmate. I was surprised he didn't piss his pants.

"What's your name?"

"Jus... I mean Seth."

"You can call me Electra," she replied.

Behind the counter, I groaned. Again with the "Magickal Name." Way back when witches were persecuted and put to death for their beliefs, what most of them erroneously referred to as the "burning times," practitioners of the Craft met in secret and used names other than their own to keep themselves safe. But here, in the twenty-first century, there wasn't much of a need for such things, especially if a person was prepared to walk into a shop like Maggie's in broad daylight. Still, some people swore by such a practice, so who was I to judge?

"If there's anything I can help you with," she said, ignoring me. "You let me know."

She turned toward me and made a face to let me know she'd heard me.

"Actually," said Jus-Seth, "there is something I'm looking for."

"Sure," she said, leading him to the counter. "What do you need?"

"Well..." He seemed to be searching for the right words, ones that wouldn't make us laugh him out of the shop. I wanted to tell him not to worry, that we'd heard it all before, that we wouldn't laugh at him, but before I could, he took a deep breath and blurted.

"The... um... Necronomicon?"

I was wrong. It took a moment for what he said to sink in, then I turned and walked quickly through the back curtain before I collapsed in a fit of giggles.

Every so often, a kid just beginning to dabble in the occult stumbled across the collected works of H.P. Lovecraft. In them, he or she found references to a strange tome, written by an insane Arab in 748 A.D., bound in human flesh, inked in blood, and containing the secrets to unlocking such powerful arcane mojo that whoever read it would become a dark god themselves, and be damned for all eternity in the bargain.

These same kids scanned the internet until they found crackpots who claimed the book was real, and they'd actually seen it, only to have it whisked away by some dark conspiracy.

There was only one problem. Those people were full of shit. The Necronomicon didn't exist. It never existed. Lovecraft himself admitted as much countless times, but that didn't deter the ones who wanted to believe. In fact, several fiction publishers contracted writers to come up with their own "Necronomicons" to cash in on Lovecraft's mysterious tome of forbidden knowledge. So every now and again, some terrified teenager with dreams of getting back at the world for some great wrong, real or imagined, would go on a hunt for the fictitious tome, only to wind up in a shop like Maggie's where the harsh truth would be revealed.

The kid was lucky someone as nice and gentle as Maggie was the one to break the news to him. I once gave a kid the old "I had it, but a man in a black cloak just bought it" routine and sent him scurrying. Maggie wasn't amused.

It took me a few moments to compose myself before I went back out, just catching the tail-end of Maggie's lesson in literature to the boy. I could tell she was as gentle as she could be, but his face was still crimson with embarrassment, and he wouldn't meet her eyes as she spoke. When she was done, she offered him a few books on real magick, and offered to answer any questions. He thanked her for her kindness and took the books. He also bought a few candles, one of which, I noted, was for drawing love. At the register, he still wouldn't look directly at Maggie or me. She rang up his purchases and handed him his receipt. As he reached for his bag, his eyes locked on the strange pages.

"Are those..?"

"Art," I said as I scooped them up and tucked them back into their envelope. "From a class at Pitt."

His eyes met mine for a moment, and in them I saw a terrified boy, but also anger. He snatched up his bag and rushed out of the shop.

Maggie sighed as the door banged shut behind him.

"That went well," I snickered.

"Hey, better I set him straight than he gets sucked up

into one of those Necronomicon cults." She wasn't angry, but there was an edge to her voice, letting me know that, funny as it was, she still respected the kid's feelings.

The telephone rang and Maggie snatched it from its charger.

"Bill?" I could hear the old man's genial voice from the speaker. "Okay," she said. "I'll send him right over."

I put the envelope in my shoulder bag and headed for the door.

"He's waiting at the coffee shop a couple of blocks down."

"Why can't he meet us here?"

"He's on his lunch break," she said. "The coffee shop is halfway between him and us."

As I stepped out into the warm summer air, my mind boggled at the concept that Bill of Evergreen actually had a job. I mean, sure, he was a normal guy, but it just seemed hard to fathom that such a powerful elder of the metaphysical community would actually have a nine-to-fiver. Somehow, I still pictured him living in a cave lit by torches and doing nothing all day but changing lead into gold and thinking deep thoughts.

I'd barely gone a block when someone struck me from behind and knocked me to the sidewalk. I hit hard, banged my knee and elbow on the way down and my face slapped off the concrete. For a moment I saw little bright flashes of light, and then I saw a pair of black Chuck Taylors in front of my face. Jus-Seth snatched my bag and took off down the street, running as fast as his lanky legs could carry him.

I staggered to my feet and gave chase. It was a futile attempt. At my age and shape, my days of distance running are over, especially if I'm chasing a skinny kid. I tried to get into shape a while ago. I even took up jogging, figuring if I was to be chased by demons or monsters, it might be good to be able to outrun them. All it did, however, was make me sore, miserable, and sweaty. It took all of two weeks for me to give it up. As I watched the kid disappear around a corner, I almost regretted quitting. Almost.

I hobbled down the street and got to the corner a full minute and a half after he turned it. Sitting there on the sidewalk was my bag, now empty. I snatched it off the ground and limped back down the block to my car. To hell with walking, I decided. My knee hurt too bad, and so did my face. I didn't even care about my stolen mail, but he didn't have to knock me down to get it.

I climbed into my car and checked my face in the vanity mirror. My bushy hair looked as out-of-control as it ever did, but the flesh under my right eye was beginning to darken, as was my right cheek. Perfect. The little jerk gave me a shiner. I cursed under my breath as I backed out.

Some people consider coffee a mere beverage, something hot and caffeinated to wake them up and get them on their way. Grind the beans, boil the water, and get on with it. To others, coffee is a way of life. Simple filtered goodness will never do, not when there's steamed milk and spice and chai and any of a thousand other things to add to the "coffee experience." I fall somewhere in the middle. I do like a good mocha every now and then, but I'd never turn down a hot, black cup of Joe. Some people are content with their automatic-drip, nineteen-dollar coffee pots. But there are others, artists in the field of jittery nerves and steamed milk. And the most talented of them work at Caribou Coffee on Carson Street.

There really wasn't much point to meeting Bill anymore, as Jus-Seth had stolen the strange package, but I didn't have a way of contacting him, and I didn't want to stand him up. Not that I thought he'd do something mystical for the offense, but I genuinely liked the man, and I didn't want to be rude. Besides, I figured a medium-sized mocha might make me feel better.

I pulled up at an empty parking space and thanked whatever powers there were for my luck. My leg throbbed as I got out and fed the meter, and I could feel my heartbeat in my cheek, but

I hobbled inside and scanned the crowd. Toward the back of the room, sitting alone at a table, I noticed white hair and a blazing Hawaiian shirt. I made my way over.

"Bill," I said, shaking his hand. Most of the members of the Evergreen Group preferred to hug, but they were still new to me. "How're you?"

"Fine, fine," he said. He smiled, but there was something in his eyes that said he wasn't happy. Something was on his mind. "I hear you have a weird package?"

"Had," I said. "Some little shit just knocked me down and stole it from me on my way here."

His smile faltered.

"Are you alright?" There was real concern in his eyes.

"I'll live." I sat down and propped my leg in the seat next to me. "Just a few bruises, that's all."

"Well, that's good to hear," he said, his warm smile back again. "So tell me about this package."

One of the baristas, a cute blonde who couldn't have been more than twenty, noticed my leg and came from around the bar to take my order. When she was done, and out of earshot, I described the pages in detail. When I finished, Bill's smile was gone. His eyebrows were knit together and he stared at the table-top, as if he were reading the future in the grain of the fake wood.

"So?"

"Well," he said after a moment. "It certainly is odd. It's a shame the boy stole them. I expect they're some kind of elaborate hoax."

"Why send them to me then?"

He shrugged. "Dunno. But if you happen to see them again, I'd love to take a look."

Something in his voice, his manner, let me know he wasn't playing straight with me. Whatever the pages were, they'd piqued his interest, but he was doing his best to downplay their importance. He glanced at his watch.

"Ugh... back to the grind," he said. I thought about asking him where he worked, but decided against it. The barista brought over my drink, I paid her, then I limped out of the shop and back to my car. Bill was long gone, and I couldn't help but wonder to where. Eight blocks to Maggie's shop, which meant that eight blocks in any other direction would be Bill's job. I decided to leave it for another day.

I sipped the steaming mocha and let it flood over my tongue and down my throat. Heaven.

When I got back to the shop, Maggie was hard at work in the back, pouring candles in the area that doubled as her workshop and altar room. A year ago, Maggie's shop was a thing to behold. Entire walls filled with herbs of every sort, handmade candles and oils, crystals, and things I couldn't even begin to guess their purpose filled the little room to bursting with everything an occult practitioner would need. Hers didn't cater to the "witch-fad" crowd. There were no cutesy bumper stickers or goth-wear. People could get that across the street. In fact, the parking sign was the only thing from the old store that wasn't strictly for the serious practitioner. Now, the shelves weren't bare, but they were a pitiful shadow of what the shop used to be. But some of her suppliers donated a few things, and Maggie was hard at work to replenish her supplies of candles and oils. It wasn't what it was, but it was growing.

"I built this shop from nothing once," she told me when we began rebuilding, her smile as radiant as ever. "And we can do it again."

I limped through the back curtain to her workshop where the scent of beeswax and lavender permeated the air. The room was larger than the front, with a wash basin and workbench on one wall. A wooden circle, outlined in metal with a pentagram etched over its surface covered what used to be a large hole in the floor. At its easternmost point was a small altar, on which sat a single shell.

"It's kind of lonely, isn't it?"

"When I find something that speaks to me, I'll add it," she shrugged, then looked up from her candle molds. "What happened to you?"

"Our friend Jus-Seth mugged me," I said, sitting on one of the barstools that flanked the workbench.

"That kid? You're kidding."

"Nope."

"Oh come on. The least you could do is lie and tell me that a gang of skinny emo-kids mugged you instead of just one."

"Hey, he pushed me down from behind then ran off. I hit my knee on the sidewalk too."

She brushed hair away from my face.

"Ooh... that looks like it hurts." She moved to the refrigerator in the corner and took a bag of frozen peas from the freezer. "Hold this on your eye. Let me see your knee."

"I can't roll my pants leg up that high," I said.

"So take off your pants," she said, raising one eyebrow. "It's not like you've got anything I haven't seen before."

"Maybe later," I said. "He took the package."

"Who, the kid?" She put her hand on my knee. At her touch, warmth flooded through it.

I nodded. "And Bill seemed... weird about it. He didn't come out and say anything, but it was like he wasn't telling me the truth."

"Bill's never lied to me," she said.

"I know. That's what makes it so weird."

"What did he say?"

"That it was probably someone's idea of a prank, that I shouldn't worry about it."

"Good," she said, standing.

"But if it's worthless, then why would someone steal it?"

She turned and put one hand on her hip.

"You're asking me why a kid who just came in asking about a fictional book would want to steal some worthless crap that got put in your mailbox as a joke?"

"Well... yeah. And do you really think a kid should have something with that much dark energy in it?"

She shook her head. "How's the leg?"

I bent and flexed my knee. It shouldn't have surprised me that it didn't hurt anymore. Maggie was very good at her craft. But it amazed me, nonetheless.

"All better," I said. "Now about the black eye..."

"I kinda like it," she said as she turned and bounced out of the room. "Makes you look like a tough guy."

Why did I have to fall for a witch with a weird sense of humor?

The rest of the day went smoothly. We finished unpacking what boxes were left and Maggie got a great start on her candles, but by five o'clock, the place still looked pitiful, to me at least. Maggie seemed satisfied, though, and declared that tomorrow would be our "official" opening day, and invited me upstairs to "celebrate."

Maggie's apartment wasn't what most people would

think of as belonging to a witch. There were no bubbling cauldrons, no thin layer of mist on the floor, no bats swooping down upon unwary guests. In fact, her apartment looked, dare I say, cute. The kitchen had a couple of little witch figurines, but was otherwise decorated with an almost frightening dedication to Betty Boop. Her living room was a den of comfort, with an overstuffed easy chair and large papasan couch flanking her big-screen television. On either side were bookshelves containing the girliest of chick flicks a person could imagine, and on the walls were "treatments," which translated to frilly things that hung and served no real purpose. Anyone who visited her bathroom would suffer from pink-overload and be overcome with the sweet fumes of potpourri in a bowl. An oil diffuser took care of the rest of the living space. There were only two things that might've tipped off the casual visitor that there was more going on here than they knew about. The first, better concealed than at my apartment, were the same types of written charms around every entrance, across the ceiling, around the power and phone jacks. Of course, hers blended in well with the rest of the decor, and didn't look like the apartment's owner went crazy with a paint pen one night. The other minor tip-off leaped up into my lap when I sat down.

"Hello, Bitsy. Miss me?"

Maggie's cat was small and jet-black, except for a single white crescent between her giant emerald eyes. She was the kind of creature that was smarter than it let on, and she couldn't let me sit without climbing into my lap. She wasn't Maggie's "familiar." Maggie hated the term. She also refused to refer to herself as the cat's owner. She just said the cat lived with her, and that was their standard arrangement, although sometimes I wondered who really owned the apartment; Maggie or the cat.

"Wine?" Maggie called from the kitchen.

"Shouldn't we be drinking champagne?"

"I hate champagne. There's beer..."

"Sold!" I called out.

I'm not much of a wine drinker, but beer's another story. Pennsylvania has the country's oldest brewery, Straub, still running, and still making damned good beer. Sure, Iron City may have been the most famous beer for the area, but none of us locals drink it. It's like asking a Texan if he drinks Lone Star.

Maggie came in with a cold bottle in one hand and a tall glass of red wine in the other. She paused in the doorway of the kitchen just long enough to make sure I was watching her before she brought me my drink.

"So," I said after a long pull. "Where should we go for dinner?"

"I have a better idea," she said, downing the last of the wine in her glass. Without another word, she got up, peeled off her shirt and dropped it behind her as she walked toward her bedroom. I stared for a moment and marveled.

Maggie may have a few extra pounds on her, but they give her body a nice shape. If she weighed any less, she wouldn't be nearly as attractive. I, on the other hand, am short and dumpy, and can't figure out why a woman like Maggie is with a guy like me. However, I've learned not to question it, and not to hesitate.

I took another slug from my bottle and decided that a big breakfast would be fine in the morning, and dinner could wait for another night.

PAGES

When I woke up the next morning, Maggie wasn't beside me. I wasn't surprised. A quick glance at the clock showed the time to be after eleven, and Maggie's shop opened promptly at nine-thirty every morning. I yawned and stretched, enjoying the luxuriousness of being naked beneath the flannel sheets that Maggie loved so much. I rolled over and buried my face in her pillow and breathed in her scent and smiled. Our relationship wasn't too terribly complicated, so long as we both agreed on a few rules. For example, Maggie occasionally used sex as a means of building power for a spell or ritual. It was part of her religion, which meant that she'd had sex with other men and women, and sometimes both at once, as part of her practice. I couldn't ask her to give up her beliefs, but I was the only one that actually got to *sleep* with her. Small consolation, I know, but she promised she'd find other ways of building energy unless it there was no other alternative. Sex to her was a wholly positive thing that could, and should, be used as much as possible, so long as all the parties were consenting and of legal age. She'd even tried to convince me to join in on one of her rituals with a rather stunning blonde, but I just wasn't ready to go that far yet. But it did guarantee that Maggie could please a person like no one else could. And besides,

I knew what she was about and I wanted to be with her anyway. Maybe I'm a schmuck, but I still loved her.

A knock on the front door got me up out of bed with a sheet wrapped around my lower half.

"Hang on!" I yelled as I stumbled into the living room.

I opened the door to find a stubbled face with hang-dog eyes I recognized.

"'Morning, Stan," he said.

Detective Matthew Taylor wasn't a normal Pittsburgh cop. In fact, he'd been on the outs with the rest of the department as of late. It seemed that sometime last year, he'd begun acting strangely, some even said paranoid. I knew why, but try explaining a thousand-year-old South American rat demon to a group of Pittsburgh's hardened finest and they'll slap you in the booby-hatch faster than you can say "yinz." When push came to shove, Taylor stayed with us, and that made him a friend.

He looked down at my sheets.

"Um... busy?"

"Nope," I said. "Just getting ready for a toga-party."

"Can it wait? I've got something I need you to see."

"Buy me breakfast?"

"Believe me, you're better off without it."

There was no humor in his eyes. Something had him spooked but good. If he was coming to me, knowing the way I was regarded by the rest of the cops in the city, something had to have given him a grade-A case of the willies.

"Give me ten minutes," I said. "Go hang with Maggie. I'll be right there."

A quick shower and change later, Taylor and I rode

in his enormous car down Carson Street, headed toward the coroner's office. He didn't say a word for the entire ride over, just kept staring straight ahead. Every time I tried to ask him how he was or what was up, he just grunted and kept going. Something was seriously wrong, but I'd just have to wait and find out what it was.

Taylor parked his car and we made our way into the building, down one level, and down a long, sterile hallway to the coroner's exam room. We went through the double doors and found the medical examiner sitting on a stool, staring at one of his sheeted exam tables, one hand folded in his lap, the other stroking his goatee. His brows were furrowed and he had the strangest look of utter bewilderment on his face.

"Clint," said Taylor as he walked in. "Take a breather. Go smoke or something."

"Gladly," said the man as he slid off his stool and walked quickly out the door. Taylor waited until the doors closed behind him, then he pulled the sheet off the table.

The body on the table was a large man, taller than me, though he looked a little younger, maybe early thirties. It was strange that he was wearing a suit and tie, as if he were already prepared for his funeral.

"Tell me what you see," said Taylor.

A human body produces an amazing amount of energy, what with electrical synapses firing all the time. It also produces another type of energy. Some people call it an aura, others call it a soul. Whatever it's called, people like me can see it. Everyone's is as different as their fingerprints, but they typically have the same basic color scheme: Blues, greens, yellows, pinks, they all mean something different according to the person's mood or personality or what their emotional and mental state is at a given time. When a person dies, there's a residue of that aura left behind for a while, but eventually, when all the cells finally give it up, the body's just a husk. The whole process can take anywhere from a couple of days to a few weeks.

I took a deep breath, closed my eyes, and lowered the walls in my perception. When I opened them again, I saw more or less what I expected to see: A lifeless shell with only a trace of energy in it, a thin corona of blue that was shrinking by the moment.

"It's a dead body," I said.

"I know," said Taylor. "How long do you think he's been dead?"

"I don't know," I said, starting to feel a little creeped out. "Couple of hours, maybe? Why?"

"His name was Jacob Owens," said Taylor, his eyes never leaving the body. "He's been dead and embalmed for five days. He was scheduled to be buried this afternoon."

"Okay," I said. "So what?"

"So this morning, at about nine-forty-five, this guy got up out of his coffin, walked four blocks to a bank, robbed it, then dropped on the sidewalk."

Coming from anyone else, I'd have called shenanigans and walked out, but there wasn't a hint of humor on Taylor's face. All I saw was confusion, and behind that, fear.

"How?" was all I could think to say.

"I was hoping you could tell me," he said. "The M.E. doesn't want to do another autopsy because he's already done one on this guy, but we can't figure out why he died on the sidewalk. More important, we can't figure out what he was doing on the sidewalk in the first place."

Taylor drove me back to the shop as he offered up theories about the how and why. Most of them bounced between improbable to ludicrous. My personal favorite was that aliens might be animating the dead in an attempt to take over Earth. I let him ramble on while I puzzled through the problem.

There were only a handful of things I knew of that could raise a dead body, either figuratively or actually. The most famous was the Haitian religion of Vodoun, which most people called Voodoo. In Vodoun, however, a person was taught from birth that another person could steal his soul, and his own faith gave an evil sorcerer dominion over him. They were called zombies, but they weren't the type Pittsburgh was famous for. Vodoun zombies were actually live people who *believed* themselves to be dead.

Another possibility was one I didn't want to think of, which was demons possessing corpses. But demons liked to feed off the energy of the living. They inhabited bodies and subjugated the soul already inside until there was nothing left of it, then they'd hop to another body. Since our boy was dead from the get-go, it didn't seem likely either.

The other option filled me with such dread that I was glad Taylor talked me out of breakfast. A person who communed with the dead, who used their energies, and could sometimes reanimate a corpse was called a necromancer. Maggie called me a necromancer, but reanimation was way beyond my abilities, as far as I knew. So if it was an evil, more powerful version of me, what was I supposed to do about it?

"I'll keep you posted," said Taylor as I got out of the car. "Let me know if you think of anything."

I waved as the land-yacht pulled away from the curb amid honks and curses from the people he cut off, then made my way back in the shop. When the bell rang, it wasn't Maggie that greeted me.

"Hi, Stan!" said the tiny nineteen-year-old behind the counter.

Andrea Bedford looked like the kind of person that would work in a shop like Maggie's. Her short pixie-cut hair was electric purple this week, and styled so it stood away from the multitude of piercings in her ears. She wore a goth version of a Catholic schoolgirl uniform, with a form-hugging shirt, red plaid miniskirt, black fishnets and knee-high boots that looked like they could crush coconuts if she stepped on them. The gauze on her left shoulder was new.

"What happened?" I gestured to the patch.

I met Andrea, Andi, a little over a year ago when I tackled her on the street and stuffed her into the trunk of Taylor's car. It's a long story. Since then, she's been working with Maggie to increase her own witchy abilities. Sometimes I think I'm the only non-witch on the South Side.

"New tat," she said as she lifted the gauze. The fresh ink stood stark against her pale skin, which made the cat juggling a pentacle look all the more intense. "Cool, right? I love it."

"Long as you're happy," I said, shaking my head.

"You okay?"

"Don't know," I said. "Where's Maggie?"

"Boss!" called Andi over her shoulder.

Maggie came out of the back room looking annoyed. Andi didn't actually work for the shop, but she hung around enough that Maggie'd put her to work. In exchange for tutoring, Andi occasionally watched things or answered questions for customers when she knew the answers.

"I'm not your boss," she sighed.

"Right, sorry," said Andi. "Most humble apologies, Oh great and powerful master!"

"I'll hurt you," said Maggie with mock exasperation.

"I'm your apprentice, aren't I?"

"Student," corrected Maggie.

"Apprentice, student, same thing."

"Ladies," I cut in. "I could use some of that sage-like wisdom right about now."

They looked at each other and snickered at their little game, then turned back to me.

When I finished telling them what I'd seen, neither one of them was laughing. They looked at each other as if expecting the other to know what the hell was going on.

"What does Taylor think it is?" Maggie spoke first.

"Aliens."

"Wasn't that an Ed Wood movie?" asked Andi.

"How do you know about Ed Wood?" Maggie cocked an eyebrow.

"What're you, kidding? I've seen every one of his movies! I even own a copy of 'Glen or...'"

"Focus, people!" I shouted. "Movie trivia isn't going to help us when there are corpses walking around robbing banks!"

"Maybe it was an isolated thing," offered Andi. "I mean, how many of these have there been?"

"Just the one that I know of," I said. "But if it happened once, it can happen again, and I don't like the thought of Pittsburgh being overrun with walking corpses."

"Okay," said Andi. "So what are we supposed to do about it?"

"You, *apprentice*," said Maggie, "need to start doing some research to see if you can find any reference of something like this happening before. I don't care when it was, but we do need to know how."

"Man... but I just got out of school for the summer!"

"Quit whining and get to it," she said. "I'll contact

Evergreen, see what they have to say."

"I guess I could go ask some dead people," I said.

"How're you going to do that?" asked Andi.

"By going to the place where a lot of them will be."

"Cemetery?" Andi looked hopeful, like she'd want to tag along.

I shook my head and headed for my car.

"You've got a lot to learn," I called back over my shoulder.

There are really only two different types of hauntings. The first type is usually found in places where the people inside had really high emotions. Not just violent deaths, like Hollywood likes to show, but just about any really strong emotion. Fear, love, joy, pain, they all do the same thing to a human body: They make that energy field around the body grow and intensify. Inside a building, enough of a powerful emotion can leave an imprint, kind of like looking at a photo negative. People who talk about seeing a ghost walk through doors that aren't there anymore, or doing the same things over and over without paying any attention to anything around them are usually seeing that imprint. It's like watching a security camera on a loop. They're not really there, but what they did left such an impression that people will see it for years to come. Some people call them residual-style hauntings. I call them echoes. Places like battlefields are notorious for being filled with echoes.

The other type of haunting is what investigators who like to sound scientific and official call a "persistent consciousness." Of course, everyone else knows them by their less formal name. Ghosts. A real, honest-to-goodness ghost is something strange and tragic, and people know even less about them than they do the echoes. It's what happens when a person dies and they don't cross over, for whatever reason. In some cases, they don't know they're dead. In others, they feel like they have something left to do, which always puzzled me because once a person is dead, the credit card bills don't really matter much anymore. In some cases, they just don't want to go. Sometimes, the spirit is hanging around, just waiting for their body to die, like if they're being kept alive on life-support. Whatever their reason for staying, they walk around, hoping someone will notice them, watching their families and friends get on with their lives. Real ghosts are some of the most tragic people I've met.

Contrary to popular belief, ghosts don't often hang out in cemeteries. Sure, people think since the bodies are buried there, that's where the ghosts are. But with very few exceptions, they don't like being reminded of what they are — or aren't — anymore. They hang out in places they loved in life, or places they would've liked to have gone. It surprises most folks how many ghosts wound up in the Pitt women's locker room ogling the cheerleaders in the showers after a game.

There are two places I know where I'll always find a few ghosts: churches and hospitals, which is one of the many reasons I avoid both.

But as I pulled into the parking lot of Mercy Hospital on Locus Street, I was looking for a conversation. If anyone would know if there were someone in town who could reanimate a corpse, I was betting the dead would know about it.

The doors whooshed open and the blast of frigid conditioned air that hit me in the face made me shiver. I walked like I was going to visit a patient and even waved at the receptionist, an older nurse with a sour expression, on my way to the one place all the souls seemed to end up. The chapel.

The room was tiny, barely twenty feet square. Heavy

wooden benches sat in rows in front of a platform upon which stood a generic-looking podium. Behind it, a large bleeding Jesus hung on the cross, his eyes open and accusing, his expression one of agonized resignation. He gave me the creeps.

There were a few people in the room already, a boy and his mother on one pew and an older man on another. I took a far seat in the back and waited. I didn't have to wait long.

A morose-looking young woman came in wearing a hospital gown. Despite her sunken eyes and frail limbs, she couldn't have been much older than Andi. She stopped in the doorway and looked around the room as if searching for someone, then her translucent body shuddered in quiet sobs.

"They're not here," she cried. "They've forgotten about me." Her body convulsed again.

I stood up and slowly walked around the pew. I could see and hear her, but no one else could. If I just started talking to her, it might make the other people in the room uncomfortable. No sense disturbing their prayers.

When I reached the doorway, less than a foot away from the crying ghost, I stopped.

"I see you," I whispered. "Can I talk to you?"

Her head jerked up in shock. I knew the tears weren't real, that her eyes really weren't streaked wet and red, but they were real to her. The emotions behind them were real. She looked confused for a moment, then nodded slowly.

The boy and his mother got up and left, giving me sad smiles as they passed by. I nodded for the girl to follow me back to the other end of the pew where we sat.

"What's your name?" I whispered.

"Heather," she said.

"Who were you looking for just now?"

"My family," she sniffed. "They stopped coming to see

me. Just left me all alone up there."

The terminal ward. Chances were good that Heather was either on life support or about to be taken off it.

"How long have you been here like this?"

"I don't know," she sniffed. "I opened my eyes one day and saw myself laying in that bed with tubes running up my nose and my mom sitting beside me. I tried to talk to her but she couldn't hear me. No one can hear me. I keep going back to my room, trying to get back in my body, but I can't do it. I just pass right through it."

"What're you in with?"

"Leukemia," she said.

"I'm sorry," I whispered.

"No need to whisper on my account," said the old man at the front of the room. He got up and walked to our pew and sat beside Heather, looking right into her eyes. He shimmered as he walked, from his pleated work-pants to his shirt with the name "Barney" stitched on the pocket. I couldn't believe I didn't realize it when I walked in, but he was a ghost too.

"It's going to be alright, Heather," he said.

"But I can't get back in my body!" she cried. "It's like I'm dead!"

"Child," he said with a tender smile. "You are dead. You're the only one who doesn't know it yet. Your family, they need to remember you as a girl who ran and laughed and played, not as a body in a bed. You have to let go to spare them the pain. You have to let go to spare yourself the pain."

"I'm scared," she said. If I could've reached out to hold her, I would've.

"I know, child," he said. "But there is peace. This isn't an end, but a new beginning. Let me show you." He reached out his ethereal hand and took hers. She almost smiled as she looked back to me.

"Be right back," he said with a wink, then they two of them faded like smoke.

I sat there for a few minutes, puzzling out what I'd seen, when the old man reappeared beside me.

"That was nice of you," he said. "Talking to her like that. She's been down here a lot in the past month."

"What did you do? Who are you?"

"I'm just here to help, Mister Cooper," he said. "I passed away a long time ago, and I decided to help others make the transition."

"What're you, some kind of angel?"

"Hardly," he chuckled. "Though if it helps for you to think of me that way, I won't argue."

"How do you know who I am?"

"I've been around a while," he said. "I remember when you were brought in here, what was it, six years ago? I was standing by the door when they brought you in."

"Why haven't I seen you before?"

"It wasn't your time," he smiled.

"I'm looking for some information," I said.

"Fire away," he said. "I'll help if I can."

He frowned as I told him about the walking corpse and the bank robbery.

"I have felt some strange energy currents in the air since yesterday," he said. "I don't know what it means, but I don't think it's a ghost taking joy rides. What they do to the bodies after they're dead, it wouldn't make much sense. When they embalm them, climbing in one isn't like being alive again. You can't feel, can't taste, can't enjoy the simple things like holding hands or kissing. Hell, seems like it would be too much trouble to try to move a corpse around."

"I kind of figured that," I said. "I just can't figure out where to start looking for answers."

"I'll tell you what I'd do," he said. "When I died, the first place I went was my own funeral. I wanted to see who showed up. Might be worth checking out. If this guy is there, he might be able to tell you about who's using his skin as a puppet."

It made sense, and seeing as I had no other ideas, I thanked the old man and made my way back out to my car.

PAGES

I hadn't been to a funeral in years, not since my father died more than a decade ago. He was a good man, honest and kind hearted. The kind of guy that was generous with his time because we never had any money. When he died, there were almost a hundred people at his funeral. I sat there in the church while people I knew and strangers got up and extolled his many virtues, but when my time came to speak, I couldn't think of a damned thing to say. I could've talked about his working-class sensibilities, his stubborn refusal to half-ass anything, even his strict discipline in the house, but no. All I could do was sit there and know that I'd never see him again, that I'd never get to ask him for advice again, that I'd never hear him complain about my hair again. All I could do was think about how much I'd miss him, and how much I hated whatever power existed that took him away from me. When the lines of people walked by, offering their condolences, I nodded and thanked them, but inside I screamed. I wasn't sorry for my father, but for myself.

As I walked down the block toward the funeral home, I ran through clever lies in my head in case anyone asked what I was doing there, or how I knew the deceased, or if I was a friend of the family. I don't own a tie or a sport coat, and the only pants I own are jeans. I don't even have a pair of dress shoes. I never needed them before. So as I rounded the corner wearing red Converse high-tops, jeans and a black bowling shirt, I was pretty sure I would stick out. Maybe it was a bad idea, but I needed answers.

I rounded the wrought-iron fence-lined corner and stopped in my tracks. Standing outside the funeral home, smoking a cigarette, stood a lanky, black-clad teen. Jus-Seth.

"You're kidding," I said to myself. I started moving forward again. When I got only a couple of feet from the gate, Jus-Seth looked up and saw me. His already pale face went chalky as he pitched his cigarette into the street and hurried inside. I quickened my pace until I was met at the door by a pair of guys that looked like they not only played on the Pitt rugby team, they *were* the Pitt rugby team.

"Private viewing," said one. He thrust his hand out to stop me.

"Just want to pay my respects," I said. Behind them, Justin stood watching from behind a doorframe. "Maybe say hello to my friend in there."

"Look, man," said the other. "This is family and friends only. You're neither. Justin told us you've been giving him trouble. Don't make us kick your ass at his brother's funeral."

A snarky comment came to mind, but for once my brain was working and I let it go. My need for self-preservation outweighed my want for more information, and from the looks of the two bruisers, they could add my corpse to the one inside without even breaking a sweat. I raised my hands and backed away, moving down the steps and down the street. I'm not much of a fighter, and I really didn't want to upset the family any more than they already were. I'm sure they didn't need some weirdo poking around after their dearly departed just went for a stroll.

At the end of the block, well out of sight, I stopped and waited. Protected or not, I needed answers. I might not get to talk to Jacob Owens, but something in my gut told me that Justin knew something. And besides, he and I had unfinished business. It wasn't so much that I cared about the stupid package from my bag, but I take it personally when someone hits me from behind and steals from me. And the power those pages put off would do bad things to him.

I waited there for nearly an hour before he came back out, flanked by his two mastodons. As they walked to their car, he saw me and grinned before disappearing into the car's back seat. I made a mental note to check with Taylor to see if he knew where I could find him. I considered going back to the funeral home, but figured I'd made enough of a scene already. Chances were, the word was out that I was around. I turned and made my way back to my car.

When I got back to the shop, it was locked for the evening. Maggie's light glowed upstairs, and I was pretty sure Andi would be up there with her, talking about the Craft and about what was going on. If I was lucky, one of them managed to find out something we could use.

As I pulled up into my parking place, I noticed a flash of color on the shop door. I figured Maggie'd left her "out to lunch" sticky note from earlier in the day, but when I got closer I saw that it was a yellow parcel slip from the mailman, letting Maggie know there was a package in her name at the post office. I grabbed it off the door and made my way for the stairs.

As I figured, the place looked like Command Central, with Maggie pacing the floor with the telephone stuck in her ear and Andi's face glued to the screen of her laptop. Maggie's eyebrows crunched together as they always did when she was deep in thought, and Andi had the wide-eyed owl look of someone who had reached "nerd-vana."

"Find anything?" I asked as I closed the door behind me. Maggie raised a hand without saying anything, listening intently to whoever was on the line with her. Andi didn't even seem to notice I'd said anything. At least Bitsy the wondercat still loved me. She wound around my legs purring while I stood like a goon just inside the door.

"I understand," Maggie said, nodding. "Of course. Thanks." She hung up the phone and turned to me.

"Hi," she said, but not in her usual, perky, glad-to-see-me voice. There was an edge of confusion that was echoed by the look on her face.

"Who was that?"

"Evergreen," she said. She always referred to them as a group, not individuals. No matter which member of the group she was talking about or with, they were one entity to her.

"And?"

"They were... evasive," she said. "They said they'd look into it."

"Told you," I said. "That's the same song and dance I got from Bill. It's like they're hiding something."

"But they've never hidden anything from me before." She sounded hurt, and I couldn't blame her.

"What about you, sport?" I turned and crossed my arms behind Andi. "Find anything?"

"Nothing but fragments of legends," she said. "Lots of nutjob cults, lots of Lovecraft scholars. Nothing documented, nothing concrete, but there's some really scary stuff in here. I did find a reference to an anthropologist who discovered what 'Zombie-Powder' was in Haiti..."

"Yeah," I said. "I saw that movie. Spooky stuff."

"But nothing about an honest to Goddess corpse

walking around. Just movie zombies."

"Keep looking," I said. "This kind of thing has to have happened before."

"Aye-aye," she said.

The three of us continued to puzzle out the problem while Maggie cooked dinner, then the conversation died while we ate. I told them about Justin Owens and the funeral home, and they both agreed that for him to know the dead bank robber, much less be his brother, was too much to be a coincidence. We talked for another hour, throwing theories about, until we ran out of steam. Rather than disturb her, I covered Andi with a blanket when she fell asleep on the couch then followed Maggie to her bedroom. With her snuggled against me, I usually felt like nothing could be wrong with the world, but as sleep claimed her and her breathing reached an easy deep rhythm, I found myself wide awake, my brain racing, trying to puzzle out what was going on.

I awoke alone again, this time to the scent of frying bacon and eggs. One of the things I loved about Maggie was that, a witch she might be, with respect for all living things, but even she knew bacon was just too good to pass up. Her and Andi's voices, peppered with laughter, filtered through the walls.

When we met her, we didn't make the best impression on Andi. In fact, we'd stuffed her in the trunk of a car in the dead of winter and drove around while she froze. I don't know how, but she and Maggie became friends after that, and closer. She wanted to know everything Maggie knew, and was prepared to spend her life learning it. Maggie saw her as a daughter half the time and a best friend the rest. The two of them shared private jokes together, usually at my expense.

But Andi was good to have around. Her skill was growing, and although she was nowhere near the spell-slinger Maggie was, she had a great deal of potential. I snuck a few glimpses at her energies while she was practicing and the power that girl could raise was significant. If she ever learned how to control it, she'd be incredible.

I sat up and ran my fingers through my hair and tucked it back behind my ears as my stomach grumbled in appreciation of the scent of Maggie's culinary expertise. I just hoped Andi wasn't the one cooking, or we'd be going out for breakfast while the apartment cleared of smoke.

I stood up and stretched, pulled on a t-shirt and a pair of sweat pants, and wandered out into the living room. Luck was with me. Andi sat at the table munching on a piece of toast while Maggie dodged splattering bacon grease.

"G'morning, sleepy head!" beamed Andi.

"Coffee," I grunted. "No talk. Coffee."

She giggled as I shuffled to the cabinet and got a mug, filled it from the pot on the counter, and sat beside her. Only after I took my first sip did I turn toward Andi and smile.

As I took another sip, there was a knock at the door. I glanced at the clock. Nine-twenty on a Saturday morning? There was only one person I knew who wouldn't think twice about banging on a door before noon, and if he was here, there was bad news.

Taylor's iron eyes and hard-set jaw stared back at me as I opened the door. The look on his face said that I was in trouble, even if I didn't know what I did to get that way. Odds were, I wouldn't get to eat my breakfast.

"You didn't happen to go by a funeral home yesterday, did you?" He didn't even wait for a greeting, which meant he was pissed off. "By the Owens funeral?"

"Why?" I turned and walked back into the room. Taylor didn't budge from the doorway. He just stood staring at me.

"Stan, please tell me it wasn't you," he said. "Look me in the eyes and tell me you weren't the guy that showed up harassing Justin Owens at his brother's funeral."

"Harassing is such a strong word," I said as I grabbed my coffee cup. "I just went to the door. They asked me to leave, so I did. Why?"

"Christ..." He shook his head and took a deep breath. "Why were you there?"

"I was trying to talk to the dead guy's ghost," I replied. Anyone else would've arrested me on the spot, maybe called the funny guys in the white coats to come and pump me up with enough Thorazine to keep me nice and drooly for a while. But Taylor knew me well enough that such a statement didn't even raise his bushy eyebrows.

"And why did you pursue Justin Owens?" he asked through clenched teeth.

"Because yesterday the little prick hit me from behind and swiped my messenger bag," I snapped.

"And you didn't report it?"

"All he took was some junk mail," I said. "I was more pissed about the lump on my head, but it wasn't worth reporting."

"Jesus..."

"You want to tell me what's going on?" I said. "My breakfast is getting cold."

"Justin Owens is dead."

I didn't feel hungry anymore. In fact, the bottom dropped out of my stomach. Aside from the sizzle of bacon, the room became very quiet.

"When?"

"Some time last night," he said. "We went around and

talked to the family, and his two cousins seemed convinced you had something to do with it."

"Why me?"

"Because, according to them, you were 'menacing' Justin at the funeral home."

"Is he a suspect?" Maggie turned off the burner off and came out of the kitchen to stand beside me.

"Officially, no," sighed Taylor. "But they described you to a 'T,' and who else do I know with a reputation of hanging around dead things?"

"How did he die?" asked Andi.

Taylor's eyes shifted from Andi to Maggie, but didn't meet mine. He reached into his pocket and pulled out a stack of photos.

"That's the other reason I'm here," he said. "He was shot twice in the back of the head, but that's not as important as... well... take a look for yourself."

The photos were poor quality, but there was enough detail to see what he meant. The body was gone, but the outline where it had been was visible, a dark puddle of red where its head had been. The outline of where the body laid sprawled across a circle, surrounded by burnt candles and a few other knickknacks. The circle itself held more than a dozen intersecting lines.

"It's a summoning circle," said Maggie.

"Yeah." Taylor took the photos back and jammed them into his pocket. "It's weird shit is what it is. And in the boy's hand, we found a couple of torn scraps of what we thought was paper. The lab boys tested it. Turned out to be mummified human skin."

I thought about the pages the kid stole from my bag and shivered. If the scraps were from the same odd-feeling pages...

I suddenly got the urge to wash my hands.

"Junk mail, you said?"

"Those pages," I nodded. "They were in my bag."

"Want to take a ride with me?" It wasn't so much a question or invitation as it was a command. One I couldn't very well refuse.

I nodded and went back to the bedroom, got dressed, pocketed Maggie's digital camera, and came back out to find Taylor hadn't left the doorway. Maggie and Andi sat at the table, neither of them speaking, but each mirroring the other's worried look.

A body can tell a lot about a person from the type of car he drives. My Chrysler has heated leather seats and a sunroof and is just stylish enough that it turns a few heads. I also take pretty good care of it, despite the occasional ding or wild creature crapping in the back seat. When rat-demon-possessed homeless people decided to use my ride as a Porta-Potty, my insurance company rushed it through to a body shop and paid to have everything fixed, so my car looks practically new. To me, my car lets people know that I take care of things, that I'm responsible, and I'm concerned with creature comforts.

Taylor's car, on the other hand, was more of a tank, a barge on wheels. The brown paint was faded in a few spots, scratched in others, and chipped everywhere else. There were dents in the bumpers and fenders, and all four wheels were missing hubcaps. The interior wasn't much better, with hard vinyl seats that carried a vague odor of stale French fries and deer piss. But under the hood, the old monstrosity had an engine that could outrun most cars on the road, and Taylor took meticulous care of all its needs. Taylor was a guy who didn't care too much about outward appearances, but when push came to shove, he was someone to rely upon.

He didn't say much as he drove, which made me nervous. Taylor was the one person in the Pittsburgh police department who trusted me, who didn't either think I was crazy dangerous or just a scam artist. He knew I was for real, even if I made him a little uneasy.

After a long silence broken only by the bumps in the road, I couldn't take any more. "Where are we going?"

"Oakland," he said. "Where he was killed. We've already been all over the crime scene and couldn't find squat. Maybe you can find something we couldn't."

I was still trying to figure out how pages made of skin had wound up in my mailbox when we pulled up in front of a section of dilapidated row houses. Now empty with the onset of summer, they were usually packed with University of Pittsburgh students. With most of them gone, the houses seemed lonely, almost haunted. I got out and followed Taylor to the splintery front door of one.

"What you see in here is still considered classified," he said.

"What're you, a secret agent? What's 'classified?'"

"I mean don't go talking about it or spreading it around. You can tell Maggie, but no one else. Got me?"

I nodded. Taylor wasn't usually curt with me. Whatever happened in the house had him spooked pretty bad. He pushed the door open and pulled a flashlight from his pocket. The inside of the bottom floor was dark, without even a sliver of light. The windows must've been shuttered or covered with something heavy, but Taylor's flashlight beam cut through the darkness revealing a floor covered in soda bottles, junk food wrappers and nudie magazines. There were also the remains of a few joints laying around.

"I don't know how long he was coming here," he said.

"He still lived with his family about two miles over."

"Looks like a while," I said, picking up one of the magazines. "This one's from last year."

"Come on," he said, heading up the stairs. I followed close behind, not wanting to be too far away from the comfort of Taylor's flashlight.

The stairs popped and groaned with every step, threatening to give up and collapse beneath us at any moment, but they held. When we reached the top of the landing, Taylor handed me the light and pointed toward a closed door at the top of the landing with yellow tape across it.

"In there," he said, fishing a cigarette and a lighter out of his pocket.

"When did you start smoking?"

"A little over a year ago," he said without looking up. He took a long drag and blew out a forceful cloud. "Let me know what you see."

The door was less than five feet away, but for some reason I had a hard time crossing that distance. Maybe I've seen too many horror movies where the plucky hero opens a door only to find some hockey-masked, chainsaw-wielding maniac on the other side. Maybe it was because I'd seen the photos in Taylor's pocket. Either way, the thought of opening that door filled me with dread.

With my heart fluttering, I pulled the tape down and pushed the door open. Light filtered in between boards nailed up over the windows, giving me a good look at the room. The walls were covered in graffiti, some of it just innocuous tags from kids, probably dared to go into the spooky old house by their friends. The rest of it, however, was a mish-mash of strange symbols and writing, some of which I recognized to be occult-related. Others, I couldn't even begin to imagine their meanings.

On the wall beside me was one piece of artwork that, had it not been so terrible, I might have considered done by a real talent. The figure was shaped like a man with decrepit bat wings unfurling from around his back. Each hand ended in cruel looking talons, as did its legs, and a long tail snaked out from behind it. Between its legs, the artist took great care to render an enormous erect penis, but it was the creature's head that I found most disturbing. Perched atop its shoulders was a glob with burning red eyes and tentacles where a mouth should've been. It was one of Lovecraft's "Elder Gods." The kid came into the shop looking for a piece of Lovecraft mythology.

"Give me a minute," I called back to Taylor, then I closed the door behind me and closed my eyes.

No matter who a person is or what they do, they leave a little piece of themselves behind. If it's a toenail clipping or a single hair, the police can usually find it and figure out what happened from there. But even if there's no physical evidence, there's something left behind. Call it a bit of their energy, call it an imprint. To me, it's a scar. It can be better than a photograph.

I closed my eyes and willed myself to lower the walls of my perception, walls that I'd built with years of practice, to make the world seem normal to me. Without them, my world looked like a constant acid trip, with colors that throbbed and pulsed around everyone and everything.

When I opened my eyes again, the room was awash with color, humming with the energy that hadn't yet dissipated. On the floor I could see the outline of the dead boy, the puddles around his head glowing with fading life. More than that, it was like looking at stop-motion animation. I could see Justin kneeling, arms outstretched, then his head jerked and he fell forward. The still image of his body jerked again then lay inert on the floor, before the whole process started over again.

Some of the words on the walls pulsed with red energy, a color that meant passion or hatred to me. The circle around the boy glowed in a powerful golden light, like most summoning circles did, but the lines that crossed and intersected in the circle all pulsed with velvety black glow. There was darkness in his intent, that much was clear.

I turned in place as I scanned the walls and the floor for more indicators of what happened. There were faint spots on the walls where blood and brains splattered, and the candles glowed as if they were lit, but even as I saw what happened, there was nothing to show me who'd done it. When I turned to face the wall with the mural, I jumped so hard that I almost fell backward. The image of the elder god shimmered and undulated, as if it were a living thing. It looked almost like a 3-D poster, except for the life of me, it looked like it was breathing. I backed away from it, turning my eyes downward until I noticed something strange on the floor.

There were two sets of footprints. For all the people who'd apparently gone in and out of the house and building, there were only two sets of footprints. The first set I assumed belonged to Justin. They seemed to be the same size as the sneakers that ran away from me, and the tread looked about right. The other pair was smaller, almost the size of a child's feet. My guess was that they belonged either to a woman or a very small man. Either way, the tracks led to where the boy was found, then stepped around the body, then left the room. My bet was they belonged to the killer, and he'd stolen the pages when he stepped around Justin's body.

But, aside from the footprints, I couldn't see the killer.

The tattoo under my watch itched as the energy of the room flowed around my own. I ignored it as I spent a few more moments looking for some little detail, some tiny thing I might have overlooked, but there was nothing.

I closed my eyes again and raised the walls and closed the doors in my mind. When I opened my eyes, I was again standing in a dim, filthy room. It took me a moment to catch my breath and regain my bearings.

Taylor was waiting for me, leaning up against a wall when I came out.

"See anything?"

I shook my head.

"I saw what happened, but I couldn't see the shooter. Just another set of footprints."

"Where? We didn't find..."

"Your guys couldn't have found them," I said. "And I'm not sure what they mean. They were smaller than Justin's, but outside of that I couldn't tell anything."

"Was the killer a man or a woman?"

"Can't tell," I said. "But look at this."

I led him back into the room and pointed to the markings on the wall.

"See these? They don't mean anything. Just graffiti and tags. But these here?" I pointed to the strange symbols and writing. "Someone put some real energy into them. I'm betting it was Justin."

"What was he doing?"

"My best guess is he was trying to summon something."

"Like what?"

I pointed over his shoulder to the mural on the wall.

"What the hell is that supposed to be?"

"I don't know," I lied. "But whatever it is, there was a whole lot of energy poured into it too. I'm betting that's what he was trying to do here."

"So can you read any of that crap on the walls?"

"No," I said, taking the camera out of my pocket. "But I know someone who might."

I made sure to get photos of all four walls, the floor and the ceiling, before Taylor and I left.

"So," I said as we pulled up into the lot behind Maggie's shop. "Am I officially a suspect?"

"You're a person of interest to the case," he replied. "Look, I know you didn't do it, but you don't exactly have a fan club at the station."

I nodded. Story of my life. No matter how much I wanted to help, all I could do was further implicate myself. How else would I know how the murders were committed if I wasn't the one who did them? I couldn't very well go in and tell the rest of the police force that I saw the murder, but couldn't see the killer, and, by the way, I thought this had something to do with the occult. Too many of them thought I was nuts anyway.

"So what can I do?"

"Lay low," he said. "Don't go poking around in this. If you get any information, give it to me. Especially if you get any more weirdo packages." He jotted a number down on a slip of paper. "Here."

"New office?"

"Cell phone," he grunted. "Damned thing'll probably give me brain cancer."

"You want to come in? Fill Maggie in on what we found?" I said as I got out of the car.

"No," Taylor smiled. "But thanks for the invitation. I've got more leads to run down. I need to make sure the other cops look somewhere besides at you for this."

I waved as he pulled away, a strange feeling creeping up my spine. Something was wrong with him. Sure, he was always off, especially since his run-in with human monsters, but he was acting especially weird today. It was like there was something he wasn't telling me, or maybe he just wasn't feeling himself today. Either way, I knew Taylor could handle it if anyone could.

We decided to go out for dinner that evening. Maggie'd been working on her shop almost nonstop all week, and Andrea informed us that if she looked at one more research article, she'd go blind and her brain would dribble out her ear. Since none of us wanted to see *that*, we decided a change of scenery would be good. Besides, after everything I'd seen and heard, I figured I could use a beer.

Carson Street had some great restaurants and good bars, but we decided a more quiet, intimate place would be better. We climbed in my car and drove into the hills to an out-of-the-way joint that had good burgers, cold beer, and played whatever sport was in season on its televisions. Even baseball.

We followed the hostess to our seats and looked over the menu, then ordered. The waitress returned with our drinks (beer for me, a margarita for Maggie, a Coke for Andi) and a deep-fried onion with horseradish, then left us in our quiet corner.

"So," said Maggie after a few moments of uncomfortable silence. "What do you think?"

"That something big is going down," I said between bites. "I think Justin was trying to raise his brother, but he didn't know what he was getting into."

"Why would he try to do that?" Andi shuddered at the thought.

"Grief?" I shrugged. "Makes people do all kinds of stupid things. Maybe he just wanted his brother back."

"Then why make him rob a bank?"

"Kid with a new toy?" I offered. "I don't know, but that's the only thing I can figure."

"Yeah, but how'd he know to come to my shop?" Maggie looked unconvinced. "And how'd he know what to steal from your bag?"

"Whoa. There's nothing that says that those pages were responsible..."

"Didn't Taylor say he had a scrap of one in his hand?"

He did, but I didn't want it to be true.

"Did you hear from Evergreen?" I needed to know more about the pages, and they were my best hope.

"They said to be on the lookout for more pages," said Maggie. "They said that what you described was most likely part of a larger book."

If the power in those pages managed to do something insane like raise the dead, then it stood to reason that the whole volume, wherever it might be, contained magick of a whole other level. Whoever had it could tap into some seriously dark mojo, and that was one thought I couldn't stomach.

"But why would someone send it to you?" Andi gave voice to the thought that was plaguing me since I found the damned pages. "Maggie's more into this stuff than you are."

Then a terrible thought struck me.

"Shit. We have to leave. Now."

It took longer to get back to Maggie's shop than I thought it would. As I careened around corners and broke speed-limit laws, I hoped I was wrong.

We pulled up in front of the shop to find the door broken, the area around the locks in splinters. Maggie was out of the car before I turned off the engine. She raced to the door and froze. The last time her shop was broken into, the demon-possessed people who did it wiped her out, destroyed everything she worked hard to build. As she stood outside the door, I saw the same dread etched over her face.

"Stay here," I said to Andi. "Get ready to run."

"Like hell," she muttered as she clambered out of the car. Sometimes she listened, sometimes she didn't.

I went to the door and put myself between Maggie and the unknown, then pushed the door open.

The shop was wrecked. Candles littered the floor, herb jars lay in pieces, books lay in piles. The glass case beneath the register was not broken, but its contents lay strewn about the floor. The register, however, was untouched.

"What... the... HELL?!" seethed Maggie.

"I don't think anything's missing," I said as I picked through the mess.

"How would you know?" she snapped.

"Because they weren't here to rob you," I said. "They were looking for something."

"What could they possibly..?"

I pulled the yellow slip of paper from my pocket.

"You have a parcel at the post office," I said. "Who wants to bet me what it is?"

Maggie figured it was best to file an official police report this time, so we called the station before we cleaned the shop. We also called Taylor, on account of he'd never forgive us if we didn't. He paced around the other cops, a plainclothes and a uniform, like an angry cat. The others dusted for prints, took photos of the damage and wrote in their notebooks, and left a bigger mess than the thief. The plainclothes guy assured us that he'd get to the bottom of it and left with Taylor close behind. No small talk, no theories shared, just straight business.

Whoever ransacked her shop didn't touch her apartment. Just as well for them, as I'm pretty sure Bitsy would've claimed a body part or two. I looked around the place with my Sight, but couldn't find anything I didn't recognize. There were a set of footprints by Maggie's apartment door, but they stopped just outside the threshold, turned, and went back down the stairs. Whoever it was, the wards on her apartment kept them out. Strange that the ones on her shop didn't.

It took us well into the wee hours of the morning to clean up the damage, but by the time the sun came up, we had the shop back into some semblance of order. Maggie sent Andi upstairs to get some sleep.

"Why my shop?" said Maggie as she swept the last remaining glass shards into a dustpan. "I mean, sure, I understand coming after me, or you even, but why do they always have to mess with my shop?"

I didn't have an answer.

"So," she said as she dumped the pan in the dustbin. "What do we do now?"

"I'm going to go get your package," I said. "If it's what I think it is, we need to get it quick before someone steals it from the post office."

"I'd like to see them try," said Maggie. "Postal workers are scary."

There was a lot of truth to her statement. Besides the whole "going postal" expression, post offices were usually staffed by folks who were damned proud of their jobs, and took their duties as an official of the U.S. government seriously, with almost fanatical devotion. The post office listed on the slip was built like a fortress, and the paranoia level there was pretty high due to terrorist threats. Even so, I wanted to get it out of there, if just so I could see the damned thing and prove to myself it was real. After a heated disagreement, I convinced Maggie to stay behind to open her shop like everything was normal. No matter what was going on, I reasoned, closing shop and hiding was not the answer. Besides, a pig I may be, but if anyone was going to risk an attack in broad daylight, I wanted it to be me, not Maggie.

I walked the seven blocks until I came to the great granite and marble building and made my way up the steps. It was still early, so the lines were short and most of the workers still looked half-asleep. When I reached the teller and handed him the slip, he gave me a strange look.

"Margarette Perry?"

"Roommate," I said as I pulled my driver's license from

my wallet with a folded piece of paper. "She wrote me a note."

The teller took the note, checked my license, and narrowed his eyes. Then he disappeared behind a curtain and returned with a small, flat envelope.

"You'll have to sign for it," he said.

I put my name on the proper form and left with the envelope in my pocket. It wasn't as big as I expected it to be. Maybe I was wrong. I sure hoped I was.

Outside, the heartbeat of the city kept a constant rhythm. People went to and from jobs, in and out of shops, all without giving me a second glance. But the tattoo on my arm itched and I felt that all-too-familiar prickle under my hair. Someone was watching me. Without breaking stride, I lowered the walls of my perception, and the city leapt into vibrant color. The people that passed glowed with beautiful shades of iridescent blues, greens, pinks and golds. A few who walked by had shades of red. Above me, the buildings hummed with life, pulsed with the people inside their walls and glowed brighter than the morning sky. But there was one color I wanted to find, one that meant malevolence and evil. I scanned the streets for anyone with more than a trace or spot of black in their aura, but found nothing.

I put my walls back up and turned to walk back to Maggie's shop.

"Got any change, mister?"

At my feet, an old man sat on the steps of the post office. His hair was greasy and long, and his face drawn and yellowed. He reached one grime-covered hand out toward me and smiled a toothless grin.

"Sorry, pal," I said. "I don't carry cash."

"Maybe something to read, then?"

The voice that came out of the old derelict's body wasn't the same as the one before. He fixed me with milky eyes and a chill shot through me. He stood slow and took a step.

"Give me the book, Cooper."

For whatever reason, the strange voice coming out of the withered body, or the realization that I was talking to a corpse, didn't frighten me nearly as much as the fact that he knew my name.

"What book?" I backed up a step.

"Give me the book," he said again. "Or you'll be up to your neck in corpses, starting with the witch and her little friend."

I don't like to be threatened, and I like it even less when people threaten my friends. Especially two women that I care deeply about. Even more so if one of those is my girlfriend. If I were a movie hero, a moment like this one would bring out a pithy response followed by one hell of a fight scene. But since I'm not...

I ran. The homeless dead guy followed, faster than any dead person should. I made it around the corner before he caught up and tackled me. My face slapped the sidewalk, the breath rushed out of me. He pulled me over on my back and climbed up onto my chest, his face inches from mine. His breath reeked of cheap booze and death, his body of urine and decay. He leered as he leaned closer.

"I'll have the book," he said. "Even if I have to kill you to get it."

He leaned down like he was going to take a bite out of my face. I raised my arm, more out of fear than some ingenious plan, and the tattoo on my wrist erupted in blue light. He howled as flesh peeled from the side of his face, then the old body sagged and dropped over on its side. I kicked and crabbed my way out from under him and kept going backward until I felt the solid wall of a building at my back.

The scene took all of five or six seconds, and in that time

traffic on the street froze to watch the spectacle. Drivers gaped while pedestrians ran to help, half me, half the homeless guy. I pushed to my feet and ran off in the direction of Maggie's shop.

When I got back to the shop, I gave the envelope to Maggie and told her about the dead guy that attacked me. After a cursory examination to make sure nothing was broken, during which she noted I'd banged my face in the same place, and that my shiner was getting bigger, we made our way up the stairs to her apartment. The whole way up, she glanced behind as if she thought someone might be following us. Inside, she locked the door behind us and opened the envelope. It was too small to hold a book, but I was surprised that inside was no note, no more pages or cryptic references. Only a small brass key. The only markings on it were the words "Station Square."

PAGES

"God damn it, Stan," said Taylor. I hadn't been back at Maggie's shop for more than ten minutes before he'd come busting through the door with all the subtlety of tornado. "I've got another stiff on the street and more than a dozen eyewitnesses that describe a person fitting your description running away from the scene!"

"He attacked me! Or did the witnesses leave that part out?"

"According to half of them he did. According to the other half, you shot him with something like a laser and he keeled over with half his face gone!"

His eyes shifted around the shop like he expected one of us to attack him. Sweat beaded off his face.

"He was already dead," I said. "The coroner should be able to tell for how long."

"But until I get the coroner's report," he growled, "I've got half the department on my ass about whether or not it was you!"

His mouth twitched and he licked his lips. Something about him didn't seem right.

"What were you doing there anyway?"

"I was at the post office," I said. "Like any other normal person."

"Doing what?"

"Getting a manicure!" I shouted. "What do you think I was doing?"

"Did you get another weirdo package?"

The question stopped me. It wasn't so much what he said, as *how* he said it, like he already knew the answer.

"No, I had to send something out," I said with a quick glance to Maggie. "For the shop." I didn't like lying to him, but as strange as he was acting, my alarm bells were jangling like crazy.

My answer seemed to agitate him, and he spun back toward the door.

"Let me know if you get one," he called as he walked out. "It's evidence!"

He brushed by Andi as if he didn't know her as he rushed back out to the street.

"Well, hello to you too!" called Andi as the door slammed. "Asshole. What's his problem?"

I didn't know, but it made me uneasy. That he lost his temper wasn't so strange. He lost it with me on a regular basis. In truth, sometimes I provoked it just to get a reaction out of the big stiff. But this was different somehow. He seemed almost desperate, angry that I didn't have the package.

Maggie held the key up.

"Should we go get it?"

"No," I said after a moment. "The only people who know where it is are us and whoever sent it. I think it might be safer for all of us if it stays there. For the time being, anyway."

Maggie nodded.

"Besides," I said as I rubbed my bruised face. "I think it's pretty clear that I'm being watched. I bet you two are too."

"So what do we do?" asked Andi.

"We need answers," I said.

"Evergreen?" asked Maggie.

As much as I hated to admit it, she was right. Evergreen was the best chance we had at finding out just how deep we were in this pile of crap.

"Evergreen." I nodded.

When most folks think of a group of mystics, a certain stereotype comes to mind. Long-robed ancients who sit in dark rooms reading many a quaint and curious volume of forgotten lore, black cats and ravens, cauldrons full of colorful bubbly liquids, and chambers lit by burning torches come to mind for me. When Maggie first took me to meet Evergreen, I admit I was scared. I didn't know what I was in for, but as she directed me to what I assumed was a highly secretive place on the side of a hill in the middle of nowhere, I was sure they wouldn't take me seriously. Imagine my surprise when that highly secretive place turned out to be a bookstore in the middle of Monroeville, their mystic chamber was the store's coffee shop, and the members were... well... normal-looking. But the collective energy of the group was staggering. I didn't need to use my Sight to recognize it. I felt it like an electric current through my bones.

We merged onto the highway just as the sun gave up and dipped below the horizon. Traffic wasn't too slow, a miracle in Pittsburgh, so it took us less than half an hour to reach our destination.

The parking lot was almost empty, which explained why the group met on Thursday nights.

"Don't mention the key," I said as I turned off the engine.

"I don't know why they're being evasive, but between them and Taylor, I'm a little paranoid."

"You don't think..."

"I don't know what I think," I said. "But the fewer people that know about the key, the better."

"Okay," she said with a shrug. "We'll play it by ear."

"I can't believe I'm finally going to meet Evergreen!" Andi bounced in the back seat. She'd been bouncing since we left Carson Street, and I couldn't say I blamed her. To her, Evergreen was like the Knights of the Round Table, people about which legends were made. To hear Maggie talk about them, I understood why. She respected them, trusted them, and it hurt like hell that they weren't playing straight with her. I didn't want to bring Andi along, but as soon as she heard where we were going, she insisted, by which I mean she got in the back seat and refused to get out.

"Try not to drool on them," I said as I climbed out of the car.

The cool conditioned air that hit us as we walked through the door smelled of coffee and pastries, so much so that the three of us couldn't help but pause and breathe it in. There were only a few patrons, none of whom looked dead to me, which was a relief. Not that they could've gotten in anyway, seeing as Evergreen had the whole shop warded against supernatural beasties.

Maggie made her way to the coffee bar while Andi scanned the room like a prairiedog. I rolled my eyes and tugged her to follow Maggie.

When we passed three long racks of magazines, the floor of the cafe came into view. Thirteen people sat at a mass of tables, all pulled from their rightful spots to form one flat-topped mass. The one I knew as "Neighbor Bob" was deep into a conversation with Bill.

"Hypnosis is a valid tool for therapy," he said. "And for regressing into the subject's past lives."

"But how many Joans of Arc have you seen?"

"I hope we're not interrupting," said Maggie as we approached.

The table erupted in surprised "hellos" and "merry mets" while everyone got up for their customary greeting round of hugs.

"Good to see you, Stan," said Bill as I shook his hand. Brea, his wife, hugged me tight.

"And who is this?" Trevor, a tall younger man with a ponytail that went down to his belt line, nodded toward Andi.

"Ladies and gentlemen of Evergreen," said Maggie with a flourish. "May I present to you Andrea."

"Andi," she beamed, and made the round of hugs with the sort of star-struck goofiness that most people only get with actors or rock stars.

"So," said Bill. "To what do we owe the honor?"

"We need information," I said. "I think you know about what."

"Bill told us about the pages," said Brea. "Have you found them?"

"Not exactly," I said. "Someone stole them from the boy who stole them from me."

"Did he describe him?" Kevin stared from the end of the table. He was a tall severe looking bald man whose eyes didn't just look through a person, they dissected him.

"He's dead," I said and let the statement fall flat.

"Oh Gods," said Brea. "How?"

"Whoever took the pages," I said. "And there's more."

I told them about the stiff who robbed the bank, about Justin's relationship to him, and about the dead homeless guy who attacked me.

"It's impossible," said Kevin. "I'm sorry, but I just don't believe you."

"I've got the bruises to prove it, pal."

"No," he said. "Not about the dead people. About the pages. There's no such book."

An almost imperceptible look passed between the members of Evergreen. It was quick and subtle, but I saw it just the same, and I knew what it meant. There was real fear there.

"Well something's making corpses walk," I said. "And if it's not these pages, then I need to know what it is."

"We could handle it," said Blossom, an Earth-mother type with large glasses and a propensity for tie-dyed t-shirts. "It isn't your fight, is it? Why not leave it to us?"

"Because someone made it my business when they stuffed those pages in my mailbox."

"Well," said Kevin. "Have you gotten any other strange packages?"

First Taylor, now this guy. The same question, twice in one day.

"No," I said. "Not yet, at least."

"If you do," said Kevin. "Bring it to us straight away. We'll put it where it can't hurt anyone else."

"I thought you said it didn't exist," said Andi.

Kevin glowered.

"If it does," said Trevor, "then we're better equipped to handle it than you are."

The rest of the group nodded, all except for Bill and Brea, who locked eyes with me. In my head, a word formed. Not so much a word, exactly, as it was a feeling.

Outside.

I agreed to bring the book to them if I got it, even though I had no intention of doing so. We stayed for the rest of their meeting, all the while Andi stared goggle-eyed from face to face. After an hour, during which time I learned more about hypnotism than I ever wanted to know, the meeting ended. More hugs ensued as they invited us to join them at the restaurant across the parking lot. Maggie made up an excuse about having to open the shop in the morning and we made our way outside.

In the parking lot, Bill and Brea walked past me at a brisk pace. I almost didn't notice the folded piece of paper Brea put in my hand. I tucked it in my pocket, got in the car and waited for Maggie and Andi. After yet another round of hugs, they climbed in the car. It wasn't until we were back on the highway that I pulled the paper out and handed it to Maggie.

"What's this?"

"Don't know," I said. "Brea gave it to me when we left."

She unfolded the paper and read it aloud.

Not safe, it said. *Traitor.*

When we arrived back the apartment, Taylor's barge was conspicuous in that it took up most of the available real estate in front of the shop. He stood by the door smoking. Judging from the pile at his feet, he'd been waiting a while.

He saw my car, pitched his cigarette into the street, and followed me around while I parked.

"Got the report," he said as I got out of the car. "You were right. The homeless guy was already dead. At least twelve hours. Coroner's flipping out, but I persuaded him to keep a lid on it. For now."

"Told you."

"But that doesn't explain why he attacked you. I mean, if you didn't have the book..."

"I never said anything about a book," I said. Maggie and Andi took the look I gave him as a cue to head for the safety of the apartment.

Taylor's face wrinkled as he stammered a reply. Flustered just didn't look natural on him.

"Well, I assumed that since you got pages, they came from a book and... Hell, I don't know. I'm making this up as I go along!"

"What's the matter with you?" I wasn't angry, but he was starting to freak me out. "You've been acting weird for a couple of days now."

He let out a heavy sigh and sat down on the curb.

"This whole thing has me rattled," he said. "Dead people are supposed to stay dead. You know this mystical mumbo-jumbo is all new to me. I'm out of my element."

I understood. When I first saw how the world really was, I hid in my apartment for days.

"So where were you guys tonight?"

"Evergreen," I said. "Trying to find out what those pages were and if they could be behind the whole stiff-walkers problem."

"And?"

There it was again, the edge to his voice that made me uncomfortable, like he was sure I was about to give him the last piece to a puzzle I couldn't see.

"Nothing," I said. "They'd never heard of them."

"Really?" It was more of a challenge than a question. "The all-powerful Evergreen has never heard of anything like this? I find that hard to believe."

"That's what they said."

"Maybe they weren't playing straight with you."

Kind of like he wasn't playing straight with me. He

wanted the book, that much was clear, but I couldn't figure for the life of me why. Or, for that matter, why I couldn't convince him that I didn't know what he was talking about.

"Maybe," I said, and let it drop.

"If you find out anything, let me know first," he said. "Understand?"

I cocked an eyebrow and snapped a salute. The look on his face told me he didn't know how to take it, so he nodded and went back to his car. I watched as he pulled away. Whatever had him spooked, it rattled him but good. I made my way inside and up the stairs. Andi was already asleep on the couch with her computer in her lap. I gently slid it out of her hands, put it on the table, and covered her with a throwblanket.

When I walked into the bedroom, I found Maggie sitting cross-legged in the center of the bed. She didn't look like she was in the mood for fun and games.

"I'm scared," she said.

I was too, but I didn't want to tell her. Some part of me, the part that looked at myself with unrealistic perception, thought I should play it strong. But a second part just wanted to hand the key over to *whoever* and wash my hands of it. I knew I couldn't. Some sense of honor, I suppose. The book, or whatever was hidden in that locker at Station Square, was dangerous. If a few pages contained enough arcane knowledge and power to reanimate a corpse, I shuddered to think of what the rest of it contained. Even if it was a recipe for soup, I was willing to bet it was *evil* soup.

I didn't know what to say, so I did the only thing I could think to do. I crawled into bed next to her, wrapped my arms around her, and held her until we both drifted into an uneasy sleep.

PAGES

I've often been amazed at just how many discoveries in my life are founded in luck. When I died, I was lucky in that I came back. When I came back, it was by sheer coincidence that I met Maggie. Luck got me the payoff from my insurance company that allowed me to buy my apartment and my car. Maggie called it divine intervention, but while I believe in some sort of higher power, I'm pretty sure his or her personality runs more toward playing practical jokes, and making me the butt of them. The rest, for lack of a better word, I call luck.

The next day, Maggie opened her shop as usual. Cowering indoors wasn't going to get the bills paid, she said, and she wasn't about to let who- or whatever was messing with us disrupt our lives.

She's strong that way. It's one of the reasons I love her.

Andi went to her Friday classes at Pitt, which left Maggie and me alone in the shop. At about ten in the morning, the bell over the front door rang. I was in the back of the shop at the time attempting to put Maggie's back-stock, what little there was, in some semblance of order. Maggie's voice filtered through the curtain as she greeted her customer. But the tattoo on my arm began to burn, and the customer's voice sounded familiar somehow. I peeked through the curtain to see what was going on.

The customer was a young woman with her back to me. Maggie smiled and chatted her up, showed her from display to display. Everything seemed kosher.

Then the customer turned around, and my stomach wriggled like it was full of worms. Though she wore dark sunglasses, I knew her face. The last time I saw it, it was streaked with incorporeal tears. The last time I saw her, she cried to a phantom janitor about being forgotten, and about her dead body in the terminal ward. Her name was Heather.

Part of me wanted to run out, warn Maggie, and push her screaming through the door. But the other half of my brain, the smart half, made me reconsider. Whatever was going on, whoever was controlling the girl's body, might not know I would recognize her. I decided to see just how lucky I was.

I came out of the back room and put on my best non-threatening smile.

"Hi," I said as I extended my hand and shook hers. "Stan Cooper. How can we help you today?"

Maggie's face turned quizzical. She knew me well enough to know I was not prone to overt acts of friendliness toward strangers. Rather than ask what was up, I was happy she decided to play along.

"This is Heather," she said. "She's here looking for... what did you say?"

"I'm just a beginner, really," she replied. She never dropped the friendly smile, the easy nature. But the corner of her mouth twitched. She knew who I was, and I made her nervous. I was right, she couldn't be the young dead woman. So who was in her skin?

"Well," I gushed. "You've come to the right place! Maggie's a first-class witch, and she's guided lots of kids through their first steps in the occult. What're you interested in?"

"Old magick," said the thing that wasn't Heather. "Something very old that is just becoming new again."

Maggie shuddered. She saw it too, the subtle shift in the girl's posture. Something told me the girl guessed I knew she wasn't Heather, and was challenging me.

"Nope," I said. "Nothing like that. Of course, if we're talking about something stupid like... I don't know... playing with dead things, I'd say you're messing with the wrong people."

"Is that a fact?" She smiled and lowered her sunglasses. Milky eyes locked with mine and my stomach clenched. Face to face with a walking corpse, again, and I felt like I was reduced to a kid sneaking peeks at a zombie flick.

The thing that wasn't Heather lunged and knocked me to the floor. I tried to get my arm with my crazy blaster-ray tattoo between us, but she pinned it beneath her leg. She latched onto my throat with her hands and squeezed.

"Tell me where it is!" she screeched. Her voice was no longer Heather's, but deeper. A man's voice. One I'd heard before, but I couldn't place.

I couldn't breathe. I struck out with my free arm, but I might as well have been hitting a sack of wet laundry. The leering smile never left her face.

My vision dimmed. The harder I struggled, the more air I lost. Without my conscious control, my perception shifted, and I was horrified by what I saw. Just like the bum, tendrils of life energy poured out of her eyes like puppet strings. The threshold of the shop was parted like a curtain to let the lights through and out into the street.

"Concusso!"

White light erupted from somewhere in the room. The ghoul on top of me pitched, its head snapped back. It screamed in agony as another wave of energy hit it with enough power to break bones. It slumped off of me, a bloody heap, while the puppet-master's strings snapped away through the door.

It took me a few seconds of deep, grateful breathing before my vision cleared. Maggie stood over the motionless corpse. Her eyes blazed with anger.

"She's dead," I said as I got to my feet.

"I know," snapped Maggie. "I just killed her."

"No," I said. "She was already dead. Been dead for a while."

"How do you know?"

"Because I saw her ghost. At the hospital."

Maggie backed away from the corpse and helped me to a stool by the register. I couldn't take my eyes off it. Heather seemed so young, so innocent. She didn't deserve to have her body used like a Halloween costume. No one did.

She stared at the corpse for a long moment. "What do we do?"

"Call Taylor? He said he wanted to know if anything weird happened. I think this qualifies."

"What'd I miss?"

We both looked up to see Andi in the doorway, eyes wide and fixed on the corpse.

"Healing skills," said Maggie. "Under his neck. Now."

Andi rushed to the back while Maggie snatched up the telephone and dialed Taylor's number. When she returned, she held a big prickly green branch that looked almost as terrifying as the corpse on the floor.

"It's aloe," she said. "Relax. It's a natural astringent and will close the cuts on your neck."

She lifted my chin, broke the branch, and squeezed green jelly from the break. Then she smoothed the jelly over the places that burned.

"He's not answering," said Maggie. "What the hell are we supposed to do if he doesn't answer?"

"Leave a message. Then, I guess, call the regular police."

"You're kidding."

"Dead girl in your store. Seems like a logical thing to do. Especially since she was already dead."

"Like, what?" piped in Andi. "A zombie? Cool!"

"No." Maggie fixed her with an icy, withering glare. "Not *cool*. And it wasn't a zombie. It was... something else."

"I don't know what, but it came in through your warded threshold, which means one of us invited it in at some point. I'm betting that's how it got in and trashed the shop."

"So it's someone we know?"

"Who from Evergreen is a customer?"

Maggie blanched, shocked at the accusation.

"The only member of Evergreen that's ever come in here is Bill," she said. "And Bill wouldn't..."

"Are you sure?"

I slid down off the stool and walked toward the door.

"Where are you going?"

"The last time I saw that girl, her body was in the terminal ward of Mercy Hospital. I want to know how she could get up and walk out."

"But the police..."

"Are already looking for an excuse to lock me away. They already think I killed the bum that attacked me outside the post office."

"But," said Andi, "he was already dead, right?"

"They're not going to buy that. Really, before today, would you? Until they find out who's really behind all this, they'll arrest me if they see me."

"It isn't a big secret where you live, you know," said Maggie. "Why haven't they come to get you already?"

"Because they don't know for sure it was me," I said. "Taylor's been running interference. But if they find another dead body with me around it..."

"Fine," she said. "Go. We'll clean up the mess."

People who didn't know her might think Maggie was angry, but I knew better. She was frustrated with the situation, with me, with the dead body on the floor of her shop. She was upset that all the evidence pointed to someone we knew, and that someone was more than likely from her beloved Evergreen group. It had to hit her hard.

"I love you," I said as I opened the door. She looked up and smiled.

"I really like hearing you say that," she said.

Subtlety is not a gift that higher powers decided to bless me with. Neither is patience. So when I need to find something out, I go to the pertinent people and ask. Blunt as a bumper, that's me.

When I pulled up at Mercy Hospital, I had a general idea of who I needed to find: the nurse in charge of the terminal ward. It never occurred to me that they switch shifts, or that they might not take kindly to some random crazy person asking about a dead body that got up and walked out. Call me silly, but the thought never crossed my mind.

After the receptionist fixed me with the dirtiest look a human could give, she informed me that only family was allowed in the terminal ward. I tried to press the issue.

"Young man," she said. "I don't give a good God damn who you are or what you're doing here, but if you stay one moment longer, I'll call security."

I raised my hands in surrender and walked back toward the parking lot. Before the front door, I ducked into the chapel to see if the phantom janitor could answer some questions. As I passed into the chapel, I let my perception shift. Instead of light and positive energy washing over me, the room was dim, silent.

Most of the energy was somehow gone, a battery sputtering for its last few sparks of electricity.

"Barney?" I whispered.

"Didn't expect to see you back so soon," came a soft voice behind me. "Though I can't say I'm surprised 'neither."

Barney's form shimmered, but was dim, less corporeal than before. His kind face looked strained with the effort of appearing.

"What's going on here? Where'd all the life go?"

"Don't know," he said. "Started a couple of days ago, just before you showed up here. Real subtle too."

"Do you remember the girl? Heather?"

He nodded.

"I saw her today, walking around in my shop."

His expression darkened.

"That's not possible," he said. "I walked her to the other side. Her body died that very minute. They took her down to the morgue and everything."

"Someone's playing with meat puppets," I said. "And they want something they think I have."

I told him about the pages, the book, the other stiffs that behaved very un-corpselike.

"What you're talking about... it ain't natural. You have any idea how much power it would take to put your will into a dead body? If it didn't kill you too?"

"What about you? You're looking dim."

"I feel dim," he smiled. "I've been getting weaker for days. Won't be long before ol' Barney just fades off."

"Whoever's doing this, he's feeding off the patients in this building." It made sense. An endless supply of puppets, energy ripe for the taking. If he worked in the terminal ward, who would question patients' deaths?

"I'm real tired," said Barney. His image rippled and wavered. "I'm going to have to rest soon."

"Go on," I said. "Recharge. I'm trying to stop this... whatever it is."

"Thanks," he said, and was gone.

"That's him!"

I turned at the voice to see the receptionist, all four and a half feet of her, pointing two large men in brown uniforms in my direction.

"I told him to get out, but he wouldn't leave!"

"Sorry," said the larger of the two. "You can't stay."

"You're throwing me out of the chapel?" I shouted as I tried to sound as incredulous as possible, and I poured it on thick. "I came in here to pray, and you're denying me the comfort of *Jesus*?"

I didn't mean a word of it, but my shouts had the desired effect. Every person in the waiting room, patient and relative alike, turned and stared.

The receptionist turned pale and the two gorillas glanced from each other to her and back again.

I turned my back to them and pretended that my giggle was a sob.

"Lord!" I cried. "Please forgive these men, for they know not what they do!"

Then I turned and made for the door. As I passed the receptionist, I muttered "Jesus thinks you're a bitch," and left her slack-jawed and fuming as I made for my car.

Outside, I felt better, but I couldn't shake how odd the building made me feel. When I got to my car, I turned and altered my perception.

The hospital should've glowed, should've pulsed with life, should've breathed like a living, vital thing. But instead, its light was dim, a candle compared to a searchlight. But the visit was not a total waste. Barney confirmed my suspicions, and even handed me the "how." The dead bodies got up out of the morgue and walked out, not the patient rooms.

I don't like cellular telephones. It isn't that I think they're obnoxious or stupid. In point of fact, I'm sure they're wonderful little devices, when properly used. My problem with them is the same one I have with hybrid cars, computers, and nuclear reactors. I see the energy pouring off of them, and I just know that kind of thing can't be good for a body. To me, all three look about the same: glowing masses that reach into a person's body and riddle them with tumors or cancer or brain-rot. It sounds silly, but cellphones scare me worse than barking dogs.

Since I gained my bizarro little "gift," I hadn't owned one. But Maggie could be very persuasive. She managed to convince me that owning a cellphone in this day and age was a necessary evil, and if I was too concerned, I should get an earpiece so I didn't have to put the thing right up next to my head. Of course, to me, that little earpiece on a cord seemed more like a straw that sucked stray energy into my ear, but after a while, she pointed out a couple of fundamental truths. First, in a city the size of Pittsburgh, it made no sense to spend all my time driving back and forth from the shop just to ask people a few questions. Second, if I were going to spend my time snooping, it might be worth my while to have a way to contact someone in case I was attacked by muggers, cops, or other-worldly monsters. Third, and most important, Maggie was always right. It was the last reason that put the final nail in the coffin of my resistance.

I popped the earbud into my ear and flipped my little red

Samsung open, then dug in my pocket until I found the scrap of paper with Taylor's number on it. As I dialed, I glanced up to see the receptionist and her two goons in the window. By the way she gestured and stared, I knew she wasn't the newest member of my fan club.

The line rang once, twice, a third and fourth time before Taylor's tired voice answered.

"Hey," I said. "I got something for you."

"The book?"

He sounded hopeful, excited even. Too excited for my tastes. In the year I'd known him, Taylor proved himself time and again of having a first-class poker face. Excitement wasn't part of his repertoire.

"No, I think I found out where the dead bodies are coming from."

"Oh," he said. "That. Where?"

"Mercy Hospital morgue. I need to see a list of the employees in the terminal ward and in the morgue. Think you can use your magic cop-powers to get that for me?"

"Why?"

"I'm looking for a name. I don't know whose yet, but when I see it, I'll recognize it."

"I'll see what I can do. Anything else?"

He sounded annoyed, like I pulled him out of the bath-tub or something.

"Yeah," I said. "I need to know if the stiffs that have come after me so far have all been from Mercy Hospital."

"Sure," he said, then the line went dead.

Apart from the whole clairvoyant thing, I'll admit I can be pretty dense. Some times, I just don't get hints. But one thing I do know is when I'm getting the brush-off. It happened to me often after I died and tried to tell my supposed friends what I saw. Every time I tried to call one of them, they all acted annoyed that I was on the line or like they were busy. I just didn't expect it from Taylor. The more I thought about it, the more irritated and worried I became. If he had a problem with me, I wanted him to come out and say it. The trouble was, Taylor never skirted issues. Not with me, anyway.

My cellphone rang. I was so angry that I didn't bother checking the I.D. window to see who it was before I flipped it open and shouted.

"You gonna hang up on me again?" I barked.

"It's Andi." Her hushed voice shook as she talked. "The police came."

"And?" I didn't like her tone.

"They're still here," she whispered. "They're looking for you."

"Me? They don't think I..."

"They want to know if you've seen Taylor," she said. "They say he hasn't been seen or heard from in, like, three days."

It wasn't possible. Taylor said he'd spoken to them yesterday, that he'd been running interference for me with the local badges. If they hadn't really heard from him, I was in trouble. Deep trouble.

"I have to find him," I said. "Something isn't right."

I hung up and punched in Taylor's new number. I counted twelve rings before I hung up on it. Odd that there was no outgoing message, that his voicemail wasn't set up. I thought for a moment, then punched in his old number. It rang twice before a pre-recorded voice informed me that his voicemail box was full.

When I died, I started seeing weird things. Then I made the mistake of telling my friends about it, and they all dropped me like a hot rock. I don't have many friends, but to those I have, I'm fiercely loyal. For most of my friends, I'd give the shirt off my back, or at least a clean one I wasn't wearing. For a select few, I'd take a bullet. But there are only three for whom I'd stand at the gates of Hell and moon the devil himself. Maggie and Andi, of course, and Taylor.

Matthew Taylor was something of an enigma, even to those of us who knew him well. He was a career cop, older than me by about a decade, and always to the point. If Taylor wanted something, he came right out and said it without preamble. Some people thought of him as rude. I found the trait endearing.

While I was busy trying to call him, I noticed a little flashing icon in my cellphone's view-screen that said I had a message. I dialed the access code and waited.

"Stan... uh... it's Matt. Listen, we're still trying to track down those pages. Uh... if you get any more, y'know, weird packages in the mail, let me know."

The timestamp told me the call came from earlier in the day, before my call to ask about morgue workers and hospital Nazis. That he tried to call me wasn't strange. That I missed the call wasn't particularly weird either, considering I left my phone in my car's glove compartment when I don't want to be bothered, which was most of the time. But the message itself gave me lots of reasons to worry.

First, he never referred to himself by his first name. Taylor was, as far as he was concerned, his first, middle, and last, end of story. Second, hinting around about the package wasn't his style. If he wanted it, if he knew I had it, he'd just come right out and say it. Something was wrong, and it was time I found out what.

I pulled out of the parking lot and headed toward Oakland.

Taylor's house sat in the middle of what was commonly known as Frat Row. Rowhouses, most of which were occupied by students at Pitt, lined the street, their yards littered with empty beer bottles and cigarette butts. Big wooden signs marked which fraternity lived in what house, and on any given night the sounds of loud music and partying filled the air. All except for one house, third from the end of the block. That house had a wrought-iron gate around the well-groomed yard and bars on the windows. Most people who passed it probably thought the owner was either an elderly woman or a paranoid conspiracy theorist. While the first guess would be wrong, the second wasn't far removed from the truth. It just so happened that Taylor's paranoia was well-founded, and nine times out of ten his theories proved correct.

I circled the block. His car was in the back parking area. Taylor was home, so why wasn't he answering? Just one more thing I'd have to ask him, right after I asked what the hell was going on.

My tires shifted when I hit the curb in front of the house. I sat for a moment, stared at the house like I was afraid it would grow splintery teeth and chew up the path. Part of me, the smart part, wanted to use my sight to check out the energies around the house. But I didn't. Sure, Taylor may have been acting weird, but he was still my friend. Still the same cop I met a year ago. The guy didn't have an evil bone in his body. A few sarcastic ones, sure, but never evil. Even so, that smart half of my brain screamed and rattled around in my skull until I opened the door and got out.

Down the street, there were parties in full swing. Music and laughter floated on the air, but died when they reached the border of Taylor's lawn. Between my car and the front door, the air was still, silent.

I marched up the walk and banged on the door.

"Taylor!" I shouted. "We need to talk!"

No answer. The smart half of my brain screamed for me to run back to the car and drive off. But I couldn't. I gave the door a half-hearted try. Taylor's house was always locked with dead-bolts all the way up the door and a flimsy door-chain just for good measure. The door swung open.

"Taylor?"

The house was dark inside, the air stale. Something stank of rotted meat and air freshener. My stomach tightened because I knew. I hoped I was wrong, but I still knew. When I cleared the entry way and saw him, I wept.

Taylor was home, his body a discarded puppet over the arm of the couch. He wore the same clothes he had on the last time I saw him. It explained how the other corpse got into the shop. I thought I invited Taylor, but I invited the puppet-master by mistake, and gave him free access to our lives. It was he who trashed the shop. I felt sick.

"Give me the book."

The voice came from Taylor's awkward form. When I didn't reply, the corpse stood up.

"I said give me the book."

"Get out of him," I snarled.

Taylor's face leered, his body jerked. The sunglasses on his face hung off one ear revealing maggoty eye sockets. How long this bastard had been playing us, I didn't know, but even a day was too long.

"What're you going to do?" laughed Taylor's body. "Kill me? I'd love to see you try."

"I don't have the fucking book. I don't even know what you're talking about."

"Don't lie to me," he said. "Or you'll see Detective Matthew Taylor's name on the news as a child rapist. And anything else I feel like making him do. Your friend's reputation will be destroyed. Think your witch-bitch friend can figure out it's not him before he cuts her throat?"

Hatred burned cold in the pit of my stomach. I didn't think. I just gave in to the rage I felt and ran at him like a linebacker. He dodged and smacked me on the back of the head as I crashed into the wall behind him.

"You're pathetic," he shouted. "And stupid. You think a fat little bastard like you could take me? In this body?"

He was right, someone like me didn't stand a physical chance against someone like Taylor in a fair fight. Which is why I didn't fight fair. I tore off my watch. The tattoo underneath erupted in blue flame.

If I were a movie tough guy, I'd have made some comment about how much it hurt last time I touched the symbol to his face. But it wasn't a movie, and I didn't have time to talk. I just wanted to hear him scream in pain again. I wanted to press the shield into Taylor's flesh and drive whoever was in there out in agony.

I made an awkward lunge, one he side-stepped with childish ease while he pulled Taylor's gun from his holster and leveled it at me.

"I have a better idea," he said. Then he turned the gun toward his face. "Explain this."

He pulled the trigger, thunder clapped through the barrel, and the back of Matt Taylor's head exploded outward and painted the wall behind him crimson. The body collapsed, the puppet-strings cut.

I don't remember much after that. I screamed. I know I screamed. My throat was raw and bloody from it. Somehow, I wound up with Taylor's broken head in my arms when the police arrived. They said I wouldn't let him go, that I cried, said I was so sorry over and over again. But it blurred together as two cops cuffed me and stuffed me into the back of a cruiser.

PAGES

10

There was a time, not too long ago, when I lived my world in black and white. Good was good, bad was bad, and the line between them was big and easy to see. But as I got older, I started noticing things that made those lines blur. A man stole to feed his family while another man donated to charity so, it would distract from his kiddie porn collection. Black and white, to me, hasn't existed for a long time. The world existed in the grey shades of intention, a gradient of purpose. It allowed for a certain moral ambiguity in my line of work. Tying a twelve-year-old to a bed seems evil, until a person realizes that I did it to help drive a monster out of the kid's body. The ends justified the means.

I sat in an eight by ten cell with my head in my hands as I tried to figure out which side of the gradient Taylor's possessor was on. Sure, I believed that everything could be justified, depending on a person's point of view, but damned if I could think of the puppetmaster as anything but pure evil.

Even more, I tried to figure out if somehow I was to blame. True, I never asked to be sent those damned pages, but I didn't have to call him. I didn't have to involve Taylor in any way. Maybe he'd still be alive if...

The outer door clanked and slid open. A big cop with a

paunch that strained his buttons passed through and made his way to the front of my cage. If looks could kill, the stare from his hate-filled eyes would've burned me to a crisp. He didn't say a word, but unlocked my cell door, threw it open, and stood staring at me.

It took a couple of seconds before I realized he wasn't here to beat me senseless. Another couple for him to realize I didn't know what to do. He swept his arm in the direction of the door, but still didn't speak. I chanced a peek at his aura. Blues, greens, brown specks. Lots of red. This guy was pissed off at me in a major way, but there was nothing at present he could do about it. Instead of saying something he knew he might regret, or be forced to apologize for, he practiced his right to remain silent as he rushed me out of the cell.

I assumed Maggie and Andi came with bail money, or maybe that the forensics team determined the time of death to be a few days before. Imagine my surprise when I emerged from the holding area to see Bill of Evergreen standing at the counter, his face lined deep in worry.

He nodded at me, and I back as the cop led me to the window where I could reclaim my personal property. It wasn't much, just my wallet, my car keys, and my shoelaces. I was glad I left the key with Maggie.

With my stuff in hand, I came around the counter where a woman buzzed me out. Bill moved to meet me. We didn't speak until we were on the sidewalk outside.

"Are you okay?"

"No," I said. "How'd you know..?"

"Maggie," he said. "She called me."

"Bullshit." I turned on him. "I never called her, and she didn't know where I was." I turned my back on him and continued walking.

Bill followed in silence for a moment, then let out a heavy breath.

"Okay," he said. "We followed you. But we only did it to try to keep you out of harm's way!"

I stopped dead in my tracks.

"Did you know?"

"Stan, I... we..."

"*Did you know?*" I spun, caught him by his Hawaiian-print lapels, unaware of the gawking passers-by. "Did you know before I went into that house that my friend was fucking dead? Did you know that some twisted fuck was using him for a puppet? Did you know?"

He didn't look afraid or even angry. His eyes dropped out of sadness.

"No," he said, his voice quiet. "We didn't. I swear to you, we had no idea."

I let him go and turned around to walk away.

"Please," he said. "Let us help."

"*Us* who? Evergreen?" I snorted.

"Then let *me* help," he said. "Please, before anyone else winds up dead. Or worse."

I stopped. Taylor's grinning face as he blew the back of his head off replayed in my mind, and I felt tired. My friend, one of the few I had, died because of a few stupid pages from a book that wasn't supposed to exist, and there was nothing I could do about it.

"Look," I said as I turned. "You want the book, you can have it. Then it's your problem, you and the rest of the superfriends. Just leave us out of it."

"I don't want the book," he said.

The statement struck me as odd. For two days, I'd heard nothing but people asking about this supposed book, which I'd never actually seen. I'd been threatened and attacked, Maggie's shop was ransacked and Taylor was dead, and for once someone didn't want the thing.

"Frankly," he said. "I hope it never gets found. I hope it stays locked up wherever it is so no one can use the power it's supposed to have. But if you know where it is, best advised to get rid of it."

"What do you get out of helping, then?"

"Please," he said. "My car's around the corner. Let me give you a lift home and I'll explain."

Where Bill is concerned, I have a hard time imagining him doing what Maggie would call "mundane" things. It's why I felt like following him earlier, when we met at the coffee house. I just can't imagine him having a job, though he obviously has some source of income. I can't imagine him shopping for clothes, though I've never seen him wear the same tacky shirt twice. I also have a hard time picturing what kind of car he drives because, well, I never really picture him driving. As far as I ever thought, he just kind of appeared places.

It's short-sighted of me, I know, but when dealing with the leader of a super-secret mystical society like Evergreen, the subject of what he does in his free time just doesn't come up. It's kind of like Santa Claus. No one considers what he does for the other 364 days of the year.

As we walked, I tried to pick a make and model of car that suited what I knew of him, and a VW Microbus was all that came to mind. When he stopped before a brand new, vanilla-colored Chrysler, I almost tripped. Where mine was a little silver PT Cruiser model, his was the top-of-the-line 300 series. Expensive, and worth every nickel.

"Get in," he said as he opened the door with his remote key-fob.

"You're kidding."

I slid into the seat and closed the door. He started the engine and pulled out into traffic.

"Like I said, I don't want the book."

"But?"

"But I don't want anyone else to have it either," he said. "It's too powerful. There's too much bad hoodoo in there for any one person to handle. Even a person with the best intentions would be tainted by it. That kind of power corrupts..."

"And absolute power corrupts absolutely. So what do you suggest?"

"We need to get rid of it."

"Great. So I'll go get it and burn it..."

"You know where it is?"

"Maybe." The key was with Maggie, but I wasn't about to let anyone, friend, foe or old-guy-I-wasn't-sure-about, know that. If the book was in the locker that matched the key, mentioning it to anyone would paint a bulls-eye on my forehead. Or Maggie's, or anyone else's who hung around us. I didn't want to lose any more friends.

"Well, don't tell me where it is," he blurted. "But I don't think burning it will work. I'd bet you anything that it's charmed against fire or water or anything damaging."

"Then what do you want to do with it? Store it?"

"Under normal circumstances, yes. But someone in Evergreen is playing for the black. We can't risk it."

"Whoever that is, I'd bet dollars to doughnuts that he's responsible for all the walking dead folks around here," I said. "And for Taylor. And I want his ass."

"I couldn't let you have him," said Bill. "Even if I knew who it was. We have our own protocols for dealing with..."

"Me too," I growled. "I kick the shit out of him and put a bullet in his head."

"Listen to me," he said, his voice tight. "I like you, Stan, I really do. But you're out of your element here. You go after this person and I promise you more blood. Not just yours."

"Are you threatening me?"

"It's not a threat!" he shouted. "I'm trying to protect you! Maggie is one of the most powerful witches I've ever seen for her age, and she couldn't hope to deal with the power we're talking about! Her apprentice? Naturally gifted, but still just a baby!"

"Thanks for the pep-talk," I grumbled. "So what do we do? Give up?"

"I don't know." He sounded tired, afraid. "But I can tell you this: He'll come again. His power is growing, and he believes you have what he wants."

We pulled up in front of Maggie's shop.

"Thanks for the warning," I said as I slammed the door. I watched as he pulled out into traffic and drove away. As his taillights disappeared around the corner, it occurred to me that I never asked how he got me out of jail. I decided I would ask him later, if there was a later.

I turned and went into the shop. Maggie and Andi both jumped when the bell over the door sounded.

"Honey, I'm home."

"Thank the Goddess," said Maggie as she rushed to me and locked me in a bear hug so strong I was sure my ribs would crack. She released me and looked into my face. Her expression darkened. "What?"

I looked from her to Andi and back again as I tried to form the words in my head. I didn't want to just blurt them out.

I wanted to find a softer way, some way that wouldn't paint the gruesome picture the way I saw it. In the end, there were no other words I could use.

"Taylor's dead," I said.

The room went quiet as my words fell. Andi's smile faded as Maggie's eyes brimmed with disbelief and tears. I couldn't hold myself together any longer, so I hugged her tight and wept into her soft hair. I felt Andi's arms encircle me from behind. We stayed like that, we three, until there were no more tears left. What was left after our sorrow was rage.

"The person pulling the strings had Taylor," I said. "He'd been dead for a while. I just didn't notice. I mean, it was Taylor. I didn't scan him any more than I would scan you two."

"Maybe you should," said Maggie. "Just to be sure."

I nodded, though I didn't want to think about either of them being possessed. I didn't want to see tendrils of energy holding them up like strings. But I understood. We had to be sure. I closed my eyes and willed the walls of my perception to lower. When I opened my eyes again, the world looked different.

To look at someone's aura, their energy signature, is like taking a peek at their soul. Their actions don't replay in front of me, but I can see what they're really like. Most people have a mix of pinks, blues, greens and yellows to their aura. It grows and shrinks according to mood, activity, health, and a dozen other factors. When my Sight is engaged, I can pick a ninja out of nightfall and I make a fair lie detector. Buildings have auras too, depending on who lived in them and what they were used for.

When I opened my eyes, Maggie's shop glowed bright with golden symbols that floated in the air and lined every wall. The walls hummed with power and love, and the energy that Maggie'd put into the building pulsed like a heartbeat. It wasn't that long ago that the building was stripped of its energies, but together, we'd brought it back.

I blinked for a moment, then turned. Maggie's aura was just as I hoped it would be. Healthy and pink. It radiated out from her and swirled with traces of blue with streaks of green and yellow. A single patch of brown, sorrow, drifted through her energy sphere. I shifted my eyes to Andi and froze.

"What?" Andi looked down at herself. "What? Tell me!"

"I'm sorry," I said. "I just... didn't realize." Andi's light was mostly pink like Maggie's. But there was one major difference. Where Maggie's aura swirled with other colors, Andi's had only one: silver. The color that happens when a soul's been around long enough to become pure, and very powerful.

"It's nothing," I said as I shifted my perception back. "You're both fine." I didn't want to tell her because I wasn't sure what to make of it. One thing was certain, however: There was more to Andi than we, or even she, knew.

We closed up shop early that day. The three of us sat around in Maggie's apartment for the rest of the evening, drinking and reminding each other of just why we cared so much about Taylor, while trying not to remind ourselves of the size void that would be left by him. Maggie's apartment was safe behind her sigils, so we let ourselves breathe for a few moments. Maggie drank beer, Andi wine. I took long pulls from a bottle of spiced rum. We laughed for Taylor, cried for ourselves, and planned what to do with the son of a bitch who killed him.

I woke up with a nasty hangover, but with a surprisingly clear thought in my head of what I needed to do. It wasn't about the book anymore. It wasn't about dead people getting up and walking around Pittsburgh. The situation was far more personal than that.

I got up and showered, dressed, and headed out the door. Maggie and Andi weren't in the apartment when I left, and I didn't really feel like telling them what I was up to. They both would've tried to stop me, and it was something I needed to do, so I left a note taped to the microwave. Then I crept down the back stairs. As I emerged into the open area behind the shop, I froze for a moment. My car wasn't there. Stupid. It was still at Taylor's.

"Where are you going?"

Maggie stood cross-armed by the shop's back door, her look equal parts reproachful and fearful.

"I need to get my car," I said.

"It's a crime scene," she said. "You get caught around there, you'll be in jail again."

"If he's there, I need to talk to him. I have to know what happened."

She nodded.

"Be careful." She turned and walked back into the shop.

As much as I hated public transport, the buses in Pittsburgh ran on a regular schedule and went within a couple of blocks of where I needed to go. It took less than half an hour to get to the Oakland part of the city, a drive that would've taken me about ten minutes, but I couldn't complain.

To most people, Oakland is the hub of the Pitt campus, infested with students and weirdoes, marked with drunken debauchery and enough petty crime to warrant its own police force. But it's actually much more. There are actually several colleges all shoehorned in together, not to mention the UPMC facility, which means at any given moment, a person swinging a stick has equal chance of hitting students, hippies, doctors, drug-dealers, and anything else one would find on a typical college campus, but with four times the concentration. A closer look shows more than just what jaded folks see. Hidden among the eateries and tanning salons, the tattoo parlors and Christian student unions, there's a real underground community. The students couldn't care less about anything but their next exam or party, but the people that worked the densely packed blocks knew each other by name. A person inclined to just wander might be amazed to find the Pittsburgh Playhouse theater, or even several museums.

When I stepped off into the street, I felt the hairs on my neck prickle and the tattoo under my watch itched.

Damn. Whoever it was, he wasn't giving up.

I cut through the Pitt campus, past the Carnegie museum, and ducked into Heinz Chapel. The massive spire always reminded me of a needle built to stab God in the eye, and the thing looked incomplete without bats zooming around it, but it was holy ground. I hoped it was powerful enough to keep the puppetmaster away, if for only a few minutes. I stood just inside the door and triggered my Sight. Maybe I could see the person watching me. A split second after my perception shifted, I realized what a stupid move it was.

I was blind. The chapel's energy was so strong, so intense and powerful, that all I could see was white everywhere.

Churches, as a rule, shine brighter than most places. It's a product of all the love and faith that gets poured into them day after day. Whether folks want to call it residual psychic energy or the Holy Spirit, it equals the same thing. The energies inside churches are incredibly strong.

Heinz Chapel was no different, except that it was older, and that giant spire wasn't used to point at God, it was more of a metaphysical lightning rod. It pulled more energy down and into the ley-line on which the church was built. I may as well have just walked up to a million-watt-bulb and yelled "hit me!"

It took some effort, but I managed to close my inner eyes again, and the building went back to being dark and creepy.

I looked around outside. The grounds were covered in students, campus police and vendors. Any one of them, or more, might have been the one watching me. I didn't have time to worry, though. I needed answers. And, besides, I figured, if he wanted to take me out, he'd have done it by now. Still, just to cover my paranoid side, I waited until I was well across the street from the chapel and triggered my Sight again.

The area around the Pitt campus held every kind of shop a person could hope for, and the whole street pulsed with life energy. Likewise, the students and other passers-by radiated their own colors. But as I scanned the crowd and down the street, I didn't see what I thought I would. No strings of energy, no trace of black. Just normal people going about their normal lives.

I tried to shake off the feeling of being watched and hurried down the street toward Taylor's house. All up and down the street, the houses radiated with the things that happened in them. A few of them looked like they were surrounded by clouds of dirt, so much abuse and anger within their walls. Others glowed of lust or addiction. Around Taylor's yard, there seemed to be a bubble. In my Sight, his house looked almost like a giant snow-globe, but that instead of white flecks there were pieces from every shade, every color, floating inside.

I flinched as I passed through the bubble wall, even though I didn't feel it. Perception made me treat it like a solid thing. As I passed through, the world stilled, just as it had the last time, only now I knew why. Taylor's home was protected in some way, though not against intruders. I'd have to think on that later.

Police-tape stretched across the front door in a large yellow "X." I nudged the door open and slipped under the tape. Inside, the place bore obvious earmarks of the forensics team. Little flags marked bits of evidence, circles marked black stains on the walls. But more, there was resonance. Taylor lived here for years, and the house still remembered him. Still remembered his daily routine, still waited for him to walk down his stairs for his morning bowl of Raisin Bran, still waited for him to sit in his now overturned chair at the end of a hard day of catching bad guys. On the floor, an outline pulsed where his body fell, and around it ghost images of myself cradling his body played over and over again. Whoever lived here afterward would have lots of stories to tell.

"I was wondering when you would show up."

The familiar voice flooded me with recognition and warmth. Taylor's ghost stepped out of a shadow. He still wore his overcoat, still wore the same ugly tie. At least his head wasn't blown open. He was dead long before the bullet tore the back of his skull off.

"I'm sorry, man."

"It wasn't your fault," he said. "You have to know that."

"How long?"

"Three days. I had to sit here and watch myself for three days while that bastard..." He shook his head. "I don't have much time. He's getting stronger. He's using the energies from the dead people to boost his own. I'm too weak to leave this house, otherwise I'd have been around by now."

"Who was it?"

He shook his head.

"Never saw him before. But he's a weaselly-looking guy. Long black hair, a little dumpy. And his eyes..."

The image of Taylor shivered.

"He stabbed me in the back. Got me right under the diaphragm. Then he stood over me so close I could smell the tuna-fish salad on his breath. He stared into my eyes as I... died. He forced me out of my body and pushed himself in through my eyes."

"Where?"

"Mercy Hospital. I was snooping."

The image flickered again and lost some of its substance.

"I have to go now," he said. If I didn't know him any better, I might swear he choked back a few tears. "Can't hang on. Don't look in his eyes. Be careful."

And he was gone, crossed over into whatever passes for the afterlife. I wished I could've asked him one more question: What he saw beyond death.

I turned to walk out of the house and froze when a large figure appeared in the doorway. With my perception shifted, I saw great arcing sweeps of crimson in his aura along with patches of brown, all surrounding a corona of green. He was angry, but not evil.

I shifted my perception and opened my eyes. It took me a few moments to recognize the tired face of Officer Appel, the man who, along with his partner, made of a habit of arresting me when I was in the wrong place at the wrong time. Like now.

He was wearing jeans and a black t-shirt instead of his usual pressed blue uniform, and he hadn't shaved in a couple of days. He had a gun in one hand and a bottle of Jack Daniels in the other, and murder in his eyes.

"I... I..."

"Was he in there?" His voice was angry, full of sorrow, but none of it was directed at me.

I blinked, unsure of how to answer.

"Was he?"

I nodded.

"I didn't have anything to do with..."

"I know you didn't," he said. "You and he were tight. I figured you came here to check on him and found him like that."

More or less.

"He said you can talk to the dead."

I nodded.

"Did he tell you who did it?"

"Never saw him before."

Appel shook his head and stepped back out onto the porch. I followed, not sure of what else to do. I cleared the doorway and found him in Taylor's porch swing.

"I don't believe you," he said. "I can't. I can't believe people can talk to ghosts and bullshit like that. But Taylor did. If you can... If he was right, you think you can solve this?"

I nodded.

He took a long pull off the bottle in his hand.

"I didn't have your car towed," he said. "Figured you might need it. Left something for you on the front seat. Funeral's at Homewood in three days. Noon."

He stood up, tucked his gun in a holster in the back of his pants, and sauntered down the path.

"Hey," I called after him. He stopped and turned as I hurried to catch up. "Look, for what it's worth, thanks for not arresting me this time."

"Don't get used to it," he said.

I watched him walk for a ways, until he threw his bottle against a brick wall. It didn't break the way I expected it to, but just bounced down to the ground before it shattered. Then I went back to my car and slid behind the wheel.

In the front seat, a manila envelope lay with "Cooper" written across it in marker. Inside was a list of everyone who worked at the hospital, organized by division and department. He knew what I was going to ask for before I asked for it. And it got him killed. I put it back in the envelope.

Thanks, Taylor.

As I reached to put my car in gear, my cellphone rang. I didn't even get the chance to say "hello" before Andi's panic-stricken voice chilled me.

"Coop! Holy shit! You've got to get over here! Maggie's holding them off but..."

The line went dead. I threw the car in gear and stomped my foot to the floor. I didn't hit the brake until I reached Carson Street.

On the street outside Maggie's shop, there were maybe half a dozen people, all pressed up against the front glass with one putting his shoulder to the door. From where I sat, I didn't know who was normal and who wasn't, so I spun the wheel hard, pulled into the alley beside the shop, and shifted my vision. A long tendril of energy snaked through the sky, splitting into five sets of strings to five different puppets. I pocketed my keys, grabbed the aluminum baseball bat from beside my seat, and ran to clear them away from the door. Inside, Maggie shouted in Latin, and the normal glow of the shop became an angry maelstrom of energy and color.

"Maggie!" I shouted as I swung at one of the walking dead, a large man with salt and pepper hair. The bat struck him in the side of the head, which cocked over sideways. He never stopped moving, but turned and laughed at me. They all laughed in unison, a strange harmony of different voices.

"The book," they said together.

Believe me, as cheesy as it sounds, it was one of the most frightening things I'd seen in a long time. I turned to run toward the back door, only to find the alley blocked by four more.

Children. Grey-skinned and milky-eyed, sure, but children nonetheless. The oldest couldn't have been older than twelve, the youngest five. They all wore pretty clothes, fit for burial, with funereal makeup on their faces like pasty clowns.

I stumbled backward, and into the larger dead man, who wrapped cable-like arms around me and squeezed. My bones ached as I fought for breath, but I couldn't expand my lungs no matter how hard I tried.

"So much easier if you just give me what I want," whispered the dead man in my ear. Shadows crept in around the outside of my vision, and I figured I was done.

"Get... away... from... *him!*"

The voice startled me, jostled my fading consciousness. When my vision snapped into focus, I saw Andi. She stood just outside the shop's side door, the broken bodies of the children strewn around her feet. Maggie leaned in the doorway, drained and weak. But Andi...

For most people, their aura is like a light from a bulb in a foggy room. It makes the body glow, sure, but it is secondary to the power of the person. In Maggie's case, the energy field reaches out a good six feet all around her, and it glows like a spotlight at night. When she's mad, it gets brighter and more powerful. Maggie's was the most powerful I'd ever seen, until that moment.

To look at Andi was painful, like the raw energy pouring off her would burn my corneas and leave me blind. White and red danced together as her rage and fear grew until, without a single spoken word, the energy in her body erupted in a shockwave of raw will. The dead man's arms spread wide and I fell to the concrete.

The man spasmed as he fell, twitched like a bug in an electric zapper. At the same time, the other four screamed, the most horrible sound, and jerked just as he did. Then all five of them fell at the same time. Andi stood for a moment, wide-eyed as her rage settled down, then a look of confusion crossed her face, her eyes rolled up, and she collapsed in a heap. Her aura was dim, but visible.

I struggled to my feet and helped Maggie into my car, then went back for Andi. I scooped her off the ground and realized just how tiny she really was. For the amount of power that came out of her, she must have damned near killed herself. I laid her gently in the back seat, then climbed in and made for the safest place I knew in Pittsburgh, where we could figure out our next move.

PAGES

I'm not stupid, and believe it or not, I do learn from my mistakes. If there was another place close by that I knew could keep all the nasties out, I'd put up a big symbol and call it my bat-cave. But there's not, which means I have to make do with what I have. So, whether I'm comfortable with the idea or not, when the metaphysical shit hits the fan, the safest place to hide is my apartment. The last time I hid out from something supernatural in my apartment, the cost was high. Too high. To the tune of the lives of everyone else who lived in my building. I still feel the loss every time I walk through the door, which explains why I don't come around much.

But, like I said, my apartment was the safest place I knew. No one from Evergreen knew where I lived as far as I knew, and if the wards I painted all over my walls could keep out demon-possessed super-rats, I was sure the walking dead couldn't take down the door. At least I hoped not. Besides, when the construction crews started the clean-up, I took a few other precautions. In the outer walls, I made sure to put sigils between the sheetrock and brick before the workers covered them up. I also put a few on the floors of all the other apartments while they were laying the carpet. It took time, patience, and determination, not to mention a large bit of sneakiness on my part, but it was worth the effort, I felt. Better to be caught drawing funky symbols with a marker than to have my neighbors eaten again.

I hadn't been to my apartment in a while for much more than to check the mail. Not that it was a bad place to live or that I was dying to get out of there. To the contrary, it overlooked Pittsburgh's three rivers, had two bedrooms, and the new families that moved in were nice, from what I could remember. In fact, the only thing I didn't like about it was the view from the second bedroom, which looked at the building I fell from when I died. But for all its simple niceties, one thing it didn't have was Maggie. Sure, I could've slept at my place, but somehow it just seemed stupid. Her life was with her shop and, as far as I was concerned, my life was with her. Of course, since I didn't spend any real time there, I didn't do little things like keep a stocked pantry.

Or clean.

I opened the door with more than a little trepidation. Nothing bad could get inside, the wards on the walls saw to that, but the smell of dust and unwashed laundry hit me in the face like a slobbering dog as scats flittered about their business. I glanced behind me. Maggie and Andi leaned against each other in the hallway. Both looked barely able to stand, much less turn their noses up at the stench. Andi's head lolled back between fits of coherence. Maggie wasn't in much better shape. I ignored the smell, ushered them inside, and locked the heavy steel door.

We took Andi to the master bedroom, which smelled more like stale sweat and feet than I remembered, and put her in my bed. Maggie slumped to the couch as I closed the door.

"What the hell was that?"

"Don't know," she slurred. "So much energy. I never expected..."

She didn't finish the thought. Her eyes fluttered closed

and left me with the sinking feeling that I was about to watch her die.

"How can I help?"

"Sleep..." she mumbled. "Food. Gotta... recharge..."

She closed her eyes again, and this time I didn't wake her. The old blanket on the back of the couch smelled just as bad as the rest of the apartment, but it was soft and warm enough. My guess was she wouldn't care if a smelly fleece Darth Vader covered her body while she slept, so I pulled it over her, then slipped out the door.

The street outside was clear. No tendrils of energy or walking corpses. So far, so good. Of course, with my luck, it was only a matter of time before a piano, ridden by some rotting naked fat person, landed on my car. Monsters always liked to mess with my car.

Out-of-towners hear the name "Strip District" and assume something akin to the red-light district in Amsterdam. They picture strip clubs lining the streets, each one more tawdry and perverted than the last. The reality is much better. At least, it is to me. It's an area of town where my one serious vice is catered to at every doorway: food. On any given day, the air there doesn't smell of car exhaust or asphalt, but of fresh bread, sizzling meat and spicy pasta sauce. It's the kind of place a guy like me can lose a couple of hours without realizing.

Since I started dating Maggie, my waistline became a major preoccupation. It took me only a few days to face a couple of facts: First, women who looked like Maggie didn't normally fall for schlubs like me. I'm not romance-novel-cover material by a long shot. Except maybe the hair. Second, I wanted to please her in every way. Her practice of what she referred to as "the Art" involved raising energy in a multitude of ways, but the most powerful ways involved full-blown rituals. Some of them consisting of chanting or dancing. A few used sex. Not just one-on-one sex, but hot-and-sweaty group encounters. It wasn't something she did often, especially now that we were together and she knew I wasn't keen on sharing, but she'd had enough lovers and partners that, to be honest, I was afraid I'd be inadequate. Not that she ever complained, but that macho-gorilla ego needled the back of my brain and made me want to ask all kinds of questions to which there were no good answers.

Things like *was it good* and *am I the best you've ever had*. Trust me, a fragile male ego may want to ask, but it really doesn't want to know.

So my visits to the Strip District and all the succulent wonders it held tapered off until I only went on special occasions. As my waistline shrank, I began to feel a little more secure about her being on my arm.

I know. I'm pathetic.

The street was packed with people, and the traffic stayed true to form in that it crawled by. As I puttered along, I glanced out the window.

So many people, and none of them knew what was going on. Few of them knew about how the world really worked. Even fewer, if any, could comprehend what kind of a shitstorm was brewing in our fair 'Burgh. And it had to stay that way. Why?

Because they didn't *want* to know. Their whole world, built on what they can see and the tangible, would come crumbling down if they were to be confronted with how temporary, how flimsy, the facade of the "real" world was. They couldn't begin to guess how much they really didn't know. Once their fears of the dark were confirmed, they would all become little children again, clutching at blankets and screaming for their mothers.

But they didn't know. They were too calm, too happy, too busy with their day-to-day lives to understand what the ramifications of someone who could raise the dead were. If only a few pages allowed him to play puppeteer with corpses, I shuddered to think what terrible secrets the whole book held. They were in the dark, and I hoped to whatever higher power listened that they'd stay that way.

I paid to park about three blocks away, but that was normal for the area. As I walked back to the enticing smells, I couldn't help but look over my shoulder. With every step, I was more sure that someone was watching me. From where, I couldn't tell, but it was like dragging kitten claws up the back of my neck. Whoever it was, he was close.

I resisted the urge to trigger my Sight. Sure, I might've found out where he was, but with so many people around, I probably wouldn't have been able to distinguish the puppeteer from anyone else on the street with any certainty. I couldn't risk it. I needed to take care of business and get back to the shop. Maggie drew her energies from the Earth and from the elements, but the lion's share of it came from her own will, her own body. It worked the same way any other exercise did, by tapping into food and energy stores locked away in fat and protein pockets. Casting spells the way she did was a more effective calorie-burner than thirty minutes on a treadmill at a fast pace.

Andi was another matter, and one that bothered me. I had no idea where she could've tapped into an energy source so great as to throw off the kind of fireworks she displayed. If it came from outside her body, all that power rushing through could've damaged her like too much electricity going through a thin wire. But if it didn't, if it came from her will alone, then we had a whole new set of problems, starting with how she could possibly recharge after such a show, or if the magick did too much damage to her body on the way out. And, for that matter, just how much power the girl held in her body sent a cold chill down my spine. I had to remind myself not to stare at her later like she was a walking nuke.

I ducked into one of the bakeries and bought a dozen hoagie rolls fresh from the oven. Two shops down, a butcher sold me freshly sliced chicken, roast beef, and pastrami. Some fresh baby spinach and a jar of local honey later, and I had the makings of a real feast in my bags. I stepped out onto the street and the kitten scratched at my neck again. My mind raced.

Maggie and Andi needed food, and quickly, but I didn't want Geppetto following me home either. I was pretty sure his puppets couldn't get past the wards I put up, but I didn't need an army of zombies milling about outside my building either. That sort of thing had a tendency to make the other tenants nervous.

I took a sharp right and headed back down the street toward my car. A block away, I ducked onto a side street and hurried down an alley. The shadow from the neighboring building gave the narrow walkway an ominous feel, but at the end was sanctuary.

Diablo's Coffees was one of those bohemian places that simultaneously didn't fit anywhere and blended everywhere. The owner, Murray, didn't care too much for "Corporate Coffee," his pet name for Starbucks, and preferred to sell his own special blends alongside unique teas. Murray was a friend of Maggie's, and therefore a friend of mine.

A bell over the door chimed as I walked through, and the feeling of being watched melted off my back. Patrons sat in the overstuffed couches and listened while a few banged on bongos that Murray provided. They smiled as I walked past to the back of the shop. True to form, Murray's lanky form swayed and danced as he filled orders in the back of the shop.

"What's up, hippie?" I barked.

Murray spun on his heel and broke into a wide grin.

"Stan the man! How's it hanging? Is Maggie with you?"

"That's why I'm here," I said. "I need some of your special pick-me-up. She and Andi..."

"Andi?"

"The student."

He nodded.

"They really blew themselves out." I held up the bags. "This would probably feed me for a week, but I bet they'll finish it inside an hour."

"Wow," he said, eyes wide. "Must've been doing some heavy mojo. No worries though. Just made a batch. How much?"

I don't drink tea. I drink coffee by the gallon, but I know nothing about how much tea goes in a cup, how to keep it, or even how to make it. That's Maggie's area.

"Two pounds?" I guessed. Murray smirked.

"You have no idea what you're doing, do you?"

"Will that be enough?"

Murray shook his head in a pitying sort of way and smiled.

"I ought to let you have two pounds, just to give Maggie a giggle."

He hefted a bag roughly the size of a throw pillow onto the counter.

"That's one pound," he said. "You're making tea for two people, not the entire Chinese army."

"Fine," I huffed. "So what do I need?"

"Leave it to me," he said. He pulled out a small white paper bag and shoveled in about a dozen spoonfuls. "It's for

Maggie, right?" I nodded, so he added another spoonful of peppermint, rolled the top of the bag closed, and gave it a good shake.

"One more thing," I said. "There's something following me and..."

"Say no more. People!"

The patrons looked up in unison.

"Let's have a deep cleansing breath! All together now!"

It was kind of creepy, the way they all closed their eyes and inhaled.

"Hold it! Now, let's have a good happy thought and blow out positive energy into the world! Ready? Three... two... one..."

The collective rush of breath sounded like an asthmatic nightmare.

"Out the back door," he said. "All that positive energy will act like an umbrella until you get to your car."

I tried to pay him for the tea, but he wouldn't hear of it and hurried me toward the exit. Once outside, I was about twenty feet across the street from my car. As I slid into the seat and turned the key, I couldn't help but smile to myself.

"I'm back!" I called out. Maggie shifted on the couch and struggled to sit up as I made my way to the galley kitchen, parcels in hand. "Fresh eats. I even got Murray to fix you some pick-me-up tea."

"Mmmm," she said as she shambled up beside me. "I knew there was a reason I loved you."

She made tea while I set to work making hoagies that would make Dagwood Bumstead cry with envy. When I was done, she took hers and wobbled back to the couch. She sat and shuddered with each bite, as if she could feel the food replenishing her energies.

"What about Andi?" I said between bites.

"I don't know," she said. "She threw off a lot of power."

"Should we wake her and try to feed her something?"

"She needs sleep now more than anything, I think."

Maggie finished her sandwich before I was even halfway through mine. Then she took her plate to the sink and made her way into the bedroom. I had a big bite of hoagie in my mouth when Maggie shouted.

"STAN!"

My sandwich fell to the floor as I rushed into the bedroom. Maggie stood over Andi's body, her face flushed with fear and concern.

The acrid smell of concentrated sweat permeated the room as Andi lay glistening on the bed. Her body shook with such violence, it seemed like it was trying to tear itself apart. Her eyes were open, but only the whites showed. She gasped as she tried to breathe.

"What the..?"

"Look at her!"

I didn't need to ask. I shifted my perception. The white-pink of her aura was now a thin corona, pale and flickering. Her life was running out, burned through by her own will.

"She's dying," I whispered.

"What do you see?"

"Her energy's fading. Her body can't heal the damage she did by..."

"No," said Maggie. "We have to do something."

"Like what? Give her a transfusion? It would take a hell of a lot of energy to push into her, and then we'd be no better off than she is. And you're weak, remember?"

"We have to try something," she said. "We can raise the energy."

"How?"

She stared at the trembling child for a moment.

"The Great Rite," she said.

For the uninitiated, the "Great Rite" means raising energy through the act of creation. Sex to normal folks. But we're not talking about normal Friday night lovemaking here. This is ritual sex at its finest, abandoned and sticky.

I'm not a prude, and Maggie is one hell of a lover. But I wasn't sure that I wanted our lovemaking to be some kind of magickal Pagan ritual. She'd done this sort of thing often before we got together, and she swore by the results. But somehow, it just seemed... I don't know... weird.

"She needs this," she said. "Or she's going to die. We can't let that happen. Not while we can help."

I couldn't argue. I nodded and she led me into the living room.

"I need salt," she said. "Candles."

I hurried to the kitchen to grab my large container of salt, then to the bathroom where, if rumor was to be believed, I was the only guy in Steel City who actually kept a bag of tea-lights. I brought them out and handed them to Maggie.

"Strip," she commanded.

I did as she said as she placed five candles at points around the room. When she was done, she pulled a lighter from her pocket, then took off her clothes and tossed them on the couch.

"Don't laugh," she said. "This is serious. I love you, and I need you to give your all to me. Do exactly as I say. Understand?"

I nodded.

"Good. Stand in the center of the candles."

She poured a circle of salt around us, outside the candles. Then she snatched a knife off the counter and sliced her finger.

"Yours too," she said. "Left hand."

That little voice in the back of my head, the one that sounded suspiciously like my grandmother, started expressing concern. Blood magick was hard-core stuff, the kind of thing that most in Maggie's world didn't dabble in. It skirted a little too close to what some called Black Magick. Of course, there was another voice in my head, one that I pictured belonging to a wicked-looking dwarf with a huge erection, that mentioned hot monkey sex, and the first voice was silent.

To use blood in a ritual, one has to give over more than their energies. He has to give over a piece of *himself*. Any bodily fluid will work, but some are more potent than others. Tears, spit, even sweat will personalize a spell. But the most powerful way for a man is semen; for a woman, menstrual blood. Blood, however, would work just fine for the both of us.

She pressed both our bleeding fingers to the circle of salt, which burned like hell, by the way. Almost at once, I felt the air around us harden, then she stood beside me, arms raised, and gestured for me to do the same.

"Hail to the guardians of the watchtowers of the East, power of air, the breath in our lungs, the wind in our faces, we invoke thee." She lit the first candle and the air inside the bubble started to hum. "Hail to the guardians of the watchtowers of the South, power of fire, passion and will, we invoke thee."

With each salute, the air inside the bubble hummed a little louder, shook a little harder, until, at the fifth candle, it was as if we were inside a hive of excited bees.

"This candle," she said as she touched flame to the last one, "I light for spirit. I call to my brothers and sisters, to the God and Goddess. Lend me your strength, look down upon us, and aid us in our task."

Okay, I know it got a little weird, but I couldn't take my eyes off her. Her nude body lit only by candlelight, sweat glistening off her curves, the buzzing energy-filled air around us, was enough to arouse my interests. I shifted my perception to See what was going on.

The air around us was alive with electric motes. They zipped around the enclosed space, pinged off the iridescent shell of air, picked up speed, and flew at a break-neck pace. Maggie's aura glowed bright and strong.

"Sit down," she said. "Cross-legged."

I did as she instructed. She raised her arms and stood to straddle my lap.

"Focus on your energies," she rasped. "Draw power into yourself through the air, candles, earth, your sweat, my breath."

Her shaved sex was right at my eye level, and as I looked up at her, she seemed more to me than a woman, more than my lover. She was, to me, the living incarnation of beauty. A living conduit of energy. Goddess made flesh.

"Constructum navitas... Constructum navitas... Constructum navitas..." Her voice was almost a growl as she panted the words, husky and full of desire. She continued to chant as she lowered herself onto my lap. I slipped inside her, and it was one of the most erotic and terrifying things I'd ever experienced. It was like having sex with a live electrical circuit. She rocked her hips in time with her chant. Sweat beaded on her forehead and breasts. She wrapped her legs around my waist and squeezed as tight as my arms around her. We rocked in unison, her voice growing in volume and pitch with each passing second. I felt my heart beat faster as release approached.

"Constructum navitas, constructum navitas, constructum navitas *constructum navitas constructum navitas!*"

She gasped as her body bucked, her eyes wide as she climaxed. It was enough to push me over the edge and I let go. All the energy in my body, all my love, all my heated passion and animal lust pumped into her in what was the greatest orgasm I'd ever experienced. She released her grip with her legs and I fell backward onto the floor, spent.

After a moment, I opened my eyes. She glowed. At some point, my perception shifted back to the normal world, but even so, I saw the life within her pulsing in time with her heartbeat. The sweat on her nude form picked up the light from her body and made her glisten like a diamond.

She stood up, the words of her chant still moving her lips, and walked to the bedroom where Andi lay inert. She closed the door behind her.

I collapsed onto the floor. It felt like I'd just run a double marathon while wired to a car battery. I closed my eyes for just a moment to savor the feeling, and was asleep before I realized it.

"Wow."

I opened my eyes to find Maggie, now dressed in my bathrobe, helping Andi out of the bedroom. It took me a moment to register what Andi said, and why she stared. I was still naked, spread-eagle in the middle of the floor.

"Um... hi..." I couldn't think of anything better or more witty to say, and frankly, I was too tired to go diving for my pants. I had no idea how long they'd been standing there, so chances were Andi'd already had a good long look at me. I did, however, roll over onto my stomach.

"Feeling better?"

"Yeah," said Andi. "A little woozy."

"You need food," said Maggie. "And so do you," she said to me.

I didn't argue. I felt drained in more ways than one. If

this was what it felt like to do major magick, it was little wonder that Maggie was always hungry.

Although my modesty was already beyond compromised, I scrambled into my bedroom and closed the door. When I emerged, wearing a pair of blue jeans and a t-shirt, Maggie and Andi were huddled around the food I'd brought home like starving vultures. I honestly thought one of them might hiss at me if I got too close.

"Sandwich," barked Maggie between chews.

She lifted a large hoagie on a plate. At that moment, it could've been prime rib or cat food and it wouldn't have made a bit of difference. My body cried out for nourishment, which was a new experience for me. I dug into the sandwich.

The first bite was pure sinful ecstasy. Those that followed were lust and greed piled together between two pieces of Italian bread. I finished it off without realizing, then sat with a dumbfounded look on my face.

"So much for my diet," I said.

"Energy work burns more calories than you can believe," said Maggie. "Keep it up and you can eat as much of whatever you want and you'll still lose weight."

"Um... guys?"

We both turned to Andi.

"Where are we?"

"My place," I said. "Don't worry. It's safe here."

"Okay... but what happened?"

Maggie and I gave each other worried glances.

"What do you remember?" Maggie took another bite.

"Those... zombies..."

"They're not zombies," I said. "They're dead. More like puppets."

"Okay, whatever. They were coming. I remember Maggie fighting them off, but one got past... got you. I remember needing to do something, anything to help. I got so angry. Then everything went white and... I woke up in there with Maggie..."

She blushed. I shot Maggie a questioning look.

"I had to feed the energy into her," she shrugged. "The best way for me to do that was..."

"I don't want to know," I said as I lifted my hands. Again, not a prude. But my mind made some very erotic and uncomfortable pictures just then, and it wasn't something I could deal with.

The apartment was quiet, save for the sound of all of us munching our food like greedy dogs. But despite our silence, I knew we all had similar thoughts in mind.

"Anyone have a clue what we're going to do?" I asked after a moment. "I mean, we can't just hole up here, and sooner or later someone's going to notice all the walking corpses running around."

"You're kidding, right?" snorted Andi. "Really? This is Pittsburgh. We're famous for zombies. We've even got a zombie-walk to celebrate it!"

Maggie stopped chewing and stared.

"When is that?"

"This weekend," said Andi. "Why?"

The bottom dropped out of my stomach.

The mall in Monroeville was the site of a yearly zombie-walk where more than a thousand people dressed up as the walking dead to raise awareness for hunger. People brought non-perishable food, walked the length of the mall, and then went home. The organizers actually set a world-record for the number of "zombies" gathered in one place. Last year, there were more than a *thousand* people. This year, I was betting there would be more, and a lot of them wouldn't be wearing makeup.

"Okay," I said. "That's not good."

"It's perfect," nodded Maggie. "He can move corpses around without anyone noticing. They'd just think they're wearing good makeup."

"So we need to find out who it is before then," said Andi.

"What do you mean *we*?" She'd already damned near killed herself protecting me. I'd already lost Taylor. I wasn't keen on the idea of losing her.

"Hey, I saved your ass back there," she said. "Don't go all *oh she's just a little girl* on me."

"Honey, you're still weak." Maggie had a way with words that could soothe even the most easily offended estrogen rage. "No one's saying you didn't help, but as weak as you are right now, another burst like that one could kill you."

"I'm not..." she stood, wobbled, and plopped back down on the stool. "Okay, maybe I am. So what're you two going to do?"

"The center of this mess is the hospital, right?" Maggie crinkled her brow in thought. "We need to find out who..."

"Shit!" I said as the other half of my brain kicked in. The envelope. Appel gave it to me, and in all the confusion, I completely forgot about it. "I ran into one of Taylor's buddies. He gave me a list of the people who volunteer at the hospital."

"Where is it?"

"In my car. I'll be right back."

The whole way down to my car, I couldn't shake the feeling that someone was watching me. Not that they were. After years of dealing with these weird abilities of mine, I learned to distinguish between genuine phenomena and garden-variety paranoia. This one was the latter. It was the same feeling I used to get whenever I left my apartment and was certain my neighbors were staring out their peepholes.

When I reached the front door, I shifted my perception

and scanned the street. No dead people, no tendrils of light, just dreary Pittsburgh sky and traffic. I hustled out the door to my car, snapped up the envelope, and sprinted back into the building. Let the neighbors wonder.

By the time I got back, Andi was halfway through her second sandwich. I heard Maggie in my bedroom rustling around. I pulled the list out of the envelope and set it on the bar. It was a longshot, a list of more than a hundred names, and I hoped we might recognize at least one of them. Five pages in, we found the one we were looking for.

"That weasel-faced son of a bitch..."

I don't strike a particularly imposing figure. I'm short and, despite my best efforts, still a little dumpy. Let's face it, when a person is being stared down by a Treasure Troll, even an angry one, it's difficult to be afraid. Maggie, on the other hand, can be downright chilling when she wants to be, and she doesn't even have to say anything. With no more than a narrowing of her eyes, I've seen her reduce burly construction workers to piss-soaked tears. When intimidation is on the agenda, or when someone has betrayed my trust, I'm always glad to have Maggie by my side.

We stormed through the doors of the hospital, right past Nurse Pickle-Face, and headed toward the elevators. As the doors closed, I heard her shouting into the telephone for security.

"You sure you want to do this here?"

Maggie didn't answer. Her jaw was rock-solid as she stared at the numbers that lit up at the top of the elevator. She had her long red hair pulled back into a tight ponytail, which only added to severity of her look. And, dressed in a pair of my jeans, a black t-shirt, and a pair of boots she'd left over at my apartment months ago, she looked like she was ready to pull someone's head off. Good thing we were already in a hospital.

The doors opened on the terminal ward. A younger

nurse glanced up from her magazine and must've seen the hatred in Maggie's eyes. She blanched and fumbled for the telephone while we stalked down the hall. I gave my best "here comes chaos" smile and followed.

Halfway through the second corridor, we saw a set of purple scrubs with a ponytail hanging down the back.

"Trevor!"

He jumped and turned. The look of shock on his face was priceless. I tried to form some pithy remark, the kind that a movie tough-guy would be famous for, but nothing came to mind.

What happened next was a blur of sparks, light, flesh and screaming. I walked in with my perception shifted in case he somehow knew we were coming. As cold recognition settled in on his features, he mouthed a few words and took off his glasses. In an instant, tendrils of pure energy shot from his eyes. At the same time, more energy flowed into him from the surrounding rooms as he fed off the waning life force of the patients. Maggie flexed and sent out her will, which caused a few of the overhead fluorescents to burst in a shower of sparks. As she ducked, five of the patient rooms opened and their emaciated occupants staggered out, each one looking more dead than alive. I chanced a look behind us and saw the desk nurse frantically trying to get people back to their rooms. When one flung her against a wall, she retreated behind her counter and hid.

Trevor smiled as he continued to mutter his chant. The skeletal fingers of the patients reached out for us, and it was all I could do to keep them from overwhelming me. Maggie had more success until one grabbed her ponytail and pulled her off balance. She stumbled backward and the mass of disease and filth closed in around us.

In that horrible, terrifying moment, I had a thought. If

Trevor controlled these things (people... I had to remember they were people), the logical course of action was to take him out. I wriggled through the tangled mass of arms and ill-fitting hospital gowns until I saw him, then I put my head down and ran as fast as I could, bellowing the whole way. I hit him with all the force of a kiddy-car gone haywire, but it did the trick. He toppled over with me on top, and the patients crumpled to the ground, their strings cut. I reared back to punch him, and made a terrible mistake. Our eyes locked.

The old saying about the eyes being the windows to the soul is wrong. They're more like doorways. Two big, open doorways with no doors to keep people out. It was what Taylor tried to tell me: Don't look him in the eyes.

I felt him like a physical thing inside my head, like we were crowded onto an elevator that was only big enough for one. In my mind, I heard him laugh as my eyes burned and my head throbbed. It was only the beginning, and I couldn't make myself break eye contact.

It felt like vicious claw-tipped fingers soaked in acid and salt latched hold of my brain and shook it. The sensation took me by such surprise that there wasn't time to scream. I tried to hit him, but my arms wouldn't respond. All I could do was watch from the inside, trapped as my body got off his and turned toward Maggie. His hate surged through my body and flooded my brain, all of it directed at Maggie.

From the inside, I begged, pleaded with my body to stop, but I could only watch as I ran at her, reared back, and punched her in the face. She didn't go down, but flailed and caught me in a bear hug. At her touch, warmth flooded my limbs, the fires in my brain cooled. Trevor screamed as Maggie forced him out of me.

"Freeze!"

All three of us snapped around to see the hospital's

inept security man, a walkie-talkie brandished in his hand. Behind him, four of Pittsburgh's finest pointed guns. I figured the guns would do more damage.

"They came in and started tearing up the place!" shouted Trevor. "My God! The patients!"

He made a good show as he scooped up one particularly emaciated old woman. The boy should've been an actor. I thought he was laying it on a little thick, but the cops were convinced. Two snaps and a shove later, Maggie and I were escorted from the hospital and stuffed into the back of a waiting cruiser.

For those who have never been arrested, take it from me. It's not a fun experience. I've had more than my fair share of run-ins with the law. Of course, none of those were my fault, just cases of me being in the wrong place at the wrong time. But I have seen the inside of several Pittsburgh station holding tanks. They're peachy. I don't mean that metaphorically, they actually have peach-colored walls. It's part of some study that shows color has a direct effect on people's moods. Apparently, a color that I like to call "faded sick orange" is supposed to be calming. The only effect it had on me was an unending wave of nausea.

"Why'd you tell them you had an alias?"

Maggie's voice sounded strange as it bounced off the concrete walls. Though they brought us here in the back of the same cruiser, the law prevented both genders being locked up in the same cell. After seeing some of the suspects in the women's tank, I wasn't sure whom the law was designed to protect.

"I don't know," I shrugged. "I figured, if I'm such a dangerous criminal, I ought to have a super villain name."

"'Captain Creepy?'"

I snickered. The truth was, the cop processing us knew who I was, knew I never had an alias, and knew that every charge ever filed against me was eventually dropped. I figured it would be funny. Of course, he wrote it down in my file, ensuring it would follow me around for the rest of my life.

"Seemed like a good idea at the time."

Across the cell from me, a fat guy in a Steelers jersey snored on a bench. Another, who looked too young to be in a holding cell, stood with his back to the bars, facing the room with shifty eyes and nervous jitters. The other guy, older and wearing rags, stood in the corner pissing on the wall.

"How're you holding up?" I called.

"Fine," came Maggie's disembodied voice. "I'm thinking of starting a book club."

I chuckled.

"How're we going to get out of here?" She sounded tired.

Good question. In the past, Taylor got me out, pulled strings and called in favors. But now...

A wave of sadness washed over me. In all the confusion, with all the chaos, I'd all but forgotten about the dead cop. He was more than that, though. He was my friend, and I didn't have many of those. I could only imagine how Maggie felt.

Trevor was more than a friend, he was like some sort of priest in her religion, a brother of faith. For him to betray her, Evergreen, and everything his religion supposedly represented must hurt her deeply. And he killed Taylor. Worse, he killed him then paraded around in his corpse like a skin-suit. One way or another, he was going to answer for that one.

"Don't know," I said. "Maybe Andi..."

"Ha! Like she has money."

"Well, better get comfortable," I said. "Looks like we're here for a while."

The thunder of rolling steel interrupted my pity-party as the door to the outer room opened. Muffled angry voices bounced against the concrete walls, followed by heavy footsteps. When they stopped in front of me, I looked up into the angry red eyes of my two least favorite people in the city.

"Officer Menold!" I beamed. "Officer Appel! What can I do for you gents?"

Appel shook his head as Menold unlocked the tank door.

"Captain Creepy?" he said. "You couldn't come up with anything better than that?"

"It fits, doesn't it?"

He motioned me out while Menold released Maggie.

"You found him?" he said.

"We found him."

"Who?" The veins in his forehead bulged and his jaw tightened. It wasn't a request, but a demand.

"Let us handle this," I said. "This is more of the 'I-can't-believe' stuff."

"I want his ass."

"So do we," said Maggie. "We'll get him. I promise."

"You'd better," said Menold. "You've been released on bail pending a full investigation."

"Who posted?" Not that I wasn't grateful, but I didn't like the feeling of being in debt to anyone.

"Does it matter?" said Appel. "Just do what you gotta do. Don't swing for that cocksucker."

Menold led us around to the processing station where we both signed away major organs on the promise of coming back or not skipping town. The officer on duty handed over envelopes with our personal stuff in them and told me where to go pick up my car. When we walked out of the holding area, we were greeted by three familiar, but unexpected faces.

"It was Trevor, wasn't it?" Bill's face still held its customary smile, but his eyes drooped. The betrayal wounded him deep, and to hunt down a member of Evergreen was probably like having to go after one of his own children.

Maggie nodded.

"I was afraid of that," he said.

"Bastard," hissed Kevin. "When I get my hands on him..."

"Calm down," said Brea.

"Oh, I think the time for calm is way past," I said. "We need to have a talk, like now."

"Yes," said Bill. "I suppose we do. But not here."

It took me almost an hour to get my car from the impound, while Bill and Brea watched. Maggie fidgeted, and Kevin paced like an angry cat. They offered to drive us wherever we wanted to go, but I'd be damned if I were going to leave my car in lockup any longer than I had to. Starship captains like Han Solo and Malcolm Reynolds had a special bond with their ships that bordered on obsessive and psychotic. I felt the same way about my car. Besides, I learned a while ago to always have my own transportation. It cut down on instances of being left stranded.

I followed them to what appeared to be a mom-and-pop coffee shop. Maggie didn't say a word for the entire ride. I could tell by the way the muscles in her jaw bulged that she was still beyond angry. I almost would've preferred a rant or angry shouts. The silence in the car, with only the bump of the road to keep the rhythm, was unsettling.

When we pulled into the parking lot, Maggie didn't even wait for the engine to die. She got out and stalked into the shop without so much as a backward glance. I locked the doors and followed.

Inside, the place was far nicer than I imagined. The outside looked like little more than an aluminum-sided shack, but inside the walls had a rich earth-tone to them, accented with dark wood paneling and furniture. The bar was far too ornate for a run-of-the-mill coffee shop, and everywhere chrome gleamed in the dim light.

"Nice place," I said.

"Most people prefer Starbucks," said Bill. "This is a good place to talk."

We took a table while Bill spoke to the woman behind the bar, who nodded and bustled off to the chrome espresso machine. He walked over to the table and sat. For a moment, no one spoke. In fact, no one even looked up. All eyes stayed down on the tabletop. I almost didn't notice when Bill broke the silence.

"What you have to understand," he said, "is that this is a very delicate subject. What we're talking about here is something that, even in our circles, we don't normally discuss."

"Why?"

"It's filth," said Kevin. "If it were real, it would undermine everything we stand for. It could start wars. It could..."

"Come on," said Maggie. "Don't bullshit me. What could possibly be so..?"

"Imagine," said Brea, her voice soft and quiet. "A caveman who just learned the secret of fire getting hold of a flamethrower. Imagine a species in the stone age being given a gun. So much knowledge, so fast, without the discipline to control it or the wisdom to never use it, would destroy that race."

"The book you're talking about isn't supposed to exist," said Bill. "There are legends about it, stories written about it, but we thought that's all they were. Stories. But the pages had to come from somewhere."

The table went silent as the waitress brought over five steaming mugs. She didn't smile, didn't look at any of us, just set each mug in front of us and walked back to the bar without a word. I took a sip and fell in love. The rich taste was something similar to dark chocolate, thick and creamy, but with enough Colombian goodness to get all my pistons firing.

"The pages are real enough," I said. "But what's so damned important about the rest of the book?"

"According to legend," said Bill, "the book was written somewhere around twelve-hundred years ago by a Jewish priest who was a direct descendent of Aaron, brother to Moses. He..."

"Wait," I said. "Moses? Like... *the* Moses?"

"Don't interrupt," hissed Maggie with an elbow to the ribs.

"According to legend, he and his brothers joined the priesthood at the same time, but while they were content to serve the church, he was more of a mystic. The legends say that, when they caught him, he'd murdered more than a dozen people and was in the throes of demonic possession."

"Tell us about the book," said Maggie.

"It's a collection of spells, incantations, dark power writings about how to communicate with the dead, reanimate corpses, and call upon the powers of heaven and hell to bend the almighty to the will of man. Supposedly, it tells the reader how to open the doors to hell and heaven, and can allow man to access either."

It all sounded very familiar, like a fairy tale I heard growing up, or worse. It sounded to me like a bunch of crazy talk.

"No doubt you've heard of it," said Brea. "Everyone and their dog has heard of something like it, though they don't believe it to be real. We have Lovecraft to thank for that."

"So what?" I said as I leaned back in my chair. "You're

telling me that this book is the Necronomicon or something?" I laughed. It had to be a joke. The most hated, feared, and, might I add *fictional* book on the planet was supposed to be real? I looked around the table. No one else was laughing.

"The book doesn't really have a name," said Kevin. "But Lovecraft based his bullshit book on those rumors and came up with a half-assed vague description that started people wondering. The more they wondered, the more rumors spread and people began looking for the damned thing. Lovecraft said he made it all up, but looks like he didn't."

"What would Trevor possibly want with something like that?"

"Think about it!" said Kevin. "Who wouldn't want that kind of power? Who doesn't think the world would run better if everyone just thought like they did? The person who holds that book is essentially a new God."

"But Trevor?" Maggie's face showed disbelief, and I couldn't say I blamed her. The guy was weird, sure, but I never pegged him as a megalomaniacal power fiend with a god-complex. He struck me as someone who would be more at home as a Dungeon Master than a demigod.

"Trevor is... was... someone with issues," said Bill.

"No shit," I said.

"When he came to us, he was just a couple of steps away from suicide. He'd lost his parents, his sister... He was in the seminary, you know. Wanted to be a Catholic priest. But then he figured that God hated him. Not that God didn't exist, mind you. He firmly believed in the Judeo-Christian deity. He honestly believed that God hated him. It took us a long time to get through to him, to work out his psychological issues. He really is a bright young man."

"Looks like you didn't work them out enough," I snorted.

Kevin stood and glared at me. For a moment, I thought he might climb over the table and choke me to death right then and there.

"Obviously not," said Bill as Brea pulled Kevin back into his seat. "That's why we need the rest of that book. If it's real, Evergreen is the only group I would trust to never use it."

"I would've said that too," said Maggie. "Up until Trevor started parading dead people around. Now, I don't know who to trust."

"No one," I said as I drained my coffee cup. "Power corrupts, absolute power corrupts absolutely. I don't think there's anyone who could resist the kind of temptation that book offers."

"We are the best qualified!" shouted Kevin.

"Who else knows how to handle this kind of thing?"

"She does," I said, jerking a thumb at Maggie. "And I trust her one helluva lot more than I trust you guys. In case you didn't notice, one of your trustworthy brethren is off playing naughty with black magick and trying to get his hands on the way to bring heaven down. And you guys didn't have a clue, did you? So you think there might not be more in your little group?"

The three of them looked at each other while Maggie turned her horrified eyes on me.

"How can you accuse them..?"

"Because I'm an outsider," I said. "I'm not part of your little political games or your little witchy social club. I'm not blinded by sentiment where you guys are concerned, and I'm telling you that something isn't right. My daddy used to say that for every snake you see, there's a dozen more you don't. For all I know, Evergreen could be one big nest of rattlers."

I'm not big on confrontations, but I'm even less on being played. I was brought up to believe in honesty, and deceit just doesn't come naturally. Frankly, it pisses me off when I find out I've been lied to. Maybe it stems from all my former friends abandoning me when I died, but my trust is hard to come by. The only thing that pisses me off more than being lied to is having my trust betrayed. For me to trust someone, I have to feel like that person is beyond reproach. But when that trust is lost, I never give it back. Besides, it makes me feel like a chump.

"We have to give it to them," said Maggie as we pulled out of the parking lot.

"Like hell we do."

"Bill's right. They're the only ones who know how to handle that kind of power."

"They're doing a bang-up job of it so far."

"Trevor... he just..."

"Just what?" I shouted. "Just found that much power too much to walk away from? Just pulled a Sith Lord move that would make George Lucas cringe? He's Dark Side now, babe."

"Nerd," she said. It was a taunt she used on me often, mostly when I made some reference to my favorite sci-fi movies.

But this time, when she said it, there was no playful giggle. It was more habit.

"The point is, I don't think he could do what he's been doing alone. I think he had help. And I don't think we can trust Evergreen anymore."

I let the sentence hang in the air like an Acme piano. I knew what was coming, but I didn't see any way to sugarcoat it.

Sometimes honesty isn't exactly the best policy.

"Bill is one of the most trustworthy people I know!" she shouted. "If you think for a minute..!"

"I said *Evergreen*. There are more members there than just Bill. How many members are there?"

"I don't know," she said. "There are the core seven, but there are about twenty that just show up every now and then."

"It's one of the seven," I said. "Has to be. The others, I doubt they'd have enough juice to work this kind of mojo. But the core, they have serious firepower. If it's anyone, it's one of them."

"How can you even think that?"

"Trevor was one of them."

She didn't say anything after that. She just sat there as I drove through Liberty Tunnel, her eyes on the dashboard.

"For the record," I said as gently as I could manage. "Bill, I trust. Him and Brea. That's it. Bill's a good man."

She nodded and smiled a little.

"Which is going to make this difficult," I continued. "I've got an idea."

Usually, in movies, when someone says "I have an idea," it's followed by ominous music and lots of blood. When I say it, I still get this tingly feeling inside like it might actually work. Most of the time, it doesn't and I wind up improvising. As plans go, mine usually suck. Which is why mankind invented good old plan "b." Of course, when that one fails too, success comes only with an obscene amount of luck. What with my being alive and being with Maggie, I often feel like I've used up all the good luck I've got coming to me. Which is why, when I say "I've got an idea," people around me get nervous.

The line rang while I waited for Bill to answer. Four rings and the line clicked.

"Hello?"

"You win," I said. "You want the book? You can have it."

The line was silent for a moment.

"If you think that's best," said Bill. "You can bring it to me or..."

"No," I said. "I want the whole group there. Someplace public with lots of people. If Trevor shows up, I want witnesses. If he doesn't, we can blend."

Okay, the whole public-drop-off gag is old, but there's a reason for that: It works. And I figured if we were going for a Scooby-Doo style trap, I might as well play it up. If I was really lucky, I might even get to do the Poirot bit and reveal the bad guy in a dramatic fashion. A guy can dream, can't he?

"But if there are lots of people around, aren't you afraid of someone getting hurt?"

"No," I lied. "That's why I want the whole group. Trevor's less likely to make a move with all of you there, and if someone else is pulling strings, he won't risk revealing himself. But I'm handing the book over to you and you only. I don't see you, I'm a rabbit. Got it?"

"I hope you know what you're doing," said Bill. "Where?"

"How 'bout your regular meeting spot in Monroeville? It's central to all of you, right?"

"Yes," he said. "That's why we chose it, but..."

"Then that's where we'll do it. Same time as your regular meeting."

"Mister Cooper," said Bill. "Are you sure this is a good idea? That book... The power in it would tempt anyone. I feel honored that you trust me enough to give it to me, but the others... I fear it may be too much for them."

"That's why it has to be with the whole group. No one will make a move if you're all there. I hope."

"When?"

"Tomorrow afternoon," I said, "Around four. I'll see you there." I hung up the phone and looked up. Maggie and Andi stared from my kitchen.

"What're you thinking?" Maggie narrowed her eyes.

"They're the only ones qualified to handle that thing, right?"

They nodded.

"And one of them is a traitor, right?"

"You don't know that," said Maggie.

"Yes I do," I said. "I just don't know which one."

"Wouldn't you be able to... you know... See that?"

I thought about that a while ago. The aura a body puts off reflects its emotional state. Most of the time, I can See pure evil as a thick black mass over a person, kind of like that person just oozes cancer. But if the person believes, balls to bones, that what he's doing isn't evil, has no actual designs of overt subjugation of the people, his aura looks pure. His intentions are, from his point of view, just, so I'm none the wiser.

"Not really," I said. "Besides, if he does make a move, I'll have you two and the other members of Evergreen there to take him down, whoever it is."

"So?" said Andi. "What's the catch? Everything you plan

goes haywire somewhere, so where's the bug in this system?"

I was quiet for a moment because I didn't want to voice that particular fear. I didn't have to worry. Maggie did it for me.

"If there's more than one accomplice," she said.

PAGES

Almost every guy wants to be Butch Cassidy, or that character played by James Cagney when he screamed "I made it, ma! Top of the world!" They want to be the kind of tough-guy who goes out in a blaze of glory, damn the odds. They want to be legends. Not me. I'm more of the type who wants to hide until it's all over and be the only survivor left to tell about it. Forget the hail of bullets or signature one-liners, I'm the guy who hears a gun go off and dives under a table. Taylor was the hero type, not me. Maggie could pull it off, wielding her magick against demons and monsters, and even Andi might be more the plucky unexpected heroine than the hapless sidekick. Me? I don't want to be anywhere near the action. But the action seems to know all my hiding spots, so I wind up in the middle of it nine times out of ten. And I get scared. Sure, I'm man enough to admit that the thought of facing down six of the most powerful mages this side of a Dungeons and Dragons game makes me want to curl up in a brightly-lit corner and cry. But being scared is normal. It's what a person does with that fear that I suppose makes them a hero or a goat. Yeah, I get scared, but when it comes right down to it, maybe I'm too stupid to run. Maybe the Scottish part of my ancestry rears its tartan-clad head and makes me too damned angry to run. Either way, terrified as I may be, I'm no coward.

Still, as I sat all the way in the back of the bookstore, I couldn't help but ask myself just what in the bloody hell did I think I was doing.

I felt in my pocket for the locker key for the third time in as many minutes. Damn. It was still there. Across the bookstore, obscured by shelves, Maggie and Andi flanked the front door and awaited the arrival of Evergreen, or anyone else who might try to take the key before I got it to Bill's hands. They were closer than the length of a football field, well within shouting distance, but I still felt like they might as well be in another state. If I was right, if there was a traitor, my plan might work. Bill could get the key, retrieve the book, and I could go on with my odd existence. If I was wrong, if the traitor just didn't give a damn about the other members, things might turn ugly fast. If there were more than one, I might be handing over the power of the world to a bunch of lunatics.

On the other hand, part of me hoped Trevor did show up, and that my theory of another traitor was wrong. The opportunity to see Bill and company kick metaphysical ass was appealing, as long as mine wasn't the ass getting kicked. Besides, Trevor needed some humbling, and I'd be lying if I said I didn't want in on it. I owed it to Taylor.

I peeked from around one of the shelves and saw a few of the Evergreens arrive. Maggie and Andi met them at the door, but there were no hugs this time, no "merry mets" or "blessed bes." The tension in the air was almost physical as my two beautiful sentries sent them to their normal place in the coffee bar. I recognized Kevin, Blossom, Neighbor Bob, and Renau, but no sign of Bill or Brea. My stomach gurgled with nerves. Maybe Trevor got to them, or maybe they weren't coming? Maybe the four that were already here were waiting for the right moment to tear us all apart and take the key for themselves. I shrank back behind the shelf and tried to breathe slow and easy. There was still time to get out, to duck through the back door and run like hell. The longer I sat, the more it seemed like a good idea.

The electronic chime on the front door sounded and I looked out again. Bill and Brea stood just inside. Maggie let a tiny smile go, her first of the evening, and pointed them to the rest of the group. Then she turned, nodded to me, and I knew there was no backing out. I got up, reprimanded my cartwheeling stomach and quivering knees, patted my pocket again, and emerged from my hiding place.

I wondered if death-row inmates on the way to the gas chamber felt the same.

The table was quiet, without a trace of the fellowship that marked their usual meetings. The warmth wasn't there, replaced by tension and suspicion. More and more, I felt like I was sticking my arm in a bear trap. As I approached the table, all six of them turned to stare. Their anger hit me like a wave of bad perfume. Maggie held my hand, her jaw set and eyes cold. I was glad she was on my side.

"Okay," I tried to say, but my throat was arid. Between it and my pounding heart, I wasn't sure I could get through the evening. A reassuring look from Maggie kept me on my feet.

"You all know why we're here," I began again. "We know Trevor is the one behind all the walking dead people. He cost me a dear friend. He killed a kid who was too stupid to know what he was getting into. He came after us at the shop. I'm out of my league. You want the book, but I want to know what you're going to do about him first."

"He'll be dealt with," growled Kevin. "It's not your fight anymore. Just give us the book."

"Until he answers for what he did, it is our fight," said

Maggie.

"We'll find him," said Bill. "He'll be held accountable. You have my word on it."

"Where's the damned book?" shouted Renau. "Give it over to us now!"

The table erupted in a string of profanities and angry voices, each demanding I hand over the book.

"Enough!" said Bill. He didn't shout, didn't need to, but his voice reverberated through the bookstore. At his word, the table went silent. Every face turned fish-eyed and snapped to him, my own included. "Mister Cooper was kind enough to bring the book to us, and we fall into bickering? Trevor will be dealt with, not only for his crimes, but for his use of dark magick. He will be stripped of his abilities, we'll see to that. After that, you can have him and turn him over to the authorities for the murder of your friend."

"Unacceptable!" shouted Kevin. "You know we can't do that!"

"Why not?" Maggie clenched my hand tighter.

"We have our own ways," said Kevin. "His punishment must be as severe as his crime, and mundane laws wouldn't even begin..."

"Then we don't have a deal," I said. "I'll burn the book and track down Trevor myself." Yes, it was a bluff, but I'd had enough of the high-and-mighty act.

"With what?" laughed Renau. "Your bare hands and this fledgling witch and her lackey?"

"*Lackey*?" bristled Andi. For a moment, I thought she was going to leap across the table and throttle the larger spiky-haired woman, and I wouldn't have risked odds on Andi losing.

"You'd be dead before the end of the week and he'd be parading around in *your* skins!"

"Like hell," I said.

The conversation wasn't going at all the way I planned. Instead of finding a second traitor, I realized Evergreen was made up of at least two people who thought they were superior to the rest of the world, two I trusted, and two more that were oddly silent.

Give me a room full of crack heads armed with razors, I at least know where I stand. One thing I can't handle is a wildcard, much less two of them.

"Blossom? Bob? You two want to weigh in here?"

The table went silent as Bob got to his feet, shook his head, and left the table.

"This is all madness," he said over his shoulder as he walked out. "Whatever you decide, count me out."

That left Blossom, who sat at the far end of the table with her face in her hands. When she looked up, her glasses were smudged with tears.

"I can see both sides of the argument," she said. "But the real problem here is the book. *I* certainly don't want it. But I don't think anyone else could possibly resist it. Except for Bill and Brea. If it comes to my opinion, I don't care what happens to Trevor, but the book has to be protected. It must be preserved, but it must stay out of hands that would actually use it. You all sound so..." She sniffed as fresh tears pooled at the edge of her glasses. "Selfish."

Bill put his arm around her and squeezed.

"That's that," he said. "Give me the book, and I swear I'll put it somewhere no one will find it, but it will be safe."

I reached into my pocket and pulled out the key.

"It's in a locker at Station Square," I said. "I think."

"What do you mean, *you think*?" shouted Renau. "You don't *know*?"

"I've been chased by dead people, arrested, and followed around town for a couple of days. Forgive me if I haven't gone to check my mail!"

"So you may not really have it at all," she said. It wasn't a question so much as an accusation.

"The writing on the envelope the key came in matched the one the pages were in."

"Give me the key," snapped Kevin. "I'll go look and you can go back to... whatever it is you do."

"Fat chance, baldy." It just slipped out, and his face twisted in fury. For a moment, a nervous giggle bounced around in my stomach.

"*I'll* take it," said Renau. "If the book is there, I'll give it to Bill."

"Why can't Bill go get it on his own?" chimed in Andi, and the whole table lapsed into insults and loud noises again.

The whole situation was out of control. I felt as if, at any second, they would jump on me, wrestle the key away, and give off an evil-villain laugh. I started to back away from the table when, out of the corner of my eye, I caught movement. A backward glance made my stomach squirm as it tried to climb up my throat.

"Uh... guys?"

The yelling stopped as all six, plus Maggie and Andi, turned to where my quivering hand pointed. In the parking lot, more than a dozen people walked toward the bookstore, all of them dead. I triggered my perception and Saw tendrils of light pouring into them all. There was so much power, it was hard to believe it came from one person. And that person was on the roof of the bookstore.

"Oh, shit."

"Don't worry," said Bill, his voice low and panicked. "We warded the store. They can't come in."

But for all the energy I Saw, I didn't See the tell-tale glowing sigils or the protective light that usually accompanied an Evergreen meeting.

"Unless someone removed the wards," I said. As if to prove my point, the first of the walking dead reached the front door, pulled it open, and strolled inside like any other paying customer. He turned, saw us, and a hideous smile broke over his face.

Sometimes I hate being right.

"Oh, roll out the barrel," it sang. "We'll have a barrel of fun..."

More came through the door and stopped behind the first. Some could've passed for living, but most of them looked like they'd been dead for a while.

"Hello, Cooper," said the first one. "Give us that key you're holding onto, and you and your chums can live."

"Don't do this, Trevor," said Bill. "Please. It's not too late. We can help..."

"Shut up!" shouted the mob in unison.

"I'm not going to ask again," said the first one. "Tick tock... tick tock... Give us the key."

"Excuse me!" The manager came from across the store at a trot. "You people are disturbing the other customers. You're going to have to leave."

I should have warned her, pushed her back, blocked her way. Something. Anything. But I stood there and stared as the dead man took her by the throat and heaved her into a magazine rack. She fell with wet squishing sound that told me she was dead.

Like someone pressed "play," everyone moved at once. The dead people let out a heart-stopping, and somewhat melodramatic, howl as they rushed Evergreen. Bill threw his hands up and the air around him thickened like water. Brea mimicked his movements and surrounded herself with a similar protective bubble. The look on Kevin's face showed pure hatred and malice as he thrust both hands out. With my perception shifted, I watched as arcs of pure anger lanced out from his fingertips into a battering ram of lightning that bowled over the first few meat-puppets. Renau's eyes burned bright as she threw her will into the mob and carved a path down the middle of them. Blossom stretched her hands out wide, made a grabbing motion, and brought her hands together in a loud clap. As she did, two of the puppets slammed against each other, leaving a conjoined pile of broken bone and torn flesh. Maggie grabbed me by the collar and Andi by the wrist and dragged us toward the back of the store.

"Move it!" she screamed.

We bolted through the shop's back door into the rear parking lot, and were greeted by more grinning faces, some rotten, others in makeup fresh from the mortician's hand. I didn't bother counting the number, but it was more than what walked through the front door. It was a trap. Trevor smoked us out like ferrets, and from the looks of things, we were hosed.

Maggie acted first with a click of her Bic lighter and a shout.

"*Flambé!*" The tiny flame erupted into a hellish fury and swept from her outstretched hand into the growing crowd of the dead. As they reeled, she shoved me down the stoop. I took off at a dead run through the parking lot with Maggie and Andi close behind. And close behind them, a shambling nightmare of singed clothes and charred flesh, grinning faces and milky white eyes.

With my car in the front parking lot, and our way blocked by a few dozen dead people, we didn't have much choice but to run in the opposite direction. In the darkness, we ran for the only lights we could see, those lighting the shops of the

Monroeville Mall. As we ran from pool of light to darkness and into the next pool, the screams of the dead behind us faded in comparison to my own labored breathing and the pounding of my heart. And behind that, the little voice in my head alternated between screaming and pointing out the obvious.

Bob left. Bob walked out before the corpses arrived.

We dodged through parked cars as we ran, determined to put as much distance between us and the dead guys as possible. Somewhere between the lamppost and the giant door, I told myself that, provided I survived with all limbs intact, maybe I should give the jogging thing another try.

By some miracle, we made it to the doors of the mall and rushed through. Headlong into a nightmare.

In front of us, a sea of decayed faces and bloody mouths, torn shirts and shambling forms, packed the mall. I must've screamed as I backpedaled toward the door, because the mass of dead flesh turned in unison to face me. Corpses in front of me, corpses to the rear. We were so royally hosed.

Then I noticed that one of them, dressed in a tuxedo, held a megaphone. He lifted to his lips and shouted.

"Alright, my lifeless! Let us shamble!"

Andi let out a nervous laugh and grabbed me by the arm.

"It's the zombie-walk!" she shouted. "They're wearing makeup!"

I shifted my perception and confirmed that what I saw was more than a thousand normal, *living* people. The energies radiating from them showed no malice, no darkness, only joy. Behind us, however, the real dead people reached the door.

"Come on!" I yelled as I grabbed Maggie's arm and dove into the shambling mass.

In hindsight, I can't think of a better place to hide from walking meat-puppets than in the middle of a huge crowd of people made up to look like them.

As I ducked and dodged my way through the crowd, I chanced a glance behind me to see the horde stymied by the mass of people. When we made it to the middle of the group, I staggered left and wound up against a wall next to a normal-looking woman with brassy copper hair and an amused expression.

"Pretty cool, huh? Seventeen hundred thirty-five was the last count. My husband and kids are in there somewhere."

"Where are they headed?" I tried to wear my best non-panicked expression.

"Down to the other end," she said. "They've got a stage set up so the band can play."

"Thanks," I shouted as we merged with the crowd and made our way further into the mall. About halfway down, we fought our way to a side corridor that had an emergency exit at its end. Once out of the throng, we paused to catch our breaths.

"Holy shit," panted Maggie. "That scared the hell out of me."

"I'm just glad you didn't blast them," I chuckled. "Freaking zombies. Only in Pittsburgh."

"They're going on everywhere now," said Andi. "This one's part of a worldwide thing."

For a moment, I thought about a world where Trevor had the book, where the thousands of zombies in the mall and all over the world were real, where the dead really did walk. It made me sick to my stomach with dread.

"We have to keep that book safe," I said. "From Trevor and from Neighbor Bob."

"What're you talking about?"

I knew her tone. It was one of disbelief and anger, but also one that said she knew I was right and didn't want to admit it.

"Bob left. He's the one who took down the wards. The

meat-puppets came in after he left. Do the math."

"I can't believe that," she said. "I just can't. I mean, he's so gentle…"

"Are you kidding?" hissed Andi. "You really think it was *him*?"

I nodded. Maggie hated betrayal almost as much as I did. Trevor hurt her on a deeper level than I would have guessed, but the thought of Bob being the other turncoat hit her harder. I squeezed her hand and kissed her cheek.

"Hey," I said. "We need to get out of here and back to my car before they find us."

She nodded as we headed through the door, but the expression on her face was one of profound sadness.

Outside, the parking lot looked just like it did any other night. Cars parked in every close space, people walking to and from the mall. From my vantage point, I couldn't see any tendrils of light or auras tinted red or black. The way seemed safe, but we still hurried across the parking lot back to the bookstore. When we came to the building, I went first. No sign of Trevor, Bob, or any of the other Evergreens, but the parking lot was awash in red and blue strobe lights from a dozen or so police cars. A few confused-looking officers took statements from bookstore patrons while others stretched police tape across the broken-out front of the bookstore. I waved Maggie and Andi forward. When we cleared the side of the building, I stopped dead in my tracks, my mouth hung open, my stomach rolled at the horrible sight.

"No," I whispered. "Those sons of bitches."

Why'd they have to go and trash up my car?

After the accident that killed me, my first thought was to buy something huge and safe, like a Humvee or a tank, gas mileage be damned. But when I stumbled onto the dealership lot and saw my Chrysler, I fell in love. Sure, it had a few dents on it, but it had low miles, a sunroof for the summer and heated seats for the winter. Plus the body shape looked sporty, like an old-fashioned gangster ride, and after I drove it once, I knew it was the car I wanted. I paid cash for it, thanks to the insurance settlement. I learned how to do minor car repair and maintenance on it myself, thanks to a fanatical online community of people who drove cars like it. I loved that car.

So as I sat on the curb near the bookstore with tears in my eyes and my cellphone in my hands, Maggie leaned in close and kissed the top of my head. The insurance adjuster didn't sound happy to be bothered at home, but he said he would come as quick as he could.

The parking lot was almost empty. Inside the bookstore, a few workers stood around looking lost. Whenever they looked toward the outline on what was left of the magazine racks, there were shudders and tears. Police still hung around to get statements, check on victims, assess damage, that sort of thing. In fact, there were only four things left in the parking lot. Three cop cars, and a broken, scratched pile of scrap that used to be my beloved Chrysler.

"We can get it fixed," said Andi.

"Air bags are blown," I sniffed. "Windows are all shattered, looks like they hit it with a train. She's gone. Those bastards killed her."

A quizzical look passed from Andi to Maggie, who waved her off. Maggie knew how I felt about my car. No replacement would be the same, no amount of paint would erase her pain.

"You don't know that," said Maggie. "Wait until the insurance adjuster gets a look at it and see. You never know what'll happen. Hell, you died, and you came out alright."

I looked away from the wreck and into Maggie's eyes. She wasn't making fun of me. All I saw was the compassion and love I'd come to expect from her.

About that time, a car with a rental sticker on the back pulled into the parking lot. A tired-looking man got out with a clipboard and a pen and asked one of the cops a couple of questions. When the cop pointed at what was left of my car, the man visibly shrank. Then the cop pointed over at me. He nodded and plodded over.

"Mr. Cooper," he said. "My name's Ken Edgar. I'm the adjuster from the insurance agency. We spoke on the phone?"

I rose and stuck my hand out to shake. He didn't take it.

"Without having to go back to the office, I can see that your car is totaled. It would cost you more to fix it than it's worth, so I've been authorized to write you a check for the full blue-book value of the car. Unfortunately, I've also been going over your claims file."

I didn't like where his statement was leading. It had an

ominous tone, but I listened without saying anything.

"Last winter, you filed a claim dealing with severe vandalism that cost our company a considerable sum."

It must've cost a lot to clean demon rat shit out of the seats.

"More recently, you've filed other claims citing damage from hail, hit-and-run, more vandalism, and most recently, a falling flower pot."

"None of those were my fault," I said.

"Be that as it may," he said. "It is the opinion of the company that you pose a significant risk to our shareholders, and that we no longer wish to insure you. We will pay for a rental car to get you back to your home, I'll hand you the check for the value of the car, and that'll be it."

"Now wait a minute!" He couldn't. He just couldn't.

"Effective immediately, we're cancelling your policy."

Just when I thought the day couldn't get any worse. I stood there slack-jawed while he scribbled out a check in his ledger, handed it over, then stormed off. He also, rather pointedly, handed the rental key to Maggie, not me.

"Come on," she said. "Let's get going. We need to figure out what we're going to do next."

I stood and followed her to the rental. It was small, white, new, and Japanese. Andi took the passenger seat as I slid into the back and lay down.

"Where to?" said Andi.

"Shop," I said. "We need to see if they did any more damage there. Then we need to make sure this key goes to what I think it does."

"If it doesn't?" asked Maggie.

"We tell Bill and hope we can make Trevor believe us. I'm more worried about if it does."

Andi crossed her arms in front of her. "What then?"

"We'll burn that bridge when we get to it," I said as I closed my eyes and tried to sleep.

One bumpy ride later, we pulled up in front of Maggie's shop. The windows looked intact, as did the door. I was surprised to see no bodies lying strewn about the street. It was almost as if the nightmare scene from only yesterday never happened.

Maggie guided the car into the parking space and killed the engine, but she didn't get out right away. She sat and stared at the door that led to the stairs to her apartment like she thought they might bite her. Andi sat in the seat beside her with an identical expression. I sat for a moment before I decided I'd had enough waiting.

"Someone's gotta do it," I said as I got out and hurried toward the door. The light inside was off, the dark glass on the door almost like a mirror. I pulled my keys from my pocket and stuck them in the lock. Behind me, two doors opened and shut. I looked up to see Maggie and Andi covering me. Their eyes darted around like nervous rabbits.

When I pushed the door open, I half expected some ghastly face to come lumbering out of the darkness. But it was quiet, nothing disturbed, nothing out of place.

"Weird," I muttered. "Who cleaned up the mess?"

I took the stairs as quick and quiet as I could, which meant a deaf man could've heard me coming. But when I got to the door, it was untouched.

"Didn't they get in here too?" I asked.

"I don't think they got in the apartment," said Maggie, "but they were all over the stairs."

Probably would've served them right if they had gotten in. Bitsy the wonder cat would've torn them limb from limb.

Maggie shoved her way in front of me, keys in hand.

When she pushed the door open, all three of us held our breath.

In movies, when the plucky hero-types open the door at the top of the corridor, usually there's some kind of payoff. A monster here, a demonic voice there, something to let them know just how stupid going through that door was.

The door swung wide, and we three non-breathing statues peered into the darkness that waited inside. But where there should've been attacking hordes, raspy threats, even a yowling cat leaping at the door, there was nothing. Everything seemed, for lack of a better word, normal.

I shot a look toward Maggie and Andi, who both looked as confused as I felt.

"I don't get it," I said. "This isn't some kind of clean-it-up spell?"

"Get real," said Maggie. "If there was such a thing, I'd use it all the time. You know how much I hate housework. Let's just get what we came here for and get gone."

It took us all of fifteen minutes to pack a couple of small bags with changes of clothes, toiletries, and a few other items. Maggie and Andi chased Bitsy into her carrier while I hurried downstairs to the shop. When we left, the windows were broken, the door off its hinges. I was sure we'd come back to find the shop ransacked and defiled. But as I opened the door, the place seemed eerie in that nothing was out of place. There weren't even any smudges on the windows.

"Curiouser and curiouser."

I made my way to the back of the shop and loaded up my bag with a few herbs and candles, checked that the back door was locked and took a good look around. Something didn't seem right. Actually, *everything* seemed right, which was *wrong*. I stood in the center of the room and made a slow turn as I tried to figure out what was out of place. There had to be something, anything, that betrayed that what we saw really happened, but the shop appeared normal in every way. I closed my eyes and lowered the walls in my mind. When I opened my eyes again, the shop looked very different, blazing bright with the energies that Maggie poured into it. Everyone who ever walked through the door left a little piece of his or her energies behind, myself included. I was used to the shop glowing bright, but what I saw made me forget to breathe for a moment or two. The walls throbbed with a pulse of light, almost like...

"Stan!" called Maggie. "We're ready!"

I took a last look around the shop, still unable to wrap my brain around what I Saw, then headed out the door to the car. Maggie and Andi took the front seats, which left me in the back with a pissed-off cat in a cage and my thoughts.

"What were you doing?" Andi stared at me from the vanity mirror.

"Nothing," I said. It wasn't a lie exactly. I was really just standing in the middle of the room. But I didn't want to say anything more until I figured out what I had seen.

"Now where?" said Andi.

"My place," I said after a moment. "Before Bitsy tears her crate apart. Then we've got work to do."

I hate being a passenger. It gives me the distinct impression that I'm not in control of things, for one. It's funny because, in all honesty, one thing I've learned in my life is that no one is in any real control of anything. Sure, we wander around with the illusion of control, think we're the masters of our own destinies, fool our-selves into believing that we have some influence over everything from the weather to when we die. But the truth is, we don't. There are too many outside circumstances over which we have no control whatsoever. Most people, myself included, either can't deal with that one simple fact, or we choose to ignore it. I'm of the latter group. Being a passenger takes that self-imposed illusion away and I feel like a kid on a family trip shouting "are we there yet" with no real say-so. I'm that way about most aspects of my life. I prefer to live with the carefully-constructed illusion that, in some small way, I'm in charge of myself.

The other reason I don't like being a passenger is that I don't have to concentrate on the road, which leaves my mind free to do silly things like think. My thoughts, most of the time, aren't unpleasant, but other times, they're downright morbid. Times like now.

The road thumped underneath us as Maggie piloted the

car toward my apartment. With every thump, my brain ticked off terrible events from over the past couple of days, the biggest one being the death of my best friend. The longer we drove, the more vivid the image of Taylor's puppet-like body became as it jerked up from his couch, how it spasmed along like a marionette, the twisted unnatural smile on his face. And the eyes, those milky-white orbs that no longer seemed hard as steel, no longer could freeze fire. The more I thought about it, the more I pictured Trevor, laughing as he made my buddy dance. Taylor's words came back to me.

His eyes.

The image of Taylor shifted and flowed into the image of the dead kid in the brownstone. Murdered for pages that he stole from me. His brother's corpse, risen from its coffin. The faces of the dead bodies that rose up, the face of the phantom janitor from the hospital, the terminal patients Trevor used against us, the look of betrayal on Maggie's face. It was too much. All the tragedy from the past few days, and so many questions remained. Sure, Trevor was our scumbag, but Bob? Why? What possible motive could he have for turning on Evergreen? And just who sent me the damned pages in the first place? And more important, why?

By the time we pulled up at my apartment, I was in a pretty dark mood. Without a word, I gathered my things from the car, grabbed the cat carrier, and headed upstairs. Once there, I put my stuff down, let the cat out, and turned to face Maggie and Andi.

"You're staying here," I said to Andi. "Whatever happens, I know you'll be safe here."

"No way!" she said. "You guys need me! I can help..."

"It's not open for debate," I yelled. "This isn't a game. Taylor's dead. They don't mind killing people. And until we know

170

more about what happened with you, you're not going anywhere. Got me?"

Her eyes were wide as she sunk down onto the couch. Bitsy leapt onto her lap and glared at me.

"You keep her safe," I said.

"Where are we going?" asked Maggie.

"First thing's first," I said. "We're going to find out which locker this key fits and make sure that what's in there is worth killing for. Then we're going hunting."

"For what?"

"Bob."

We didn't speak for most of the drive to Station Square. Maggie kept her face forward, but every now and again I felt her gaze crawl across my cheek. I knew why. She was worried about me. But at the moment, I was less concerned with myself than with paying back the son of a bitch who killed Taylor. Everything else, the car, the shop, would have to wait.

"Stan," she said. Her voice was soft, soothing, like she knew she risked getting bit if she poked too hard. "Are you okay?"

"No," I said. "I'm about as far from okay as I can get."

"Andi only wanted to help."

"You think I don't know that? I'm not putting her at risk any more than I already have."

"She's an adult, you know. She can make her own decisions."

"So, what? I should've let her come? Let her face off against Trevor and Bob? You think she'd survive two seconds against them?"

"No, but..."

"I'm not going to lose her. I'm not going to lose any other friends. Not now. Not because of some moldy book."

"You let me come."

That stung. The thought of losing Maggie terrified me. My life was empty before she came into it, one long spiral of self-loathing and doubt. But then she came, shook me out, took me in. Without her, I didn't know what would've become of me. I loved her, more than I could ever express. But I also knew her abilities. If there was anyone I needed by my side, no matter what the obstacle, it was Maggie.

"That's not fair," I said. "You can fight back. You could hold your own against them. She doesn't know what she can do or how to control it yet. Besides..." I took a deep breath. Confession time. "When you're with me, I feel like I can do anything. I feel stronger. With her, I feel like an overprotective parent."

She nodded and took my hand. It was enough.

We pulled into the parking lot at Station Square, paid the attendant, and found a spot close enough that we could get out quick if the need arose. For a moment we just sat and stared at the old station, neither of us wanting to move.

"The lockers are in the back," she said. "Behind the shops."

I nodded. "Lots of people around."

"Good," she said. "Maybe that'll make it harder for him to see us if he's here."

"He's here," I said. I hadn't seen him, didn't feel him, but somehow I knew Trevor was somewhere nearby, watching.

We got out and walked, hand in hand, across the parking lot to the entrance. Before we went inside, I paused and closed my eyes, opened the doorways in my mind, lowered the walls. When I opened my eyes again, the mall glowed like neon. People passed by, their auras shades of happy pinks and blues, excited yellows and whites. This was a happy place, a place where people came to enjoy themselves. I breathed a silent prayer that, after we left, it would still be so.

Once inside, we made a quick beeline to the last shop, a tobacconist, and around the corner to the lockers. It didn't take me but one glance to see the one we wanted. It stood out from the others in that the edges of its door glowed gold and silver, and across the front were sigils that no one but me could see. To the average person, the locker looked innocuous, just like all the others. To me, it blazed like it was on fire.

I reached into my pocket and pulled out the key.

"Wouldn't it be funny if what was in there wasn't nearly as dangerous as that book?" For a moment, I almost had hope.

"Like a nuclear bomb?" giggled Maggie. Nerves always gave us both a case of the giggles.

The key fit snug in the lock, and I held my breath as I turned it. I half-expected the locker to explode, or at least be guarded by some ankle-biting beast with a million fangs and a huge appetite. But as I slowly opened the door, nothing leaped out, no bright lights, no fireworks. I peered into the cavernous hole. To me, the inside burned with sigils etched along every metal wall of the locker. At its core, however, trapped by the hidden symbols, was cold darkness in the shape of the book. The power that rolled off it was enough that it made Maggie gag and made my hands tremble. Without thinking, I reached in and grabbed it.

"Wait! Don't!"

My mind flooded with images of death, mutilation, every deviant practice known to man, and a few I didn't know we'd invented yet. Beneath it all, rage flooded into me. Damn Trevor and Bob. Damn Evergreen for their flaccid ineptitude. No one understood, not the whore Maggie or her simpering little sidekick. They all wanted it for themselves, all the power, all the knowledge. I'd show them. It was sent to me, wasn't it? By some blessed benefactor who chose *me* to keep the book because *I* was the only one worthy to have it. If they wanted it, they could try to take it! Even Maggie would fall, and she would watch while Andi satisfied my every carnal...

"Stan!" Maggie punched me hard across the jaw and sent me sprawling to the tile floor. For a moment, my only thought was to leap up and strangle her with my bare hands, but the urge faded like smoke and left me feeling bewildered.

"What the hell was that?"

"I'm sorry," she said. "You got this weird look on your face, and you started breathing fast and..."

"It's okay," I panted. "You did right. Holy shit! I've never felt anything that strong before."

"What happened?" she said. "Is it the right book?"

"I *hope* it's the right one," I said. "If something more powerful than that exists, I don't want to know. It filled me up with such... hatred. For everyone. Even you."

"So what do we do with it?"

I kicked the book with the toe of my shoe until it was all the way back in the locker, then I closed the door and locked it.

"We leave it here," I said. "Nothing is getting past those wards, and this way we know where it is."

"Is it safe?"

"Safer than leaving it in my apartment where curious fingers can get to it." Andi was a bright kid, and very sweet. But she was also insatiable in her thirst for knowledge, even if that meant looking where she ought not.

"Point taken," she said. "Now what?"

"Now," I said as I tucked the key back into my pocket. "We go find Neighbor Bob."

Finding Neighbor Bob proved to be a lot easier than I expected. In all honesty, when I said we were going to find him, I had no idea where to start. I knew next to nothing about the man, had no idea where he lived, or even if he was still in the city. For all I knew, he walked out of that bookstore and hopped an airplane to Amsterdam. But my gut told me he wouldn't leave, not with so much power at stake. That left us with the tiny problem of finding him in one of the largest cities in the United States.

It was Maggie who had the brilliant idea of trying to track him down through Bill. If anyone knew where he might be found, chances were Bill was the guy.

He answered after two rings. After the usual greetings and panicked inquiries about how we were and how we managed to get away, he got down to the meat of the matter and told us where we might find Bob. He didn't even mention the book, which earned him brownie points in my book. After he made us promise to be careful, he hung up and we were on our way to the tiny town of Pitcairn.

PAGES

Like every other major city, the majority of Pittsburgh's population doesn't live there. Sure, a few reside among the glass towers and storefronts of Pittsburgh proper, but most people live in the tiny outlying towns that, really, are just suburbs of the big 'Burgh. While some of them, like Monroeville and Moon Township prospered, there are others that didn't fare so well. Boarded-up shops and crumbling houses mark their borders, and for many, that's as good as it gets. Still, the citizens are fierce in their pride, and fight to keep the larger townships from swallowing them up. And even though they flood or the yearly snows wear away at their little scraps of land, they refuse to leave because, dammit, it's their scrap of land.

Welcome to Pitcairn.

We pulled onto the main street, the only business street in the tiny hamlet, and scanned up the side streets for Bob's address. A left up the hill and we found what we were looking for.

Pitcairn might not've had much in the way of industry or shops, but it did have an abundance of one thing: churches. For a town that teetered on despair, it was little wonder that churches dotted most every residential corner. Hope was in short supply, and people needed something upon which to cling. Of course, there were just as many bars as there were churches because, while some people found their faith in Jesus Christ, others found theirs in Jose Cuervo. When the churches shut down due to financial issues, the bars flourished. Go figure.

We pulled up in front of a gigantic Gothic structure with boards on the windows and chains on every door we saw. It was, at one time, a beautiful Catholic church. But like so many others, it closed and it sat neglected as decay and apathy claimed it.

"You sure?" I looked up at the behemoth. "*This* is the place?"

Maggie nodded. "This is where Bill said we'd find him."

"So how do you suppose we get in?"

She shrugged and walked up the front steps to one of the chained doors. For her, it would be easy to mutter one of her spells and force the lock. Very easy, in fact. Too easy.

I didn't even have time to shout before there was a loud pop, a flash of gold light, and Maggie fell back on the pavement in a sprawl. I rushed to her side as she groaned and sat up.

"Yeah," she said as she rubbed her elbow. "This is the place."

I closed my eyes, lowered my walls, and took a deep breath. When I opened them again, I Saw pretty much what I expected.

Churches, even those that are old and abandoned, are wells of energy. It's not that the Almighty takes up residence in a church. For all the different denominations and all the buildings in every town, God would have to be like a roving district manager or something, traveling from church to church to check in on his employees. But what does take up residence is the collective energies of the faithful. Every prayer, every blessing, every "Hail Mary" and "Our Father" pours energy into the foundation, the walls, the mortar. Faith is a powerful thing, enough to cure disease and stop a bullet. The trick is, not everyone's faith is strong. Most folks go to church once or twice a week, beg forgiveness for their supposed sins, and then go out to commit a few more. But the truly faithful, the ones who have no need for proof and no doubt, they're the ones who give the church its power. I don't know if what they believe in is right, but I suppose that energy could be called God. As a consequence, the older the church, the more love and faith it sees, the more powerful it is.

The church Bob hid in I guessed to be around two hundred years old, but the energy that shone from it made it seem much older. The walls crackled with it, hummed like a live wire. Where a normal threshold was like a curtain, this one was more like an electric fence.

"We're not getting in that way," I said as I helped Maggie up. "Anything broken?"

"My pride," she said as she rubbed her butt. "I should have known better."

We made our way around the outside of the building, through a broken section of fence, to the back. The windows stared down at us, questioning and judging. It gave me the creeps.

"Door," said Maggie.

In the wall of gold and silver light, there was one small door, plain and rough wood. The energies covered it, but it wasn't as bright as the ones in front.

"Isn't there a way around a threshold? I mean, what if someone just *had* to get past one? How could they?"

Maggie raised one eyebrow and thought for a moment.

"I need something from inside the church," she said.

"How're we supposed to get something from inside when we're out here?"

She whipped her head around until she saw a Dumpster toward the back of the churchyard. Without a word, she marched to it and climbed in.

"Uh... Maggie?"

From where I stood, she just disappeared into the giant metal trash bin. I couldn't even see the top of her head over its walls. But from inside, paper and refuse rustled and heavy objects banged about as she searched for...whatever it was she was searching for. After a few very pregnant moments, during which I felt the church's gaze on me like an angry nun, her head popped up.

"Got it," she said. "Gimme a hand."

I trudged over to the bin took her hands, and pulled while she struggled to climb out. Once on the ground, she held up her prize and grinned.

"I don't know if this'll work," she said. "But it's worth a try."

In her hand was a tiny burned votive with less than a quarter inch of wax left to it. The blackened wick stuck up only a fraction of an inch, and the thing just looked pathetic and useless. She walked back toward the church with purpose in her stride.

"I need my purse," she said as she sat.

When Maggie said "please" or "could you..." I always had the option of saying no. In those cases, she asked. But when she said "I need," she meant "now, and no arguments." I hurried to the rental, grabbed her purse out of the back seat, and headed back at a half-jog. When I got back through the hole in the fence, Maggie sat chanting, eyes closed, the sad-looking votive on the ground in front of her. Without opening her eyes, she stuck out her hand.

"Athame."

I dug in her purse until I found her witch's dagger, double edged with an onyx handle inlaid with a pentacle. The thing looked dangerous, but to her it was nothing more than a tool, a symbol around which she could focus. It was also very pointy.

She drew it from its sheath, opened her eyes, and picked up the candle. On its bottom, she carved intricate lines and shapes and poured her will into the crevices.

"What..?"

"It's a sigil," she said. "Key of Solomon. The candle was one of those prayer candles. It was blessed at the church. I'm hoping it, combined with the key, will let us in."

"Mind if I just stand back here while you try it?"

She shot me a scowl and pulled her lighter from her pocket. When she lit the candle, the air around her crackled. Then she walked slowly toward the glowing door. I held my breath as she reached out toward the door. To my surprise, the wall of energy split around the candle and let her through.

"Come on!" she hissed. "There's not much of this thing left!"

I hurried to her side and grabbed her hand while she guided us through the energy wall and into the hallway beyond. She stumbled and almost fell, and it took me a moment to realize why. With my perception shifted, the hallway was lit by the faith that still lived in its walls. But to Maggie, the place was pitch black.

"Let me go first," I offered. "I can see fine." For once, she didn't argue.

It didn't take us long to find Bob. The hallway led straight to the main sanctuary, where he sat at the altar. What was once a beautiful piece of architecture stood empty and eerie, the pews long since gone and every vestment of the church taken with them. All that remained were the stained glass windows and the dirty outline of a crucifix on the wall.

Bob knelt, his back to the door, facing the missing cross. His wore the dark flowing robes of a Catholic priest.

"Please come on in," he said without looking at us. "Been expecting you."

"You're a... priest?" I stammered.

"Was," he said, rising. "Long time ago. Lost my faith in the church, but I figured now was as good a time as any to give it another shot, what with Trevor and all."

"We know it was you," said Maggie. Red licked through her aura. "You're the one working with Trevor."

He sighed and slowly got to his feet, then turned to face us. In the darkness, I bet he looked menacing. A defrocked priest in an empty church before a Christ that didn't exist. But his aura told a different story. There was no darkness in the man that I could see. He shone silver and white, pure and earnest in his love and understanding.

"You think so, huh?" he said. "Why me?"

"You took down the wards when you left, didn't you?"

Power swelled in her. The energies surging in her body made the hair on my arms stand up. If she wasn't careful, her rage would kill Bob, and I wasn't sure she would care.

"I did no such thing," he said, his voice calm. "I just couldn't be there for all the bickering. That book shouldn't exist, and anyone who has it is just asking for trouble. I don't want it, but I don't want anyone else to have it either. Bill included. No one can handle that much power."

"Liar!" she shouted.

"Maggie," I said. "I think he's telling the truth."

She turned her blazing eyes on me, and for a moment, I thought she might burn me to ash where I stood.

"It had to be him," she shouted. "No one else left! There's no one else it could be!"

The anger in her surged forward in an uncontrolled wave of heat and pain. It built in her eyes before it leaped out of her body and toward Bob. The old priest never dropped his smile, and for a moment, I was certain he would hit the ground as a charred husk. But the energies of the church burst from the floor like a shield in front of him.

"You can't hurt me here, child," he said, his voice soothing as a warm bath. "This church and I, we're old friends."

It was at that moment that I realized something about the church. So much energy had been poured through the old building in the past that, somehow, it was no longer just a church. It pulsed, reacted, protected. The building had its own life force. For lack of a better term, the place was *alive*.

Maggie dropped the candle and rushed him, her hands out in front like she wanted to claw his eyes out. When she came to the barrier, it bowed, slowed her, then threw her backward onto the stone floor with a heavy thump. More silver light erupted through the floor and cocooned her until she could do nothing but lay and wiggle.

"No!" he shouted. "Don't hurt her!"

If Maggie heard him, she didn't seem to care. She thrashed until she was good and tired. The shell around her contracted with every jerk until it seemed about to crush her.

"Stop it!" I yelled. "You're killing her!"

"It's not me," said Bob. "She attacked me. I told you, this church is my friend."

Friend or not, the life of the building tightened around Maggie until her face melted from rage to panic. The light around her body flashed in spastic bursts as she fought to free herself, but every strobe flashed a little dimmer. And damned if I could think of anything that wouldn't leave me on the floor beside her, but I had to try.

I took off my watch as I ran to her side. The tattoo on my wrist glowed bright blue. It burned as I forced my arm between the pulsing bonds of energy and Maggie's failing body, like the bone of my arm was on fire. I screamed and pulled hard, opened up a little space so she could breathe. Her eyes rolled and her head fell limp. I forced more of my will through the sigil on my arm and felt the bonds retreat a little more.

Bob stood by, the sad smile never leaving his face. He made no movement toward us.

"Come on!" I shouted at him. "Don't just stand there! Get off your ass and help me!"

"I can't," he said, his voice just above a whisper. "You don't understand. It's the church that has her, not me. I can't help."

"You could at least try! She's your friend for, Christ's sake!"

He bowed his head for a moment, like he was shamed. Then his head snapped up, his eyes cold pits of blue fire. He took two steps toward us and the power radiating from his body hit me like a hot wind.

"Do *not* take the name of the Christ in vain!" He swung his arm in an arc and his righteous anger knocked me backward, away from Maggie. I scrambled to my feet and backed away.

"She's your friend!"

"She attacked me! She didn't bother to ask, only assumed I was the Judas!"

The blue and white flames around his body shifted, darkened to shades of red. I'd pissed him off plenty, and it seemed like I was going to pay for it in spades. But I wasn't scared. I was more concerned for Maggie than I was about whatever Bob wanted to do.

"Fine!" I shouted. "I'm sorry, okay? Just make it stop hurting her!"

"Why?" he said. "Why should I help a..."

"You smug bastard! Do unto others, remember? Do no harm? Doesn't your faith preach forgiveness? Tolerance? Isn't that what Evergreen is all about?"

His expression faltered and his eyes went wide, then he spun to face Maggie on the floor. Her light was weak, her breathing shallow. He knelt and slapped the floor and sent his will through the stones where it bounced like shockwaves. The bonds around Maggie broke apart and sank back into the ground. Maggie lay gasping for breath.

"I'm sorry," he said. "It's this place. I sometimes forget myself." He placed his hands on her still body and closed his eyes.

For some, faith healing is the Holy Spirit moving through their bodies to work miracles. For others, it's all a bunch of psychological mumbo-jumbo. But to see it in action, I don't know if it's the first, but it sure as hell isn't the last.

The energies from his body flowed into her, soothed her body. The power came from inside him, not on high, but it was his faith in that power that made it so powerful.

I suppose it could be called the Holy Spirit, but to me it was the same type of magick Maggie used whenever I got beat up or when one of her clients was in pain. Physical, emotional, it didn't matter. She poured love through her hands and somehow, she made things better. Bob did the same, and as the color came back into her cheeks, he smiled and sat back on his knees.

"I used to be a priest, you know," he said. "Left the church because of bigotry and hypocrisy and... I just got disgusted with the whole lot of them. I found out something when I left. All the religions? They're all right. And they're all wrong. No one has it completely right yet."

"Listen," I said. "I'm sorry to bust in on your musing, but if it wasn't you, who the hell took down those wards?"

"I don't know," he said. "But I've known the members of Evergreen for years. They're all capable. They've all got a dark side to them."

Maggie groaned and Bob helped her to sit up.

"I'm sorry," he said. "You okay?"

"What the hell did you do to me?" she said. "It was like I was being squeezed by a giant python."

"Wasn't me," he said. "It was the church. What can I say? She likes me."

She glanced to me and I nodded. Of course, I saw the whole thing whereas she didn't. To me, it was terrifying in its beauty. She didn't get the pretty light-show, however.

"If it wasn't you," she said as she rubbed her neck, "then you might not be safe here."

Bob chuckled and cocked an eyebrow.

"I think you just proved that I am," he said. "No one can get in here without my say-so."

"We did," I said. My words hung in the air as Bob's smile faded to a frown.

"Yes," he said. "About that. How?"

Maggie tossed the spent votive to him.

"Prayer candle," she said. "Found it out back in the bin. I figured it was blessed here, so it was part of the church. A little carving and it works like a key. And I'd be willing to bet that if I know how to do it, so does Trevor."

"I see," he said as he turned the candle over in his hands. "That does present a problem. Looks like I've got some cleaning out to do."

Bob jerked his head up like a dog listening to a whistle. Maggie shot me a glance, but I didn't hear anything. Whatever it was, Neighbor Bob was the only one who sensed it.

"Oh, my."

He ran to one of the windows not made of cut stained glass and stood on tip-toe to look out. Maggie and I followed him over.

"That's interesting."

"What?" said Maggie.

"See for yourself," he said, and stepped aside.

I had to jump to see out the window. The brief look I got made my heart flutter and my fingers tingle. Outside, a large crowd gathered in the street surrounding church. How many there were, I couldn't tell. But one thing I did see was the ribbon of energy that went into their eyes, split between them.

"They might have a hard time coming onto holy ground," said Bob. "Unless they were part of this parish. Then..."

As if on cue, a half dozen of them staggered forward and onto the churchyard. Maggie gasped from the window, then her features grew hard.

"Trevor..."

"You do have the book," said Bob. "Right?"

"No," I said. "But we know where it is. We could bring it here..."

"Don't you dare!" he shouted. "The power contained in it will corrupt whatever is around it. I don't want it here. As powerful as this church is, imagine what it could do with that book influencing it!"

I admit, I didn't think of that. As much raw energy coursed through the building, it would be like throwing gasoline on a burning house. The fire would burn hot and bright, and would spread.

"So what do we do?"

He turned away from us and hurried to the altar. With a quick stomp, he broke a few pieces of it off and came back to us.

"Take these," he said as he handed a piece to each of us. "I'm going to empty that bin today and hope Trevor didn't think of it. But I would like for you two to be able to get back in. Use them like you did the candle."

"Uh... thanks," I said as I turned the piece of wood over

in my hand. "That doesn't exactly help us now, though, does it? How in the He... heck are we going to get out of here?"

"Fight our way out?" suggested Maggie.

"Leave that to me," said Bob. "There's another entrance under the building. One that no one knows about. It leads to the house across the street."

"Why would a church need..."

"Impious priests," he chuckled. "That house used to be a brothel."

Despite our situation, and how juvenile I felt, I couldn't stifle a snort of my own.

"What about the people who live there now?" Leave it to Maggie to be the pragmatist in the face of a near-perfect half-assed plan.

"It comes up in their basement," said Bob. "I don't think they know about it. I'll have to close it off once you're through."

"Good enough for me," I said. "Where?"

Bob pointed to the altar. I hurried up the steps and found the opening. The worn spots on the old carpet told that the door was right below the pulpit, where the priest stood to deliver the Sunday lesson.

"What about you?" shouted Maggie. "Are you coming?"

"I can't leave my church," said Bob. "She needs me as much as I need her. Hurry now. They're trying to get in."

Who was I to argue? I lifted the heavy door and climbed down the ladder. The floor stank of mildew and stagnant water, and there was no light to speak of. Even with my walls down, it was dim.

I have a fear of enclosed spaces, especially tunnels. Something about nearly getting torn apart by human rats while climbing around in the Pittsburgh storm drains makes me really nervous about tunnels. The darkness is bad enough, but it's the smell that really freaks me out. One whiff of that odor makes my heart pound, my stomach convulse like I've drunk rotten milk, and gives me the urge to stop breathing. I wouldn't call it an irrational fear. To me, it's perfectly rational. To me, dark tunnel equals monsters, which equals death.

Still, it was better than what was upstairs waiting for us. Maggie scooted around in front of me and raised her hand.

"*Candere*," she whispered. The ring on her hand glowed softly in the darkness and lit the tunnel for a few feet. It wasn't perfect, and it didn't at all diminish my sense of impending doom, but it would have to do. I closed the trap door behind me and followed the light, and prayed we wouldn't have to be underground for long.

In the darkness, I couldn't tell how far we'd gone. A few feet, a mile, it all seemed relative, but I kept my eyes locked on Maggie's glowing blue ring. The only sounds were our own breathing, our shuffling footsteps, and the constant drip of water from the outside. Armageddon could've been going on topside, we wouldn't have known.

The tunnel ended at a solid wall. Maggie motioned me forward and, together, we gave it a hard shove. Bricks ground against each other and the wall moved. Light peeked in around the edges of the door, followed by the sounds of things crashing to a concrete floor. Lots of things. So much for being quiet.

We hurried through the doorway and found ourselves, just like Bob said, in a blessedly normal-looking basement. A washer and dryer, piles of don't-know-where-it-goes, and a bunch of musical equipment dominated the room. In one corner, an electric guitar stood in front of a speaker set so large it was guaranteed to give anyone within twenty yards hearing damage. In front of the hidden door was a tipped-over plastic container, its contents scattered across the floor. I grunted and pushed the door shut as the sound of running footsteps came down the stairs.

"Who the fuck is down there?" shouted the footsteps' owner.

"Sorry!" I shouted. "Didn't mean to... uh... we come in peace?"

The kid appeared from around the stairwell, a good foot taller than me with long hair and a linebacker build. He brandished a hockey stick at us.

"Don't make me fuck you up!" he shouted.

"Sorry!" I said again. "We didn't... this is a mistake..."

"You're fuckin'-a right it is!" he said.

"We don't have time for this," said Maggie, exasperated. She set her jaw and stepped up to the kid. "Get out of our way."

He towered over her, was way more physically imposing than her. But when she spoke, the look on his face went from anger to fright. He clutched his hockey stick like a teddy bear and backed away from the outside door. He never took his eyes off her as she passed.

"Do yourself a favor," I said. "Stay inside. Don't go out there. There's weird shit going on."

He nodded and I followed Maggie out to the yard. She stood just behind the fence peering across the street. Our car was still there, undamaged. It was also surrounded by walking corpses.

I glanced behind us to find the kid leaning out the door, hockey stick still in hand, his terrified eyes locked on Maggie.

"Get back inside!" I hissed. "What'd you do to him?"

"Nothing," she smiled. "Not everything requires magick. Sometimes you can get by on attitude alone."

"Got enough to get us into our car and away?"

"No," she said. "What we need is a diversion."

I thought for a moment.

"Kid!" I whispered. "Hey, kid!"

The kid's head bobbed through the door.

"That your guitar rig in there?" He nodded. "What's your name, kid?"

"Zack," he stammered.

"You any good?" He nodded again. "Okay, Zack. Play me something. Something loud and long."

"But... my mom says..."

"Come on," I said. "Is she even home? Crank it up to eleven. Let it rip for once."

He nodded and shuffled back inside.

"What the hell are you doing?" Maggie eyeballed me suspiciously.

"One reversed diversion," I said. "Coming up."

I heard an electric buzz, followed by an open chord. The volume swelled and the kid launched into the loudest, most impressive solo from "Freebird" I'd ever heard. The corpses all turned and stared our way.

"Don't move," I said. Maggie froze under their stare. I think she even held her breath. After a few tense moments, They turned back toward the church and resumed trying to get in.

"So what was that?" she said.

"Now they won't care about noise coming from over here," I smiled. "His sound'll mask us sneaking up, and they'll be none the wiser till it's too late."

I turned and went back to the door. The sound coming out from that basement was physically punishing. Every note pinged off my skin like musical pellets. When Zack saw me, he stopped playing.

"Awesome!" I yelled. "Keep it up!"

He grinned and nodded and fired off a machine-gun hail of notes that I was sure would leave me brain damaged. But I didn't care, so long as it kept the dead guys across the street from looking this way. I took Maggie's hand and opened the gate. I wish I could say it squeaked open, or closed with a clang, but just those few moments in close proximity of Zach's playing left my ears ringing and I wouldn't have heard an elephant if it snuck up behind me and trumpeted.

We hurried across the street toward the car. So far, so good. The church's glow pulsed as it repelled every attempt to get inside. We got within a couple of feet of the car when one of the attackers turned and saw us. In unison, the rest turned and advanced. Maggie fumbled with the keys.

"You *locked* it?"

"Bad neighborhood," she shouted as she struggled to fit the key in the lock. I put my back to the door, tucked my watch in my pocket and got ready for the fight. The shield on my arm might hold them off long enough to let Maggie get in the car. I just hoped she didn't drive off without me.

As the first leaned in, the smell of rot filled my nostrils. In the winter, the cold might help to keep the stench down, but with the summertime heat hitting us, these things were putrid. I swung my arm and connected with the side of his head. Without the shield tattoo, he might've shrugged it off, but with Maggie's magickal sigil on my arm, there was a pop and a burst of blue light and the dead man fell in a crumpled heap, the light tendrils snapped back, and for a moment, I thought I might get away easy.

Silly me.

In the time it took me to knock one flat, four more reached me, with even more close on their heels. Cold fingers grabbed my wrists, my neck, my legs, pushed me against the car. One of them leaned in close, his breath the smell of rotten milk and low tide.

"The book," it said. "Give us the book."

I kicked and flailed, but the harder I fought, the tighter the dead fingers held me against the car. I heard buzzing and the solid mass at my back slid away. Then a hand snaked into the back of my pants and pulled.

"Dammit, get in here!"

With my butt, half my legs, and half of my back sticking through the window, Maggie gunned the engine and hit the gas. My sudden movement caught the dead guys off guard and they lost their balance. I flailed and kicked until I was free of the last of them, then wriggled my way into the passenger seat of the car as it picked up speed, my dignity injured but otherwise intact. By grabbing my pants, Maggie saved my ass. Again.

We sped down the hill to the main street and out of Pitcairn with the howls of the walking dead in our ears and the stench of rancid breath in my nostrils.

PAGES

There is a moment, one every adrenaline junkie experiences, where the rush of impending death brings a weird sense of euphoria, a rush beyond anything that can be explained to someone who hasn't experienced it. It usually manifests as uncontrollable, inappropriate giggles.

So as we roared down the road in the now scratched and dented rental, I didn't think much of it when Maggie started with a little twitter. But the nervous laugh turned into a roaring cackle that shifted into uncontrollable screaming. She pulled off the road, across two lanes, and straddled three parking spaces at a Dairy Queen. Her knuckles on the steering wheel were bone white, her eyes wide. As her face contorted I couldn't ignore the notion that I was watching her have a nervous breakdown.

In all honesty, I felt like having one myself.

Dead people, their spirits, I could handle. But the bodies themselves, walking around and attacking, was a little too much for any sane person to hope to bear. The horror movies had it wrong. People didn't often become heroes in the face of weirdness and adversity. Most people cracked, their minds unable to reconcile what should be and what was. Maggie was the strongest person I knew, saved my ass too often for me to count, and was the one person I could count on in a pinch. If she lost it, what hope did I have?

"Hey," I said. "Thanks for pulling me in back there."

Lame, but it was all I could think to say. I touched her rigid hand and gave it a gentle squeeze. She breathed hard and turned her tear-stained face toward me.

"They were dead," she said. "All of them."

"I know."

"How? How is he doing it?"

I took a deep breath and told her what I saw, the tendrils of energy that poured into their eyes.

"They look like individuals, but they're all him. It's his will."

She shook her head.

"They can't be at rest," she said. "Not with their bodies walking around like that." Fresh tears followed the streams down her face. "It's inhuman."

Taylor said as much. He couldn't hold on, his soul sucked away until there was nothing left. For every person killed, every body resurrected, was there then a soul that just blinked out of existence? Did they feel pain? What was it like, death for the dead? I shivered with fear and rage. It didn't matter anymore what happened to me, what happened to Maggie or to anyone else. Taylor didn't matter, and neither did Justin Owens. In my mind's eye, I imagined what the world would be like if Trevor got hold of the book, if its powers warped him even more than he already was. There wouldn't be any need for religion because, when a person died, there'd be no debate. Blink, gone, nothing. And his corpse would still walk around to do Trevor's bidding.

"We can't let him win," I said softly. "If he gets that book, the worst parts of every horror movie will come true. And no one will be able to stop him."

She nodded.

"I need you," I said. "I need you strong and sane. I don't think I can do this by myself."

"I'm here," she said. "I need you too, you know."

By the time we got back to my apartment, my brain was a cyclone of details, all of them geared toward trapping Trevor and whoever his partner was. The more I thought about it, the more convinced I was that he couldn't pull off such heavy mojo on his own. Maggie wouldn't believe it at first, but my argument won out in the end. First time for everything.

Taylor's words came back to me: *Don't look him in the eyes.* The dead people had tethers of energy through their eyes back to the source, who always stayed just out of sight. It made sense that Trevor imposed his will through his eyes and into theirs.

Of course, knowing how he did it didn't give us a single clue as to how to stop him, but the thoughts did come. Everything from blinding to blindfolding him ran through scenarios in my head, and they all came up short. In every case, the questions came as to how we would first find the little bastard and then how we would get close enough to execute any sort of plan.

I opened my apartment door to find Andi sitting cross-legged on the floor surrounded by candles. Naked.

"What is *with* you people?" I shouted as I covered my eyes.

To be clear, I have nothing against a naked nineteen-year-old girl in my apartment. In fact, girls who are shaped like Andi are the stuff of which wet dreams are made. But I'm a one-woman guy for starters, and, to me, Andi's more like a kid sister or an adopted child. Seeing her naked just feels... ew.

"I'm meditating." She sounded irritated that we inter-rupted her. "I got bored."

"*This* is what boredom does to you?"

"You guys just left me here. What'd you expect? I was just doing what Maggie taught me."

I shot Maggie my best incredulous look.

"The body is nothing to be ashamed of," she shrugged. "Going skyclad is a good way to connect with the Goddess and God."

"Fine," I said. "Could you give a little warning next time? Please? At least hang a sock on the doorknob, for crying out loud..."

"Whatever," she said as she got up and headed into my bedroom. She slammed the door as I hurried to the refrigerator. Just my luck. No beer.

When she came back out, she seemed sullen, but at least she was dressed. She sat on a stool with Bitsy in her lap as we filled her in on the day's events, about Neighbor Bob and the church, and about the book in the locker. I left out the part where we got away with my butt in a car window and my arms and legs wriggling out of it like fish.

"So what do we do?" asked Andi.

"*We* don't do anything," I said. "*You* are staying put where it's safe."

Andi's expression darkened and the kitchen lights dimmed a bit. It only took me a second to figure out that I'd pissed her off but good. She shot up from the stool with Bitsy under her arm and stormed into the main living area, snatched up the remote control, and plopped down on the couch. The television buzzed to life and she turned the volume up.

"You hurt her feelings," said Maggie.

"I don't care," I replied. "She can be mad all she wants. I don't want her out there where she can get hurt."

"She can make her own decisions, you know."

"She's just a kid."

"She's nineteen. And she wants to help."

"Uh... guys?"

We both turned our attentions to Andi, who sat staring at the television.

"You'd better come see this."

The WBGN banner at the bottom of the screen said that the images were live. A frightened-looking man held a microphone on the corner of Wood Street and First Avenue. In the background, I spotted my apartment building. Around him, a crowd made up of people who looked either angry or tearful gathered. Officers Appel and Menold flanked him to keep the crowd back.

"...but the reports just keep coming in. The police are overwhelmed with reports of missing invalids and violence that are reportedly perpetrated by recently dead relatives. Police say that, while they would normally write off such reports as a hoax, the city coroner has gone on record as saying that seven corpses have disappeared in the last two hours."

"Turn it off," I said. My mouth went dry as I stared at the image.

"In every case," continued the newsman, "cryptic messages about a book have been left at the scenes of the attacks. One such message included the name of a person. While the police declined comment on that person's name, we have learned that the building behind me is his residence. His involvement, whether as an accomplice or a potential target, is unknown at this time."

"Son of a bitch." I ran to the window and looked down. More than a hundred angry faces stared up at my building. I didn't need to see their auras to know what they were thinking.

They were afraid, angry, ready to lash out at any potential focal point. The reporter would, most likely, get penalized for turning the public on me like that, but it didn't matter. The damage was done. If I lived through this fiasco, I was going to sue the pants off the television station. *If* I lived through it.

"They look really pissed," said Andi. I turned to find her still captured by the television.

"You get a better view from here," I said. "They're right outside."

"We can't stay here," said Maggie, her voice tight with fear.

She was right. History was full of examples of what happened when Mob Mentality took over. None of them were pleasant. If we tried to stay, chances were the building would be attacked. If we left, we would be attacked. Of the two, I knew there was only one choice. If we stayed, everyone else in the building would be put in the line of fire. I couldn't have that on my conscience, not again.

"Get down to the car," I said. "We're going. Now."

"Good thing it's a rental," said Maggie.

It took us less than five minutes to scoop up our things, and most of it was spent chasing Bitsy back into her carrier. Every door we passed on the way to the elevator made the same sound, the dull clicks of deadbolts being turned. As the elevator door opened, I half-expected it to be full of angry villagers, complete with torches and pitchforks. But our luck held and it was empty.

Once we got to the bottom floor, we all stopped. We needed a plan.

"Isn't there some kind of cloak or something that you two can use to make yourselves invisible?"

Andi rolled her eyes. "Look who's been reading Harry Potter," she said.

"No," said Maggie. "The best way is just to not attract attention."

"Okay," I said after a moment. "We go out one at a time, real slow and easy. Maggie, you go first so you can get the car started. Andi, you next and take Bitsy. Both of you in the front seats. I'll go last."

"Why would you want to do that?" Andi's eyes were wide and disbelieving.

"Because if we all go out together, they'll spot us for sure. When it comes to my turn, have the door open because I'm going to be running like hell."

Maggie locked eyes with me and nodded. Then she took a deep breath, let it out in a forceful blow, and walked out the side door toward the rental.

It was painful to watch. Every step seemed to take minutes, and with every footfall, I was certain someone would notice her. But no one did. She made it to the car, got in, and started it up. I breathed a little easier.

"Your turn, kid," I said. "Walk slow. You're not running for your life, you're going to the grocery store. Got me?"

Andi's hands shook with fear, her eyes wide. For all her bravado and attitude, she looked like a scared bunny, not a burgeoning witch. I couldn't blame her. I was pretty sure I was doing a fair impression of a Parkinson's patient myself. I stepped back away from the door as she cleared her throat, cleared her expression, a trick I wished I could do, and walked to the car, cool as a cucumber. One or two people noticed her leave, but didn't raise a fuss. Then it was my turn.

"You can do this," I whispered. "Walk in the park."

I put my hand on the door and my stomach dropped. Too late to back out, I hitched up my drawers and walked through the door, head down. The first five or six steps went fine, considering the angry mob that wanted my head on a platter. Lots of shouts, angry and fearful, found their way to me. I did my best to ignore them. But then one shout blew my cool.

"That's him!"

I didn't know who said it, or even care. In the space of two heartbeats, I shifted into high gear and ran as fast as my out-of-shape body would let me. The roar of righteous indignation that came from the crowd was more like a bloodthirsty howl as it surged in my direction. My heart already pounded a punk-rock rhythm, but with the added threat of the lynch mob, it picked up speed to double-time. The car sat ahead, the back door open, and I puffed and wheezed and dove through the door before anyone got to me. A squeal of tires and we were out of the parking lot.

"Where are we going?" shouted Maggie.

I tried to answer, but I couldn't stop panting long enough for the words to come out.

"Shop," I croaked. "Fast."

"The shop," she cried as the car careened around a corner. "Are you crazy? They'll find us there for sure!"

"Shop!" I rasped. "Trust me!" My throat felt like sandpaper and my chest felt like it was going to explode. I lay there in the back seat, wheezing like my lungs had a slow leak, while Bitsy yowled in my ear. Andi shook with silent tears, but said nothing during the ride, and Maggie had a cold look of determination that only accompanied anger. I closed my eyes and tried to will my heart to slow down.

By the time we arrived at the shop, the sun was almost down. My chest still hurt and my head felt like it might split with pressure, but at least I could talk again. Maggie pulled the rental into the parking spot behind the shop, threw the car in park, and turned to stare at me.

"Why are we here?" she said. "They already trashed the place once. We know it's not safe."

"Maybe," I said. "But it's the only place I can think of. Unless you know of somewhere else where no one will get hurt."

"We could just keep driving," she said. Andi nodded without saying a word.

"I don't think we have to," I said as I slid over and opened the car door. "Andi, I need you."

The look that passed between them was strange, one part fear, one part confusion. To her credit, she got out of the car and followed me to the back door.

"I need you to trust me and open the door," I said. "Maggie! Come here. You need to see this."

She got out and walked slowly over to us, the same look of mistrust on her face. I turned back to Andi.

"Listen carefully," I said. "When you open the door, walk in and say 'I'm home.'"

She gave Maggie one more backward worried glance, then unlocked the door and walked in.

"I'm home?" Her voice trembled when she said it, and it didn't come out as more than a whisper, but when she spoke, the lights came on and warmth flooded the room.

"What in the Goddess' name..?"

What I saw before, the pulse of energy, the rhythmic thrum of power wasn't just *like* a heartbeat. For all intents and purposes, it *was* a heartbeat. Like the living energy of the church, the responsive life force that gave the place its power, this building now was, for lack of a better word, alive.

I walked into the shop behind her, followed by Maggie, who stood goggle-eyed at the room as if she'd never seen it before.

"I knew it," I said.

"What just happened?" Andi stood and stared at the walls.

"Do you remember that massive energy burst you let off that almost killed you?"

She nodded.

"When you did that, the energy had to go somewhere, right? You poured that much of your life and soul into that one attack. All that residual energy, combined with all the love and work and passion already put into this place and you kind of brought it to... life. I think."

They both stared at me. From the looks on their faces, I guessed they were trying to figure out if my hamster wheel finally came off the spindle.

"That's not possible," breathed Andi. "Is it?"

"The church," said Maggie. "It was... but this can't be... it's..."

"Think about it," I said. "The church got so much energy and living force that it developed into something more than bricks and mortar, right? You've loved this building for how long? Put all your heart and soul into it? All it needed was a push. Andi gave it to us."

"I don't believe you," she said.

"Andi, please ask the shop to do something. Something simple."

She looked around as if she were afraid the walls might bite her.

"It's a little warm in here," she said.

A cool breeze blew from the front of the shop and the temperature dropped by a few degrees. Andi smiled a little.

"Thanks," she said. "That's perfect."

A strange sensation passed through my body, not temperature or electricity, but a feeling of joy.

"What do you feel?"

"Welcome," said Maggie. "Happiness."

"Me too," said Andi. "I can feel it. It wants to please us."

"Not it." Maggie's eyes went wide and a hint of a smile crossed her lips. "She. I can't believe it. I'm a mother to a city block."

"Not quite," I said. "We all put ourselves into this building, but Andi gave it the spark. If anyone, Andi's the mother."

Andi's smile melted as her jaw hung open.

"We're more like the favorite aunt and uncle."

I let the comment hang while I ran back out to the car and retrieved Bitsy. She paced in her carrier, but didn't hiss or spit as I came through the back door and pulled it closed. Once inside, I set the carrier on the ground and opened the door. The cat took a few tentative steps, then started purring loudly and bounded into the main room. I followed and found Maggie and Andi standing and looking around.

"Wow," said Maggie. "Who cleaned up in here?"

"*She* did," said Andi.

Bitsy jumped up onto one of the front window ledges and rubbed her face against the brick, then turned in a circle and went to sleep.

"She can feel it too," I said. "I wonder how far it goes?"

"Like, maybe, my apartment?" Maggie looked toward the ceiling. "Wow."

"Guys," said Andi. "I don't mean to... I mean this is... but what are we going to do? Will we be safe here?"

At her question, the windows darkened to opaque.

"Somehow," I said. "I think we will be. At least for now."

PAGES

Life can be funny sometimes. I don't mean funny-ha-ha, but funny-weird. A man wakes up one morning and discovers everything he's ever believed about life, death, and the world around him is wrong. His life gets turned on its ear, and no matter how hard he tries, he can't right the wagon. From that point on, for better or worse, that wagon still runs, but on its side.

When I went to check my mail a couple of days ago, I had no idea what was in there. I was secure in my abnormal little life with a few trusted friends, dead people hanging around, and while I can't say I liked it that way, I was at least used to it. Just enough excitement to keep the blood pumping, just enough to keep me on my toes. But now one of my best friends, my only friends, was dead and my home was alive. How's that for a boot to the head? I didn't know the implications of the latter, but the former filled me with rage and guilt. Justin Owens came looking for guidance and I laughed. Taylor tried to protect me and it cost him his life. Now it seemed like the whole of Pittsburgh was looking for someone to blame for all the weirdness on the streets, and my name was at the top of the list of scapegoats. Part of me felt like, somehow, I deserved it. The more rational side of my brain fumed and boiled because it knew who was really to blame, and the only way to get myself out of this mess was to catch him.

The only problem was I didn't have any idea how to accomplish that little feat.

In the past, Evergreen was our lifeline. When things got too hairy, when the metaphysical shit hit the fan, Evergreen swooped in to save the day. But now, with the group splintered and a traitor amongst them, we couldn't call on them. Even Bill, for all his strength and wisdom, was out of the question.

If Taylor were still around, he would come up with a plan. We could always rely on him for heavy artillery. A blunt instrument maybe, but in a pinch there was no one else I wanted by my side besides Maggie. But he was gone. Not just dead, but really gone.

"Hey." Maggie knocked on the open door. I sat in the bedroom at the edge of our bed. My hands wouldn't stop shaking, no matter how hard I told them not to. My tear-slicked face felt hot, and for the life of me, I couldn't figure out what I was supposed to do.

"You okay?"

I nodded.

"I think the shop reaches up here too." I gestured to a cup of hot tea on the nightstand. "She's been trying to comfort me."

"That could be awkward," she said.

I smiled despite myself. Maggie sat down on the bed and put her arm around me. She felt warm, safe, everything I wanted to be, but wasn't.

"Why me?" I couldn't look at her. "Why'd they send that damned thing to me? They could've sent it anywhere else in the world, left it lost or buried in a closet, even thrown it into the ocean for all I care. But no, they had to send it to me, and because they did, Taylor's... Why? What's so damned special about me anyway?"

There was a long pause, the kind that usually meant she was looking for the right thing to say.

"I don't know," she said. "But there must've been a reason. Right now..."

"Right now we have to figure out what to do about Trevor," I said. "I don't know how we could cut off his power. There are too many old and sick people for him to draw on. Whatever he's pulled out of those pages made him plenty strong. I don't know how to fight him."

"Maybe we don't fight him." We both looked up to find Andi in the doorway. "Maybe we turn him against himself."

In the grand scheme of things, I pretty much stay clueless. Sure, I delude myself into thinking I'm a rational and intelligent guy, but when it gets right down to the nuts and bolts, I can be pretty thick. Computers, for example, befuddle me. I know that a few keystrokes and mouse clicks brings up news, blogs and porn, but I have no idea how they really work. I also can't figure out the "sport" of curling. And I've resigned myself to the certainty that I'll never figure out the intricacies of the female mind. That goes double for *teenaged* females.

When Andi's plan began with "we lure him to a mall," I snorted and dismissed it. There were so many drawbacks to her plan that I almost didn't know where to begin.

"First off, there are too many innocent bystanders that will get hurt. Second, what're you planning to do? Distract him with a shoe sale? Third..."

"Will you let me finish?" she huffed.

"He's right," said Maggie. "We just can't put that many innocents in danger. Besides, how would we..?"

"Let me finish!"

We both stared and, almost in unison, crossed our arms and gave our best "impress-me" looks.

"Thank you! We need to turn his own power against him, right? So how is he projecting his will into the dead bodies?"

"Through the eyes," I said. "He opens their eyes, looks into them, and a piece of him goes into the body."

"Right, so how can we direct that against him?"

"Blindfold him?" Maggie shrugged. "Poke his eyes out?"

"Maybe we could just hold up a big mirror," I snorted.

It was a joke. I should learn to keep my mouth shut.

"That's the idea!" she said. "We get him into one of those 360-degree mirrors in one of the department store changing rooms and he won't be able to look anywhere! If he sees his own eyes..."

"What," I said. "He'll possess himself?"

"Think of it as a feedback loop," she said. "Ever point a video camera at its own monitor? You get that weird psychedelic hyperspace looking picture. I'm thinking he'd get something like that."

"That's ridiculous."

"Actually," said Maggie, "She might be right. It's worth a try."

"Time out. Did you miss the whole 'going-to-the-mall' thing? He's not just going to let us lead him into the changing room. And, oh yeah, there's the other problem with all the dead people he's got walking around in front of him. Even if we could get him there, which I doubt, what makes you think he won't send his ghouls to do his dirty work for him?"

"Have you got any better ideas?" shouted Andi.

"No," I said. "But just because I don't doesn't mean we should go with a really bad one!"

"This isn't helping!" Maggie slapped the table. The sound echoed, and a low rumble followed it. The tiny apartment shook, not hard, but enough that we would notice.

"I don't think She likes it when we argue," said Andi.

I looked from wall to wall, ceiling to floor, like I expected the sentient shop to somehow make an angry face.

"Sorry," I said. "But even if you're right, I don't know how we would get him there to start with, and I still think getting him inside a mall is a bad idea. Too much can go wrong."

"Then you come up with a plan," she said.

Thoughts bubbled and churned in my head. I didn't come up with a plan, so much as I did a vague idea.

We couldn't rely on traditional methods to gather people. Trevor might be listening in on our phone calls for all we knew, but we still needed to get the word out to a few trusted people. In the past, that number would've been limited to the three of us, Taylor, and Evergreen. But those numbers were seriously depleted. As it stood, there were only five people I trusted, and the rest of the population of Pittsburgh that I didn't.

We sat in the back room of the magic shop, each of us throwing ideas at the others. No matter what the plan, how stupid or childishly simple, it all boiled down to one simple fact: The three of us weren't going to get it done. We couldn't. We didn't have the resources, and no matter how much power Maggie and Andi had, none of us had confidence that it would stand up against Trevor and the pages. Not to mention the mysterious "other."

Once we figured out there was no way around asking for help, the question came of who we trusted. Sure, we knew a few good people, people who would gladly help out in any situation. But the problem, one we couldn't justify in our hearts and minds, was that anyone who signed on to help us ran the risk of winding up dead. Or worse. The ones who didn't know much about our world would never recover, if they survived. The ones who knew would be damned silly to sign on for what was likely a suicide run against the deepest darkest.

"There are only two people we can call," I said, though I was loath to put them in harm's way.

"We can't," said Maggie. But she knew I was right. Bill and Brea were the only two people in Pittsburgh with power enough to possibly help, and they were already in the sewer up to their eyeballs. It took a couple of minutes to convince her, but after some gentle persuasion, she nodded and let out a defeated sigh.

"Okay," said Andi. "We call them. How?"

"I'll go," I said. "I can..."

"Like hell you will," growled Maggie. "Trevor's looking for you. And besides, you don't even know where they live."

"Do you?"

She shook her head.

"I don't know where any of them live. I only know phone numbers."

"So we call them," said Andi.

"No," I said. "Too dangerous."

It was ridiculous. Call them and we run the risk of Trevor intercepting the call. Call to arrange a meeting, more innocents get put in the way. But if we didn't, we were as good as dead. The puzzle of how to contact Bill and Brea rolled around in my head, without solutions, until my brain hurt.

"There has to be some other way."

"Maybe there is," said Andi. I lifted my head to see her eyes darting around the room, just above floor level. The expression on her face told me that wheels were turning in her head. "The scats."

Scats are weird little metaphysical creatures. They exist only in the periphery, just out the range of normal vision. Normal folks see them all the time, darting around rooms like little shadows, but when they stop and try to get a good look, they're gone. There are lots of theories as to what they really are, but no one really knows. All we know is that they're created by the living energy that surrounds things, like a living byproduct. To my knowledge, no one's ever caught one, and no one's ever really figured out what they do. They just kind of... are.

"What about them?" said Maggie without looking up. Her voice sounded weary, exasperated. She needed sleep. We all did.

"They're energy, right?"

"As far as we know," I said. "Why?"

"Ever watched them move?"

The question struck me as odd. Why would I? They didn't really do anything, didn't bother anyone. They just kind of ran around and did whatever it was they did.

"Look," she said, her eyes darting around.

I closed my eyes and concentrated until the doors in my mind opened and the walls lowered. When I opened them again, the shop pulsed with its golden heartbeat. Scats ran from side to side, up one wall and down another.

"Look," she said again. I was about to ask what she meant when I noticed what she was talking about.

There was a pattern to their movement. They didn't just scamper in random paths. They moved in arcs, waves. Some moved in unison with others. It was almost as if they moved with purpose, an intelligence to their motions.

"How did you..?" People didn't see them, at least, not from straight on. But Andi did.

"I don't know," she said after a moment. "I just do. But that's not important. Look, it's like they communicate, right?"

"Yeah. So?"

"So maybe we can use them. Y'know, like to relay messages or something."

"Excuse me!" Maggie stood by the table with her hands on her hips. "What the hell are you two talking about?"

"Scats," said Andi. "We might be able to use them to get a message to Bill."

"First off, how the hell can you see them?" Maggie crossed her arms across her chest. "Second, what makes you think we can get them to do what we want? It's not like they talk! You can't catch them!"

"Have you tried?" It sounded stupid and childish, but the more I watched them, the more convinced I was that there might be something worth pursuing here. Besides, we were fresh out of ideas.

"Fine," said Maggie. "What do you want to do?"

It took us a few minutes to gather together a few supplies from Maggie's workroom. Five candles, a piece of chalk, and her athame. She drew a tight circle on the floor in the center of the room, then set the candles at points around it. When she was done, she stepped back.

"Well?" she said to Andi. "It's your theory. I don't know what you want to do."

Andi glanced at me and nodded.

"You want to stay and watch this?" she asked.

I rolled my eyes. I knew what she was going to do, but I was too curious to let modesty get the best of me. I nodded.

"Just get on with it," I said.

Andi kicked her shoes off and shed her clothing. When she was naked, she shivered.

"A little warmer, please," she said. The shop complied with a warm breeze. "Thank you."

Andi stepped into the center of the circle and sat on the floor, cross-legged.

The room darkened as the windows went opaque. Andi lit each candle in succession, her lips moving in silent prayer. Her energies glowed from her core and built with each candle lit until it pulsed in time with the shop's heartbeat, the candles flickering wicks. With the last candle lit, she settled back, rested her arms on her knees, and closed her eyes.

Most other times, when a person builds power, her energies pulse and grow until it reaches what I like to call "critical mass," when it seems that they will leap out of the person, or maybe that she might explode.

Andi's energies built, but settled into a steady rhythm. I turned my attention from her to the rest of the room, and was startled by what I saw. The scats stopped moving. For as long as I knew about them, I'd never seen scats do anything but zip around rooms. But now, they were still, as if they were paying attention to Andi, listening to the silent hum of her energies.

"I'll be damned," I whispered.

"There're so many of them," echoed Maggie. I turned to find her slack-jawed and goggle-eyed at the sea of tiny motes that lined the room. With my perception shifted, I Saw them all the time, but for Maggie, they were like they appeared to everyone else: little darting shadows. But now that they were still, their shapes were plain, their numbers evident. I closed my eyes and forced my perception to shift back to the normal world. When I opened them again, the scats were still there, little blobs of shadow, now held rapt by the naked girl seated on the floor.

A ripple went through them toward Andi, and her body tensed. Maggie made to move toward her, but I stopped her. Another perception shift and I saw Andi's energies pouring off her like water from a fountain, washing over the strange little creatures. Stranger still was the wave passed over them, then returned to her, flowed into her body, and back again.

"I... can hear them," she said, her voice quiet. "And they can hear me." She blew out a forceful breath, and another wave of energy flowed out of her and into them. In a space of time the width of an eyelash, all the scats moved as one and scattered in every direction. Andi pulled her energies back and opened her eyes, grinning.

"That was cool," she said as she looked from Maggie's eyes to mine.

She put out the candles, saluted each of the deities or watchtowers, the stood and picked her clothes up from where she dropped them. As curious as I was, I couldn't bring myself to stand there and stare as she got dressed, so I scooped up the candles and went to put them back in the workshop. By the time I got back, the girls were seated at the counter. Andi flapped her hands as she explained what just happened. Maggie stared, hung off every word.

"They're not just energy," said the girl. "They're intelligent! They're connected to everything, everywhere!"

"So," I said as I took a seat on the other side of the counter. "What? They talk?"

They both turned and stared at me with identical looks that questioned my I.Q. It seemed like a perfectly reasonable question, up until that moment.

"No," said Andi. "But they communicate with feelings. Seriously, when I was jacked into them, I could sense every inch of this building."

"So?" said Maggie. "You told them to go find Bill and Brea?"

"I think so," she said.

"How do we know if it worked?"

"We wait," I said. "And hope."

An hour passed, during which Andi tried to explain to Maggie and me how she managed to communicate with the scats. She tried not to show it, but I'm sure Maggie was a little jealous that she'd never even heard of such a thing before, much less tried it herself. It made sense to me, though, using them like a giant fiber-optic network. If the world was a circuit board, scats were like the little electrical impulses that raced down the copper leads. If it worked, it solved our biggest problem.

It also raised more questions. How could Andi see them when Maggie couldn't? What even gave her the idea? Why had no one done something like it before? And the big one: Just how powerful was Andi, anyway?

"The strangest thing just happened," came a voice from the shop's door. We looked up to find Bill and Brea in the doorway. Brea looked around the shop, her expression growing more and more confused by the second. Bill stared at the three of us, his face a mirror image of his wife's.

Andi squealed and jumped from her chair, arms above her head in a joyful victory dance.

"It worked!" she giggled.

Maggie went to the doorway and ushered them inside,

then closed the door.

"What happened?" she said.

"Well," said Bill. "I was at home, watching TV..."

My brain snapped off. Television. Bill watched *television*?

"When the shadows in the room started doing the most peculiar things. It took us a moment to figure out that it wasn't the shadows, but the scats. They flashed and moved and formed a message, to come here, then they were gone. But how did that happen?"

"Back up," I said. "*Television*? You're one of the most brilliant metaphysical minds on the planet, and you watch *television*? What could possibly entertain you?"

"BBC America," said the old mage. "I like *Doctor Who*..."

For the second time in as many minutes, my brain snapped off.

"Um..." Brea continued looking around the room. "Am I missing something, or..."

"Yes," said Maggie. "The shop's alive."

"My," said Bill. "You *have* been busy."

It took us the better part of an hour to explain everything from the scats to the reason why Maggie's shop was alive, all the while I sat and stared at Bill and tried to reconcile the fact that he was *human*, and a little nerdy, in my head. Bill and Brea offered their blessings on the shop, which sent a ripple of happiness through the main room, then we sat on Maggie's oversized sofa in her workroom.

"So," said Bill. "Do we have a plan?"

"Not so much a plan," I said, "as a vague idea. His power manifests through his eyes. We need to cut that source of power off."

"You're not suggesting we blind him!" said Brea. "Twisted he may be, but he's still a human being!"

I thought about arguing the point, but it wouldn't do any good.

"No," said Maggie. "But maybe if we direct it back toward him, like a feedback loop..."

"My idea!" chirped Andi.

"We could keep him from creating any more puppets. If we could trap him in something with reflective walls, like maybe an all-around mirror, then..."

"And where are we supposed to find something like that?" Bill raised his eyebrows at her. "At a mall?"

"That's what I said!" said Andi.

"No." I fixed her with a steely gaze. "Too many innocents, too much potential for mayhem. We need to lure him somewhere safe, away from most people. Somewhere we can rig to trap him."

"With mirrors." Bill cocked an eyebrow.

"It's all we have," I said. "Unless you've got something better. I'm all ears if you do."

He let out a long sigh and sat back, his brow creased in thought. Brea stroked Bitsy's back and between the ears. The cat smelled her loving nature the moment they walked through the door, and never turned down an easy mark. The moment Brea sat, the cat was in her lap.

"I have an idea," she said after a moment. Bill shot her a horrified look, but she put a reassuring hand on his knee. "But how to get him there. That's going to be the difficult part. He'll send his puppets first, so we have to separate him from them, then make sure he continues on into the trap."

"Wait," I said. "First off, where are we going to find somewhere out-of-the-way enough that we're not going to get a thousand people killed? Second, how're we going to get the little coward to show himself?"

"I don't know about part two," said Bill. "But part one, I

think we've got covered."

Before, when I asked Maggie about an invisibility spell, I was joking. I know how the laws of magick work, and I know the difference between B-movie physics and actual spell-slinging. Still, I often find myself hoping against all sanity that movie-magic works.

Sure, we were safe inside the shop, but I figured Trevor would have the place staked out. Bill and I stepped outside into the darkness, and the pin-pricks under my hair started straight away. Somewhere, just beyond the pools of lamplight, Trevor's goons were watching. He was smart enough to make them keep a healthy distance from the shop, but I felt them. If I shifted my perception, I knew I'd See them. But I didn't want to. Bad enough I knew they were there. They wouldn't dare attack with Bill by my side. At least, I hoped they wouldn't.

We climbed into Bill's car. Maggie, Andi and Brea stayed in the shop to plan.

"They're watching us, you know," said Bill.

"Yeah. Where're we going?"

"Someplace Trevor knows nothing about," he said. "In fact, no one except Brea knows about this place. You'll be the first person to see it in twenty years."

I didn't say anything else for the drive. Bill looked lost in thought, and I didn't feel like pushing him. Whatever it was, I'd see it soon enough. But the farther we drove, the more bizarre images popped into my head. It was Bill. His love for British television notwithstanding, he was still the closest thing to Merlin I knew. For all I knew, we were headed to the secret holding place of his metaphysical doomsday device.

Part of me hoped so.

The Strip District was dark, all the shops closed. It occurred to me that, should Trevor get his hands on the book, I might never walk those succulent streets again, never taste the fresh bread, never sample those incredible flavors. To get the book, he'd have to kill me. Whatever Bill had up his sleeve, I hoped it would be good.

At the edge of the Strip District, we came to a long row of warehouses, surrounded by a chain-link fence. Bill pulled up at the gate and punched in a code. The gate groaned and squealed as it opened.

"What're we doing here?"

"I own it," he said. "At least, part of it. We rent most of the buildings out to businesses. But one of them I keep just for me."

We pulled around to the back of the lot and parked in front of a big steel building that looked like all the others. There were no distinguishing marks on it, no big "Keep Out" signs, no trolls guarding it. The only thing that even showed it was in use was a big shiny padlock on the front door. Bill killed the engine and got out and motioned for me to do the same. As we got to the door, he stopped.

"I wasn't always... whatever I am," he said. "I had a lot of jobs before I formed Evergreen, and I didn't always have the same beliefs I do now. Please, don't think less of me."

He unlocked the door and stepped inside. I followed him into pitch darkness. A moment and a series of clicks later, my jaw hung open at what I saw.

Carnival equipment.

From one end of the warehouse to the other, stacked high and deep, were carts and wagons, rides and booths from another era. From the ceiling hung a giant cloth banner with the words "The Amazing William" in fancy script. The man below the words was younger, but there was no mistaking who it was supposed to be.

"You were a huckster?"

"Carnie," he said. "I was an entertainer. A sideshow magician. I owned the carnival, but my act was stuff like sawing a lady in half, that kind of thing."

My mind reeled. For all his power, all the things I'd seen him do, Bill was, more or less, a bullshit artist.

"Of course, that was before I met Brea."

He pointed behind me to another hanging poster of a beautiful woman with long flowing hair and a crystal ball in her hand. "Madame Brea," said the words under her image.

"I could pull quarters out of children's ears, link rings, do card tricks... I hired Brea as a fortune teller. It only took me a month or two to realize she was the real thing. Brea was the one who showed me how the world worked. She introduced me to real magick. Kind of like how Maggie introduced you."

He was wrong. I didn't have some gentle, loving hand to guide me into the ways of energy and death. I had my eyes ripped open, my world forever changed the day I died and came back. No one guided me down the warm and fluffy path of enlightenment. I was pushed screaming into this nightmare of a world, terrified of the things I saw and abandoned by everyone I loved. He was right about one thing, though. Maggie saved me. She lifted my broken soul back up and pieced it back together with love and kindness. That he showed me his deep dark secret rattled my image of him, but it also made me feel closer to the man. We were more alike than I thought.

"So what are we doing here?"

"You said you wanted to trap him with mirrors," said Bill as he walked further toward the back of the warehouse. "If you can get him inside, I think I have just the thing."

I followed him to a trailer draped with dark cloth. He gave the cover a tug and it fell away, revealing the words "House of Mirrors" in faded yellow and red paint on the side.

"It'll take me the better part of a day to set it up, but if you can get him in there, he won't be able to look any direction without locking eyes with himself."

"And that's going to be the hard part, isn't it?" Trevor may have been first-class, grade-A crazy, but he wasn't stupid. It would take some really fancy footwork to get him anywhere near the trailer, much less inside. "Where?"

"Why not here?" said Bill. "We can use the rest of this junk as distractions."

I nodded. It wasn't a great plan, but it beat trying to lead him to the mall. The only thing left to do was set the trap and pray like hell that it worked.

Bill took me back to Maggie's shop. It was well after midnight, but Trevor's puppets still held their vigil. Of course they did. Dead people didn't need to sleep, and neither, it seemed, did Trevor. Bill got out of the car and hurried inside. I got out and walked to the rear of the car, then I shifted my vision and took a good look. There were six of them on the street, hidden by shadow and garbage. The corona of the shop's aura reached just past the sidewalk and kept them at bay.

"Trevor!" I paused for dramatic effect. "I know you're watching, so listen up. You want the book? You got it. Send one up where I can see him!"

The shadows shifted and a tall, emaciated man with long stringy hair shambled forward. In the darkness, he might've been just another homeless person, drug-addled or strung out. But the streetlight revealed his milky white eyes, the bruising where blood pooled. Even without my perception shifted, I'd have known he was dead. Tendrils of light led into his eyes and split off to the other five who kept watch over us.

"That's far enough," I said as it reached the edge of the shop's protective bubble. The creature stopped and swayed. "The book's not here."

"I know," croaked the thing. "I've been watching you. Is it still at the post office? Did you hide it?"

"First, I want your word that Maggie and Andi won't be harmed."

"You have it."

Of course I knew he was lying. I'm not stupid.

"Bill and Brea, too."

"Alright."

"We give you the book, you give us seventy-two hours to get out of town. Deal?"

"Seems fair," croaked the puppet. "Now where is it?"

"It's safe," I said. "We'll meet you someplace private. We don't want any more innocents getting hurt. Agreed?"

"Yes," it said. The puppet bounced, as if it were excited.

I gave it the address of the warehouse and a time, then I turned my back on the puppet and walked as calmly as I could manage back to the shop. I didn't breathe until the shop door was closed behind me.

"It's done," I announced as I walked in. "Now what?"

"Now," said Brea. "Bill and I have work to do. What about the puppets out front?"

"They won't bother you anymore tonight," I said.

"Good," said Bill. "We'll contact you when it's ready."

They said their goodbyes like they were going off to war, which, in a way, they were. There would be no guns or bombs, but magick and mirrors. The phrase "fighting spirit" took on a whole new meaning. The stakes, though, were just as high. Higher, even. In a war, only the bodies were at risk. In this case, dying was just the opening act to horrors unimaginable should Trevor win.

We spent the next day in Maggie's apartment. Every so often, Andi went downstairs to the shop just to touch the shelves and talk to her "daughter." But for the most part, we stayed in Maggie's living room. We didn't talk much, didn't watch television, just sat with the comfort of each others' company. When Andi fell asleep on the couch, Maggie and I retired to her bedroom where we lay in bed and held each other like it would be the last time. For all we knew, it was. As the day stretched on and darkness approached, we all grew tense. Just like children, we were again afraid of the dark, and for good reason.

The first rays of light broke the night sky, and I was awake to see it. I was tired, but my mind raced with images that wouldn't let me sleep. Behind my tired eyelids flashed armies of the walking dead, slimy things reaching out of the clouds, and burning cities. Over them all on a throne made of skulls sat Trevor, the king of the wasteland. Worse, I kept imagining what would happen to Maggie. If I died, I had no doubt her life would move on without me. But if Trevor killed her, I wouldn't have to commit suicide. I'd just die there on the spot. It occurred to me to lock her in the bedroom and hurry to meet up with Bill, and hope she didn't kick my ass when she got out. But I needed her beside me.

Andi snored on the couch, her tiny frame barely a lump under the blanket. So much power, so much raw talent, it boggled my mind to think how powerful she might grow. And it terrified me.

As the sun came up over Carson Street, I watched the other shopkeepers unlock their doors and set their sandwich boards out. A few pedestrians trickled down the sidewalk. None of them knew. They were better off. Otherwise there'd be a thousand faces like mine staring out windows like it was their last days on Earth.

"Hey." Maggie slid her arms around my waist and kissed my shoulder. "Did you sleep at all?"

I shook my head. "Couldn't."

"Heard from Bill yet?"

"Nope. What's he going to do? Call us?"

Andi sat bolt upright on the couch, eyes closed. The shadows around the room swirled and joined into a large wave that undulated like a tentacle. The scats moved as one, shifted toward Andi, and moved under the blanket, across her legs and up her arms. It was creepy, like watching her being eaten by ants, but they didn't bite and she nodded her head, listening to sounds only she heard. Then the scats retreated and scattered and again became little things that most people don't see. Andi opened her eyes.

"That was Bill," she said. "They're ready."

Performance artists and people like me have precious few things in common. One of those things is that we're both used to being stared at. For a performance artist, it's a case of "what's he going to do next" or "look at that weirdo." For me it's the same thing, but with more fear involved. For both of us, there comes a point where we just don't care. People can think what they like, but I'm going to do what I do.

So, although people on both sides of the street stared at the three of us, it didn't make me feel the least bit uncomfortable. As to *why* they stared, it could've been anything. My hair, the way we were dressed, the way we walked like we had a real direction and purpose. Might've even been the full-length mirrors we carried. Okay, it was probably that last one.

While we got dressed, Andi mentioned that she didn't like the idea of walking out defenseless. In my sleep-deprived state, the thought of carrying mirrors around seemed reasonable enough, so I agreed. Maggie had two in her apartment and one more in the shop downstairs. It took only a couple of seconds to pop them off the walls. She took a paint-pen and scribed wards on the backs of them, and violà! Shiny reflective shields. We also had to take the rental car back the day before, which left us without transportation. The plan, as ridiculous as it sounded, was to take the city bus. We had a few hours before I told Trevor to show up, so it gave us time to get there and plan out where everyone needed to be. For a moment, I felt like General Patton as he drew up battle plans. Of course, Patton had his own swarm of tanks. He never had to take public transportation.

When the bus pulled up, the look on the driver's face was partly surprised, but mostly irritated disinterest. The other passengers, however, showed no interest in us whatsoever. They were, I assumed, all too absorbed in their own lives and situations to be concerned with three weirdos on the bus with mirrors. After fifteen minutes of stop and start travel, Andi poked me in the ribs.

"Everyone's so quiet," she whispered.

"So?"

She rolled her eyes. "Have you ever even *been* on a bus? They're never this quiet."

Maggie and I glanced toward each other. The kid was right. Except for the asthmatic growl of the engines, the squeal of the brakes, the bus was silent. No radios blaring, no crying children, no arguments or half-heard conversations over cell-phones. It was as if everyone on the bus were...

"Oh, crap."

In unison, two dozen heads turned and stared at us. My stomach tried to wriggle out of my nether regions as they spoke.

"Give us the book, Cooper."

Maggie reacted first. She jumped to her feet, the mirror held in front of her like a makeshift disco-shield. Andi followed suit, one hand on the shield, the other bowed back behind her like she was going to deliver a knockout punch. I didn't need my sight to know they were gathering power, drawing it from deep inside them in equal parts fear and panic. For a moment, no one moved, a Mexican standoff. We had to be careful. One wrong word, one twitching finger, even a loud fart, could set things into ugly motion.

Leave it to the bus driver to pull the proverbial trigger.

"Hey!" he shouted as he looked in the rearview mirror. "Sit down or I'll kick you off the bus!"

Two dozen mouths opened and gave the same breathy roar, then the bodies came at us.

I dropped the mirror and rushed forward, my shield tattoo held high and blazing. I'm not sure what I was thinking. No matter how I looked at it, we were still up against the back end of a moving bus with more than twenty corpses bottlenecking down on top of us. Maggie and Andi had power, but they had numbers, and eventually we'd have to make a choice: Either get crushed by them, or jump out the emergency exit onto the busy freeway where we'd get squished by a tailgater or two.

"What the fuck?" shouted the bus driver. "Get your asses back in your seats! What's wrong with you people?"

We fought a futile fight, but none of us wanted to go down without taking a few of the putrid bastards with us. A wave of heat burst forth from Andi, knocking a few of them back over the seats, but for every one that went down, there was another to take its place.

"We've got to get out of here!" she screamed. She turned away from the advancing horde and slapped at the safety glass behind us. Panic had her, and I wasn't far behind. But in that moment, I noticed something. I don't know how amidst all the screaming and slashing, but I noticed one seat's occupant still seated, a large brown stocking cap pulled over his head. I blinked and forced my perception to shift.

As I expected, tendrils of light flowed into each of the dead people, affixed to their eyes. What I didn't expect was to see those tendrils combine into a double rope of pure energy and descend onto the guy in the hat.

"Trevor!" I yelled. I should have known. He had to be close to them to keep control. In every other place, I knew he was hidden nearby, but it didn't even occur to me how he would control so many on a moving bus. He would have to be *on* the bus with them.

The stocking cap turned and revealed Trevor's wire-frame glasses over the seat. He grinned before his face twisted into a mask of hatred.

"Kill them!" he screamed.

The bus gave a violent shift that almost knocked us all off our feet. It took me a moment to become fully cognizant that the driver was screaming bloody murder. The bus shimmied again and for a moment, everyone, living and dead alike, stopped fighting. They must've felt it–I know I did–the moment when a person knows that something is about to hurt really bad.

The right front side of the bus tipped down as it ran off the road and down the embankment. As it rolled onto its side, I slammed into several meat-puppets on my way to the side, which was now on the ground. The energy tendrils snapped back to Trevor and the corpses went slack, their strings cut, and they became a single mass of loose limbs flapping as the bus pitched and slid. I landed on a few of them. Andi's scream stopped short with a loud cracking noise. I caught sight of one of Maggie's shoes as her legs flew out from under her and she tumbled to the last place I saw Andi.

The bus skidded to a stop and, for a moment, nothing moved. The only sound I heard was my heart pounding in my ears and my own heavy breathing. I smelled gasoline and fear, rot and panic mingled with the smell of burned rubber and oil.

"Maggie!" A groan answered me. "You alright? Where's

Andi?"

"She's hurt," moaned Maggie. "I think I landed on her."

"Gimme a second. I'll get you out."

"Get Trevor!" she shouted.

I rolled over and saw him crawl over the mountain of bodies, toward the busted front windshield. Blood trickled from his lip, but he looked otherwise uninjured. If I caught him, that would change.

I struggled over the bodies and made my way across the seats to the front of the bus. The driver had a nasty cut across the forehead, but his eyes were open in his bewildered face.

I touched his shoulder and crouched by his face.

"What's your name?"

"Gary," he said. He looked like he wasn't really sure he was talking.

"Are you hurt?"

He shook his head, though he didn't look convinced. It would have to do.

"Okay, Gary. You need to get out of the bus. My friends are in the back. If you can help them out, I'd appreciate it."

"The... other passengers..."

"Are dead," I said. "It's not your fault. They were already that way. But my friends are alive back there. They need your help. Can you do that for me?"

He nodded.

"Thanks, Gary." I scrambled out the broken windshield and went after Trevor.

PAGES

I've said before that I'm out of shape. In most cases, I'm not the kind to run or chase anything less than an ice cream truck. Unless, that is, whatever I'm chasing has pissed me off. What I lack in actual stamina and speed I more than make up for with bull-headed determination and single-minded fury.

Trevor managed to kill one of my only true friends, terrorize the city, cost some poor deluded kid his life, and tamper with the very laws of nature. Because of him, Andi and Maggie were laying in a pile of bodies, injured, in the bus. And he destroyed my car. When, not *if* but *when*, I caught him, I'd either give him the worst beating of his life, or die trying. With the amount of power he'd been demonstrating, the latter seemed more likely, but I didn't care. Trevor had to answer for his crimes, and there were no police around, which meant he belonged to me.

I triggered my Sight and scanned the area. It didn't take me long to find his tracks. His shoes left an impression, one of panic and pain. He was injured in the crash. Good. Part of me—a large part—hoped he was slowly bleeding to death.

It took me a few seconds to recognize the area where the bus went down. Far from the warehouses near the Strip District, we'd gone the other direction in what was to be a loop, miles away from Bill and his carefully laid trap. So much for plan "A." The steep embankment gave way to thick trees and vines. We were somewhere near one of the smaller towns, which suited me fine. There were fewer people around to get hurt, fewer for Trevor to press into service. I hoped it would also make it harder for him to hide.

I pushed my way through the brush and came to the road that passed under the highway. To one side stood a giant converted steel mill. To the other, two blocks' worth of a town's decaying corpse. Houses with rotted and buckled roofs, missing doors, and rusted cars in front beckoned. The only twitch in the dying town's leg was a lone mongrel running up the center of the road. Appropriate, but Trevor's tracks said he went the other way, toward the mill.

I hurried to the door and went inside. It slammed behind me and echoed against the sheet-metal wall. The inside still smelled burnt, like the old smelting furnaces could kick back into production at a moment's notice. But it was cold, more so than it should've been. As I crept into the main area, I raised the walls and closed the doors in my head.

The energy-Sight thing can be really good for tracking, but places like old mills have long memories. Images of the people who worked there, some who died there, still linger, still go about their daily routines. In some places those echoes are so strong that, for me, it's hard to distinguish the living from the dead, and the dead from the memories.

The great track still loomed overhead, waiting for molten steel to carry from side to side. Across the open way, renovations made crude concrete walls and sectioned the open spaces into cells, businesses of an industrial sort. I stopped and listened for something, anything that would tip me off.

Heavy breathing, shuffling feet. I took off at a run straight for the sounds and caught sight of a closing door. Without thinking, I hit the door at top speed. Trevor was waiting with a fire extinguisher. It struck me at the bridge of my nose and sent me sprawling. My head swam and my tears flooded my eyes. For a moment I couldn't see, but when the dark clouds cleared, I caught sight of his hat as he disappeared down the stairs.

I staggered to my feet and went after him. The stairwell echoed our steps and wheezes. My legs and lungs burned, but I kept going. He was the fox, I was the hound, and there was no way I was letting go without my pelt. Below me, he hit the door with a loud bang. Mad as I was, I didn't want another encounter with the fire extinguisher.

See? I can learn.

I slowed at the bottom of the stairs and crept to the door, then pushed it open a crack. Trevor waited in the large open area beyond the makeshift shops. In one hand, he held the pages. His other hand he stretched above his head like he was trying to pull the smelting rig from the ceiling. He was mumbling.

For the most part, the whole concept of "magic words" is malarkey. It doesn't matter *what* a practitioner says as much as the *intent* behind those words. But there are cases, rare as they may be, where words do have power. Not implied, not assigned, but real fire-and-brimstone power. Most of those words are lost, forgotten in languages that haven't been spoken in thousands of years. And for the human race, losing those words was a real species-saver. But every now and again, someone finds those words, and those of us who know about them tremble.

When Trevor spoke, I didn't recognize the language, but I felt their effect. Waves of heat poured off of him. My skin prickled and the hairs on my arms stood on end. The stench of ozone stung my nostrils. It was electrical, power drawn from every light, every plug, even the static in the air. Trevor drew it all toward him and channeled it. When he let it go, it was like lightning struck the earth in front of me.

Every electrical system in sight went haywire. Those that couldn't handle the charge popped and fizzled. Those that could revved their engines, roared with infused life. He smiled as he curved the fingers of one hand into the shape of a gun and pointed them at me like a cowboy with a six-shooter.

"Bang."

I dove to the side, curled up with my arms over my head when the arc struck. The tattoo on my wrist lit up like a Roman candle and I howled in pain. I smelled burning hair and the melted rubber of my sneakers, singed cotton from my pants and shirt. But I was alive. The tattoo did what it was supposed to do. I hurt, felt like someone wired a car battery to my face, but I was alive. Trevor looked shocked. No pun intended.

I scrambled to my feet before he could ready another blast and cut the distance between us fast. When I hit him at the waist, the air rushed out of him in a loud *whoof* and we both tumbled to the ground. The pages went flying. I wish I'd had the presence of mind to think of something snappy to say, something that would've made a good action-hero line. The truth was, I was too scared to think beyond getting him to the ground and pounding him in the head until he couldn't read anymore. Ever. I scrambled on top of him, but when I postured up to try to turn his face into hamburger, I made an awful mistake. I locked eyes with him.

In an instant, I felt him try to climb into my mind.

For anyone who's dealt with possession, an invading spirit isn't very comfortable, but in most cases it tries to back-door its way in. It's smooth, sneaky, it whispers things to the victim and eventually, the victim lets it in. It feels like putting on a hat that's adjusted one click too many. Tight, uncomfortable, but not painful and not something a person can't learn to live with, or even ignore.

Trevor didn't waste time with subtleties. He didn't whisper in my ear or try to worm his way in. It felt like he hit my skull with a chisel and tried to pull the two halves of my head apart to climb inside. I tasted blood before I knew I was screaming, felt my elbow crack against the concrete floor before I realized I fell. I clawed at my head and face as if I could somehow physically drag him out.

"You're mine now," he said.

Somewhere, past the pain, past the fear, I saw him. There was no factory, no concrete floor, no shops. Just Trevor and me, standing inside my head, neither of us willing to give up position.

"Give me the damned book," he said. "And I'll let you go. I'll let you all go. Otherwise, I'll do you like I did your buddy Taylor, and feed on you until there's nothing left."

"Then you'll never know where it is," I said.

"I'll peel the memories from your brain and make you scream while I do it."

Inside a person's mind, the real and unreal sort of intertwine. A person sees his own self-image, and for most folks it's a grotesque caricature of what he *wishes* he were. For some people, the self-image is a knight in shining armor. For some, it's Superman, complete with a cape and whatever their first initial is stenciled on their chests. It's a manifestation of what they want to be.

Trevor, or his self-image, stood in front of me like a dark angel, some kind of demon with horns that jutted from his forehead and bat wings, dressed in a long tattered black robe. His hands ended in long wicked claws and he towered over me with burning eyes and blood drooling from his mouth.

I, on the other hand, looked like... well... me.

My own self-image isn't a product of self-delusion, or some egocentric puffery. It looks exactly like I do in the physical world, complete with big unruly hair and red canvas high-tops.

Trevor laughed at the sight of me, deep and throaty, then he lunged. Claws ripped through the air and his mouth stretched wide. The wind that came off his wings stank of rot and burned meat. He didn't want to scare me anymore. He aimed to swallow my soul. If he did, everything I knew would be his, every ounce of energy that was me would add to his. I'd be his meat puppet.

But climbing into my head was a mistake on his part. The average Joe Bagadoughnuts didn't have Maggie to teach them about the ethereal world, didn't have years to try to piece back together a life once lost. Not everyone could tell the difference between what happened in their minds and what was real in the physical world.

He expected me to quake in fear, to piss my pants and cower in some dark corner of my mind until he sucked down every breath of mine. But anger mixed with my fear, turned my dread to rage. All around me, memories of Maggie and Andi beneath the pile of dead bodies, of Andi's shivering frame on my bed, of Taylor's slumped corpse played. All of it together fueled so much hatred in my heart that, instead of running away, I ran straight at the nightmare version of Trevor. For my efforts, one giant clawed hand backhanded me sideways and sent my metaphysical self sprawling.

"Tell me where it is," he whispered. "Or else."

"Eat shit!"

Trevor's ethereal form shivered with laughter as his arms encircled my body and held me tight like steel bands.

"You think you're tough?" he hissed. "You'll tell me. I'm going to enjoy breaking you."

Everything around me blurred and shifted until I found

myself in a storm drain beneath a city street. The cold air bit my arms as half-frozen water seeped into my shoes. Behind me, something not quite human let out an ear-piercing scream. I remembered the scene all too well, one year ago, surrounded by human rats, and the king rodent wanted to tear my head off.

When it happened for real, I ran. I managed to trap the rat and escape with burns and a deep-seeded hatred for underground tunnels. But Trevor held me tight, locked my head in place so I couldn't even turn away from the nightmare version of the demon-possessed anthropology professor as he stepped out of the darkness. In the real world, he looked like someone's kooky grandfather. In my nightmare, however, he looked more rat than human, with eyes that burned red and vicious yellow teeth that looked sharp enough to take an arm in a single snap. His body bristled with nails and needles, and his shrill cry sounded high enough to shatter crystal.

I held my ground. Fear was something I got used to a long time ago. His distorted face hovered near enough to mine that, even though it was all in my head, I gagged against his garbage-rotten breath, but I still held my ground.

"Not enough?" Trevor gestured and out of the darkness tumbled two figures. They didn't look the same as they did in the real world, rather idealized versions of themselves, but I still recognized Maggie and Andi as they fell bleeding at the shrieking monster's feet.

It wasn't real. I knew, at least on some level, that my two favorite people in the world were nowhere near, that the king of the rat demons was dead, but when it lunged at them, I couldn't stop myself. If I had, I don't think I could've forgiven myself. I tried to throw my body between theirs and his, but my feet stuck in the muck of the drain. I sprawled face-down in the putrid water, scrambled to get up, but the muck held my hands, sucked my feet like thick mud. The harder I struggled to reach my screaming friends, the tighter it held me. In the end, all I could do was watch as the nightmare creature tore into their bodies and rutted in their steaming carcasses.

I lay in the slime and sobbed, cursed and screamed at Trevor. He leaned down, his mouth by my ear.

"Tell me what I want to know and I'll make it stop. Otherwise, you get to watch your friends die over and over again. And don't think I can't come up with some really nasty shit to do to them. I've had years to think up some whoppers."

"You son of a bitch!" I howled. "You'll never get it! Not from me! It's not real! None of it is real!"

"Still some fight?" He chuckled. "We'll see about that."

I blinked and the slime let go of my hands and feet. The storm drain vanished, and I found myself on all fours on the concrete outside a bar in Squirrel Hill. Traffic crawled by to a heavy bass beat that came from inside. I knew the place, though I'd not been back to it in years.

"You okay?"

I looked up into the eyes of a stranger who wore a white pressed shirt and black slacks. The club's bouncer.

"Yeah." It all seemed so real, so familiar. "Yeah, I just tripped is all."

"You sure? Don't need no one puking on my sidewalk now."

"I'm fine," I said as I struggled to my feet and brushed his hand off my shoulder. "Don't be such a jagoff."

I left him behind me, probably angry, but I didn't care. Everything about the club, the atmosphere, seemed right. I remembered the place, down to the color of the leather on the seats and the posters on the walls. Houlihan's. Where my friends and I hung out.

The door swung wide as I walked in and scanned the crowd. It was packed, but my friends had a table already. They always did. The same table. We might as well have carved our names into it, gangster-style, as often as we sat there. Sure enough, I spotted them and made my way over. For a moment I let myself believe that the last six years of my life never happened, that it was just another Saturday night in the 'Burgh with my closest friends.

"Hey!" I said when I reached the table. No one looked at me.

"Hi, Stan," said Robbie. He never called me by my name. Always "Stan-the-man" or "Coop," or even "Short Round," but never just "Stan."

"What's going on, guys?"

The others' eyes stayed glued to their drinks. Linda and Trish gave each other wide-eyed giggles, but wouldn't say anything otherwise.

"Guys?"

"Yeah..." said Clint. "Where are your new friends?"

"What... new friends..?"

"The dead ones!" blurted Linda, which sent the whole table into peals of laughter.

"Go on," brayed Robbie. "Tell 'em how you can see ghosts now! You fucking loser!"

I remembered. The bar wasn't real either, but that didn't make it any less painful to relive. Rather than let the whole scene play out, I turned to leave. Once was enough for me, thanks very much.

"They should've checked you for brain damage!" cackled Trish. Her laugh infected other patrons, who turned and pointed at me, whispered and then broke into rolling laughs of their own. I ducked my head and ran for the door. They were so cruel, so gleeful. No sympathy, no understanding. Not one even entertained the thought that I might've been telling the truth.

I threw the door open. A friendly face waited on the other side.

"Maggie!" I sobbed as I pulled her into a tight hug.

"Get off of me!" she shrieked. Then she pushed me to the sidewalk.

"But..." Of course. She didn't know me then. Before the accident, I probably wouldn't have been very nice to someone like her. "Maggie, it's me. It's Stanley."

"I know who you are, loser," she spat. "How could I forget the worst lay of my life?"

"Don't..."

"All those men I've been with, you think you even come close? Please."

"Maggie... don't do this. Please, help me."

"Freak. Why would I want to be with a short, fat, goofy-looking little loser like you?"

It wasn't her. It couldn't be. The Maggie I knew would never say anything so hurtful. She loved me. At least, I thought she did...

"You should've stayed dead," she said. "You're nothing but trouble. If you'd stayed dead, they wouldn't have wrecked my shop. Taylor'd still be alive. You're like cancer. You should just die before you get anyone else hurt."

"You're not Maggie," I muttered.

"You know when you died? How you only saw black? That's because there's nothing on the other side for you. No one ever loved you, no paradise, no afterlife. You may as well have never existed."

I always suspected as much, but I never told anyone. All those people who saw their families, saw Heaven, saw Hell, there had to be something after death for me. But there wasn't. Not for me. I was a waste of skin, not even worth being called a blight. I was nothing, and nothing was all that waited after my life was over.

"That's not true," I wailed. "It can't be!"

"Aww..." She patted the top of my head. "Poor widdle baby thinks he's special. Newsflash, hotshot. You're shit. You're worthless. You don't deserve a woman like me."

She gave me a hard shove and left me in tears on the sidewalk as she marched into the club and joined the hyenas.

In movies, heroes left on the sidewalk turn their faces to the sky and scream out the name of the person who hurt them. For me the best I could do was curl into a ball on the sidewalk and let everything out in a guttural moan. My former friends, I could handle. That part came from memory as much as it did the twisted funhouse mirror of my perspective. But Maggie, even if it wasn't really her but some nightmare waved in front of me by Trevor, was too much. The real Maggie would never say things like that, but somewhere deep inside me, that little voice told me she might think it sometimes.

"Tell me where it is," hissed Trevor in my ear. "I'll make it stop. I'll let you die quick and no one else will have to get hurt."

My breath quickened as my heart slammed and rage flooded my mind. Bad enough to dredge up the pile of dripping shit that was my life, but to drag the one bright spot in my existence through the filth was depraved.

"No? This is getting fun."

Wind whipped past my ankles and sunlight blinded me for a few moments. When my eyes adjusted, my heart skipped and stuttered. The open Pittsburgh skyline stretched out around me in every direction. Around my legs and waist, my old safety harness felt snug, the way it did before. The rooftop looked just like it did in my nightmares, exactly like it did the day I died.

"Remember this place?" taunted Trevor.

I turned in place to see him standing at the roof's edge. Bound and gagged on either side of him stood Maggie and Andi.

"I'm telling you, I can keep this up forever," he said, then kicked Andi square in the stomach and sent her over the edge.

Real or not, the look of terror on her face would haunt me for the rest of my life.

"You want to see your bitch die too? Tell me where it is."

It felt so real. The air I wasn't really breathing smelled like exhaust and roof tar, with a hint of the three rivers. The heat from the sun made sweat bead on my forehead, and wind whistled in my ears. What if it wasn't in my head? What if we were in the real world and he'd just killed Andi and Maggie was about to die if I didn't tell?

It didn't matter. Real world or not, if I told him where the book was, they'd die anyway. He'd kill them and me out of spite.

"Fuck you."

Maggie's face contorted in disbelief and fear as he shoved her over the edge. The gag in her mouth muffled her scream, but I heard it all the same. All the way down, until it stopped short, and I knew she was dead.

"This is boring," said Trevor. He grabbed me by the front of the harness and dragged me to the edge. Below me, the city opened up like a hungry chasm. Real or not, I remembered the sensation of falling, and it hit me again, with interest. Maggie's broken body lay on the concrete so far down that she looked like a doll. The pool of blood around her grew and joined with the one that spread out beneath Andi.

"Last chance," he said. "You tell me, or I drop you and peel what I want to know from your mind while you die."

It didn't matter. Maggie, Andi, Taylor... I was alone again.

But Trevor didn't know me very well. Sure, there was a time when I wallowed in self-pity. Once upon a time, I might have crawled into a hole, just given up and let the bad guy win and surrendered to the terrible black that I knew came after death. But that was a long time ago. My friends did for me what therapy, medication, and doctors who didn't believe me never could. They gave me strength. Replaying the horrors from my past didn't break me. It pissed me off.

Trevor shoved me over the edge, but I clamped onto his arm like a crazed ferret.

"You're coming with me!"

Real fear flashed across his face, and I knew I was on to something. As he lost his balance, my stomach fluttered and the air opened up behind me. But I didn't scream. At least, I don't think I did, but I know I wore a maniacal smile as I stared into his terrified eyes.

I counted... five... four... three... in anticipation of that instant of agony, then release as my body died and sent me into the darkness. The pain came faster than I thought, but not from my body having a meet-and-greet with the sidewalk. I felt a jerk at my middle, my spine strained, and I found myself very much alive in unfamiliar surroundings.

I lay face-up on something coarse, matted. Over my head, a dingy ceiling fan turned against a dark gray ceiling. For a moment, I thought I was back in the real world, but as I struggled to sit up, I realized how wrong I was.

In front of me, a long dark hallway stretched to a vanishing horizon. Along both sides, doors of every shape and texture dotted the walls. Light came from bare bulbs above that flickered and buzzed. Down the hallway, I heard screams, voices. In the space of a few breaths, I realized where I was: Trevor's mind.

Which meant I was in a whole new world of trouble.

When I grabbed him, he retreated and pulled me back too.

"You can't be here!" screamed a voice from down the hall. A door ahead of me slammed, and I took off at a run. Real world or not, the only way to put an end to Trevor's madness was to catch him.

I reached the door, old and warped with the number 4 stenciled on it, and turned the knob. The room beyond was dirty, its walls stained with cigarette smoke and water damage. On a bed in the corner sat a woman in black underwear and a see-through robe.

"Hey, honey," she said. "Wanna party?" She was drunk or stoned, I couldn't tell which. She stank of sweat and piss.

"No, thanks," I said as I checked behind the door. "You see someone run through here?"

"The kid?" spat the woman. "Can't get no work done with him around. You want him? You pay me, you can have him for an hour, if that's your thing."

"Trevor..?"

"Yeah, that's him," she said. "I ain't seen you before. How do you know him? He been selling it on the side and not giving me my cut? That little bastard! I'll wring his scrawny neck!"

I backed out of the room and pulled the door shut. Memories. The doors all lead to memories. Which meant that woman was...

"Get out!" His voice came from down the hall. "What'd you see? Did you fuck her? Did you?! Did she try to sell me to you? How much did you pay her? How much?! Get out! You can't be here!"

Another door slammed further down the hall. As I ran toward it, my mind raced. His mother. Poor kid, sold to pedophiles by his own mother. The knowledge made it harder to hate the guy, but he still had to be brought down.

The next door looked more like a wooden gate. I unlatched it and pushed it open. Dead animals lay strewn before me, their carcasses ripped open and splayed like they'd exploded. Flies swarmed and settled again as I backed out and struggled not to throw up.

The game continued for what seemed like hours in the same way. An open door, another atrocity, a glimpse and a taunt. Behind every door were horrors, each more demonic than the last. Crushed hopes, tortures at the hands of relatives and high-school bullies, rivers of blood where he cut himself to try to get some attention. As I continued down the hall, I realized he wanted me to see them. He was leading me, explaining to me in his own weird way why he was the way he was.

I came to one door that looked like one from inside a church. When I opened it, the room beyond was dark, save for a large cross in a pool of light in the center of the room. The cross was upside down, suspended from a ceiling I couldn't see, and on it a man bled pools onto the ground. I knew it wasn't real, but I still ran to the man's side to try to help. When I realized it was Bill who hung on the cross, I jerked back.

"I tried," he whispered. "I tried to save him."

I backed out of the room and pulled the door shut as a wave of anger hit me. For every bad thing that happened in his life, Bill tried to help Trevor. And for his efforts, Trevor betrayed him.

I turned and saw another door, this one pink and covered in paper hearts, like a child's valentines. I pushed the door open and stared. The room beyond was a shrine, a stalker's paradise. Photographs stretched from the floor up into the darkness and covered every inch of the walls. In the center of the room sat a wooden stool, a candle, and a straight razor. That there was a room dedicated to someone special didn't surprise me. To whom it was dedicated made me sick to my stomach.

"You don't deserve her," came Trevor's voice. "She's too good for you."

Maggie's face stared back from every wall.

"She should be mine!"

The voice was close, right behind me. I spun in time to see a door across the hall slam shut. Without another thought, I followed Trevor and hit the door hard. It burst open into a room very different from the others.

Gray and blue walls, adorned with penciled windows that twisted at impossible angles, met with the filthy blue carpet. Against one wall rested a mockery of a dresser. Across from it, a tiny bed, its mattress enclosed in a barbed wire cage. Broken toys littered the floor. It was his room, a child's room as drawn by a child.

In the corner, across from the bed, stood the artist in a filthy long nightshirt. For all his sadistic glee and bravado, his projected magnificence, his real self-image was a pathetic sight, skinny and sickly.

"Get out!" The voice that came from the child didn't match his body. Where it should've been high-pitched, pre-pubescent, it still had the harsh growl of Trevor's. The look of hatred on his little face had the same comedic effect as it would on any blustering ten-year-old. It was all I could do not to break into a fit of giggles and give the kid a spanking right there.

"Trevor?"

"You can't be here!" he screamed. "Get out!"

He swept his hands forward. Broken toys and torn papers flew at me in a gale. Not enough to do any real damage, but enough to give me pause. His mind, his rules, which meant the laws of the outside world didn't necessarily apply here. His child-like stature suddenly seemed more threatening.

Imagine a child's world, where anything is possible, ruled by a child's imagination. And make that child a spoiled brat. Or a frightened, bullied kid, abused for his entire life and suddenly drunk with power.

"You ruined it!" he shrieked. "You ruined it all!"

Around me, the distorted furniture fell over as more broken bits of toys and blocks bounced off my arms and face. I stood my ground as he stepped toward me, both hands in front as if he were trying to tear me to shreds. In any other situation, I might've walked away, ignored the tantrum until the child calmed down. However, seeing as I was in his *head* and had no clue of how to get back into my body, the subtle approach wasn't on the menu. So I took a page out of my father's guide to parenting.

"That's enough!" I bellowed as I unbuckled my belt and slid it off. I folded the belt in half and whipped it into the palm of my hand. The crack echoed off the walls more like a gunshot than a belt-pop.

Trevor's eyes went wide as he backed up a step.

"You've been a very bad boy!" I took another step forward and snapped the belt into my hand. The pop thundered in the tiny room, and Trevor retreated further, until he was pressed into a corner between his bed and dresser. Tears poured from his terror-filled eyes. I felt sorry for him. It was a terrible thing to do, to play on his psychological scars, but he was still a kid with a gun, dangerous to himself and everyone around him. For everything he'd done, everything he wanted to do, he had to be stopped.

"I didn't mean to!" he wailed. "He *made* me do it! It's all *his* fault!"

Trevor!

The voice rumbled through the room like an earthquake and sent the sniveling little boy into hysterics. I followed his line of vision to a drawing of a door on the wall. Bigger at the top than on the bottom, it was how a child might draw a door if that child were insane. From around its edges, darkness latched hold of the wall like fungus. The front of the door bowed and moved as if it were breathing. I turned back to the child in time to see his dirty feet disappearing as he scrambled under the bed.

"What is that?" I shouted. He didn't answer. I knelt down and looked under the bed. The child was pushed as far into the corner as he could go, legs drawn up under him, his grimy thumb in his mouth as he gently rocked and muttered.

"Not my fault... not my fault... not my fault..."

Trevor!

Heavy footsteps accompanied the voice.

"*Trevor!*" I spat. "Who is that?"

"Master," he whined.

It made sense. The whole bid to take over the world might've been right for someone like Trevor, but the power had to come from someone else. Nothing I saw in his mind indicated the kind of power he needed to pull of his shenanigans. The rage, the drive, yes, but not the power to make his wishes reality. There was another, someone else from Evergreen. It never occurred to me that, while he was busy possessing other people, someone was controlling him.

"Who is it?" I shouted as the thundering footsteps grew louder and closer.

The child closed his eyes tight and shook his head, hands clamped around his ears. Blood trickled from the edges of his mouth where he clamped his jaw shut and bit his lips.

A clawed hand tore through the doorway as if it were made of cardboard. Through the rip, darkness spilled like heavy smoke, and through it a pair of red eyes glowed. They locked with mine.

"Cooper," it growled. The fact that it knew my name

shouldn't have surprised me, but to hear it said by its voice, which sounded like a thousand locust wings beating against broken glass, scared the hell out of me.

I've said before, I can be kind of slow on the uptake. Occasionally, things just slip right by me, or I tend to forget things that I ought to know. But when those things do click, when all the pistons fire, I use everything I can to my advantage.

In my own head, I should've known that I could, more or less, control what happened. Sure, Trevor was busy ripping my mind to pieces, but it was still my mind. But if Trevor could create chaos in my mind, what was to stop me from doing the same in his, and directing at this dark monster?

Inexperience, for one thing. I knew I could do it *in theory*, but I had no idea how. I stood my ground, put on my best tough-guy face, and hoped for the best.

"Back off!" I shouted.

The eyes wavered for a moment, which I took to be a good sign, until I realized the low rumbling sound I heard was its laughter.

A smoky black tendril shot out and knocked me sideways while another upended the bed and threw it across the room. Trevor screamed, and I couldn't do anything but watch as his child-body was swallowed up by the darkness. He shrieked and fought with all the strength and determination of a ten-year-old, but the darkness held him fast.

Despite everything he did, the lives he ruined, and the ones he cut short, I couldn't let the little bastard just suffer. Call me a sap or stupid or whatever, but even though I should've just let the dark-thing strip his bones clean, I couldn't. Maybe it was because he looked like a child, or maybe it was because he was forced to do those awful things, but whatever the case, I struggled to my feet, threw up my tattooed arm, and ran to put myself between the glowing embers of eyes and the screaming child.

In the real world, my shield manifests as a bright blue light that erupts from the tattoo on my arm.

In Trevor's head, however, it took on my interpretation of it, which was an actual physical shield, complete with a star in the center and leather straps around my arm. I ducked down behind it, put my shoulder forward, and held my ground. The power coming off the dark thing was heavy, strong. I never moved my feet, but it pushed me backward all the same.

"Who are you?" I bellowed.

It laughed at the question, which, to be fair, I didn't really think would work.

"The book," it said.

"Master, I tried," Trevor wailed from inside the creature's darkness. "Please! I tried!"

"You failed me again," said the creature. From inside, Trevor screamed from the bottom of his soul.

I put my foot against one flimsy wall and pushed off, toward the swirling mass. The darkness flowed around the edges of my shield. Where it touched me, it stuck like tar and burned cold.

"Let him go!"

The creature's eyes turned toward me and narrowed.

"I'll deal with you later," it growled.

Pain lanced through my skull in electric arcs as the world around me spun in a nauseating panorama of color and sound. My stomach churned as I fell, farther than from the building that killed me. More than my own screams, Trevor's cries of agony echoed through my mind and heralded my way out.

The flat, cold concrete behind my back did nothing to cushion my fall back into my own mind. Though my body didn't move, it still felt as if I'd slapped the ground from high above.

Everything hurt. Even breathing was a lesson in pain. My eyes throbbed in time with my heartbeat until I was sure they would burst. I rolled to my knees and vomited what felt like every dinner for my whole life onto the floor, then collapsed with heaving breaths.

Trevor lay inches away, his eyes open, his body twitching. The grimace he wore showed a few teeth, broken from the pressure of biting down, I guessed. Foamy spit and drool ran down the side of his face. He was gone, burned to his core by whatever, *whoever* the dark presence in his mind was. I closed my eyes against the thrum of my own heartbeat.

Against the black of my eyelids, those burning eyes stared.

I'm coming, they said. *I have plans for you.*

They faded, moment by moment until only the memory of Trevor's screams filled the darkness, and I gave over to it.

The hard concrete beneath my back was replaced with something only slightly less rigid with the faint scent of plastic and disinfectant. I opened my eyes to find the ghost janitor staring down at me.

"Thought you bought the farm that time," said Barney.

"Did it work?" My throat felt like I'd scrubbed it with a bottle brush made of razor blades and tried to wash it down with gravel.

"Feels different," said Barney. "Better, I think. I'd say whatever you did worked, yeah."

"Good. How'd I get here?"

"Same way as last time," he said. "In the back of an ambulance, through the Emergency Room. Docs say you have symptoms of a mild concussion, but they can't figure out how."

"Yeah," I croaked. "Funny about that."

"Your lady-friends are here too."

"Maggie? Andi? Are they..?"

"Young'un has a broken leg. The other one's got some scratches and bruises, but she's okay. Lemme tell you, son... You sure can pick 'em." He waggled his incorporeal eyebrows and grinned.

"Don't go peeking," I smiled. If not for the pain in my head, I'd have laughed.

"Ain't my style," he chuckled. "I'm just making an observation. I'd better go. Got lots of folks to help cross. You take care now."

"Don't take this the wrong way, but I hope I don't see you again soon."

"See who?" Maggie stood in the open doorway to my room. Behind her, Andi balanced on crutches.

"Just a friend," I smiled. I tried to sit up, but the pressure in my head doubled and I slumped back to my pillow.

"Easy," said Maggie. "Don't push yourself. How's the arm?"

It didn't occur to me until that moment that I couldn't feel my left arm. Not that it didn't hurt, but I couldn't feel it at all. I looked down to find it wrapped in bandages with a tube snaking beneath them.

"The doctors said the skin will heal, but the nerves won't grow back. They said the burn damage goes all the way down to the bone."

"Can you move your hand?" Andi's voice trembled. I looked down and willed my fingers to wiggle. Nothing.

"What the hell..?"

"The shield," said Maggie, her voice calm. "It exploded. It saved your life, but..."

"But it cost me my arm?"

"We don't know that," said Maggie. "I can try to fix it. We can figure out..."

"Don't," I said. "Just... don't."

"At least you got the guy responsible," said Andi. "Right?"

"I got Trevor," I said. "But he wasn't the one. There was someone else."

I told them about the things I saw in Trevor's mind. The abuse, the torment, all of it contributed to create an unstable man. I left out the part about the shrine to Maggie, but I did tell them about the other entity, the dark presence and what it did to Trevor.

"So we're no better off than we were before this whole thing started?" Andi's voice shook, choked with tears.

"We know the traitor's real," came another voice from the doorway. Bill and Brea stepped into the room. Bill's normally jovial face looked more careworn than I'd ever seen it before.

Brea hugged her husband tight.

"How're you feeling?" asked Bill.

"I'll live," I said. "Next time we'll go with your plan. It think it'll save me getting my ass kicked."

"We're so sorry you got dragged into this," said Brea.

"Thanks," I replied. "That means a lot." It came out as sarcasm, but I was sincere. Bill and Brea would never have done anything to hurt any of us. To see us all banged up must've torn them apart. Taylor's death at the hands of one of their own weighed heavily on them.

"If we can help in any way," said Bill. "Please, do call us."

They turned and shuffled out of the room. As they cleared the doorway, two more figures walked in.

"Was that him?" Officer Appel stood at the foot of my bed while his partner hovered by the door. "Was that the fucker that did Taylor?"

I glanced at Maggie.

"Yeah," I said. "That's him. Where is he?"

Appel let out a long frustrated sigh.

"He's in ICU. They can't find anything physically wrong with him aside from a few broken teeth and some bruises. But..."

"But?"

"His brain activity is nonexistent. He's dead from the neck up."

"Your handiwork?" Menold glared at me.

"Yeah," I said.

"Did he suffer?"

"Plenty," I said. The sounds of Trevor's screams still stuck out in my memory as if they were playing on a loop. No matter what the police or judicial system could've done to him, he got far worse. I wasn't sure even he deserved it.

Appel nodded. "Good."

The two cops turned and left the room. Maggie and Andi turned to leave too.

"Wait," I said. "Please. Don't leave me."

The images of their deaths still played over and over in my head. Maybe it was silly, but to have them here, with me now, was like a security blanket. I just wanted to hold them both for a while to make sure they were real.

"Stay," I said. "At least until I'm asleep."

Maggie smiled and took my dead hand in hers.

The doctors released me the next day with an entire pharmacy's worth of prescriptions for nausea, swelling, pain, and anything else they could think to bill me for. All the scans came back with no physical signs of injuries, with the exception of my arm, which they wrapped in some kind of synthetic skin and bandaged up tight. Then they made sure I made several followup appointments, which I had no intention of keeping.

As they wheeled me down the hall toward the doors, I wondered how I would get home. Maggie didn't own a car, and mine was a giant paperweight. Andi, even if she had one, couldn't

Scott A. Johnson

drive with her leg in a cast up to her hip. When Bill's monster Chrysler pulled into the turn-around, I was surprised. Even more so when Maggie got out of the front seat to greet me. Bill was nowhere to be found.

She helped me into the front seat. When I got the seatbelt buckled, which was more difficult one-armed than I expected, a pair of slender arms slid around my headrest and hugged me tight. Andi's cast was already covered in signatures and artwork, some magickal in design, others cartoons and doodles.

"Bill loaned you his car, huh? Good guy."

"No," said Maggie. "He said he felt bad about your car and about everything that happened..."

"No. I can't take his car. That's nice of him, but..."

"He said you'd feel that way. That's why he gave it to me."

"But..."

"It's a done deal," chirped Andi. "If you give it back now, it'll hurt his feelings. Besides, this thing has heated seats!"

I sighed and sank down into the leather. It was a nice gesture, but one that I didn't feel was necessary. After all, it wasn't his fault that someone sent those pages to me, was it?

"Let's get you home," said Maggie. "I want to start working on that arm."

"You really think you can help?" I glanced down at the bulbous mass of gauze in my sling. "Docs said there was no chance in Hell."

"I don't believe in Hell," smiled Maggie. "And they've never met me."

I smiled and closed my eyes for the rest of the ride home.

"We're back!" called out Andi as she crutched her way into the apartment. The air warmed a bit and the scent of lavender drifted through the room. The teakettle in the kitchen whistled. Bitsy looked up from her sunbeam in the window, yawned, then put her head back down. Nice to know some things never changed.

"Now," said Maggie. "Let's have a look at that arm."

"Can it wait? I need a shower. I feel gross. Then we have something we need to do before Taylor's funeral."

"You're going?" Andi's mouth snapped shut as if she wanted to suck the stupid question back in.

"Yeah," I said as I moved toward the bedroom. "I have to. I can't let him go without saying goodbye."

The shower in the bathroom snapped to life before I finished the painful and complicated task of getting undressed. One-armed, I could manage the shirt. But the pants proved to be too much. With Maggie's help, I managed to get my clothes off, then she put my withered arm into a giant plastic bag and left me to my shower. It felt wonderful, just the right temperature. Maybe the whole living-house thing wouldn't be so bad. After a few minutes alone, the bathroom door opened.

"You okay in there?" Maggie poked her head in.

"Yeah," I said.

The shower curtain slid aside and she climbed into the shower behind me. Her body felt good pressed against mine, made me feel safe and loved. She wrapped her arms around me and kissed the back of my neck.

"You scared me," she said. "I thought maybe I'd lost you. I need you too, you know."

The thought never occurred to me. Always so wrapped up in my little insecurities, I always assumed the world would get by if Stanley Cooper just fell off it one day. It never dawned on me that she relied on me as much as I did her. Maybe, as much as I loved her, she loved me.

She washed my shoulders and my hair, then helped me dry off and get dressed. Then we made our way to the living room where Andi sat with her leg propped on the coffee table and a cup of tea in her hand.

"C'mon," I said. "We've got an errand to run."

The key fit snug in the lock and I held my breath. Bill peered over my shoulder, his face a mask of nervous anticipation. Behind him, Brea stood with a rune-covered satchel at the ready. Maggie watched the corridor for signs of trouble. We weren't expecting any, but one thing we learned over the last few days was to be careful at all times.

"Thanks," I said. "For everything."

"It was the least I could do," said Bill. "You lost so much trying to help us, what's a car? I can always buy another one."

"What exactly do you do for a living?" My curiosity burned whenever I looked at him.

"Lots of things," he said with a smile. I wanted to press the issue, but his eyes told me I wouldn't get a straight answer. It was an argument better left for another day.

"You sure you want this?"

Bill shook his head. "No. I really don't want it, but it's not fair that you should have to keep it either. I'm better equipped for it than you are."

I'm not sure why, but a small part of me took offense. Maybe I wasn't the right guy, but someone sure thought I was. Otherwise, they wouldn't have sent it to me. Maybe I was supposed to give it to Bill all along.

"You asked for it," I said. I turned the key, pulled the locker open, and stepped aside for Bill.

The book was gone. In its place, a folded piece of paper hung from a string attached to the locker's ceiling. Bill looked confused as he pulled the paper out and unfolded it. It was a note, typewritten with no distinguishing marks.

"The book is no longer here," he read aloud. "I see now that no one can be trusted with something so powerful. For now, at least, the book is safe."

He looked up from the note, his face a mix of confusion and horror.

"How?"

"I don't know," I shrugged. "It was there before. Whoever sent it to me must've come and got it."

He looked from me to Maggie and back again, the confusion easing off his face.

"That book is dangerous," he said. "Are you sure?"

I nodded. He gave a sad little smile, took Brea's hand and walked away without another word. Maggie let out a long breath.

"That went well," she said.

Of course the book wasn't there. I moved it hours before I called Bill. After what we'd seen, I couldn't be sure who to trust. As much as I wanted to believe Bill would do the right thing, I couldn't take that chance. We still didn't know who the other traitor in Evergreen was, and Trevor wouldn't be doing any talking for a long time, if ever. So I put it in the only safe place I could think of. My apartment.

In all of Pittsburgh, there was not a safer place against magick, evil, or any of the big nasties that would get hold of something with that much hoodoo attached to it. Maggie and I installed a steel plate over the window and double-warded my extra bedroom, and there it sat, on a shelf, where I hoped it would stay until I could figure out some other way to be rid of it.

Bill knew I was lying, but I had to give him an out. If anyone came to him asking about it, he could honestly say he didn't know where it was. He could also honestly say that he didn't know for sure who had it. I hoped it would keep him safe, at least until our mystery person revealed his intentions. For it to be in my building was a horrible notion, but if Maggie and I were the only ones who knew it was there, maybe we could keep the other people in the building safe too. It was a nice thought, anyway.

In movies, it always rains on funerals. Crowds of mourners sit and wail, cry and dab their noses beneath black umbrellas while a preacher drones about how precious life is. For a cop, there are supposed to be uniformed pallbearers with white gloves and military precision, and the whole thing is supposed to be capped off with a twenty-one gun salute.

But the sun shone in a clear blue sky on the day we buried Taylor in Homewood.

Cemeteries are peaceful places, quiet and reverent. If one looks at the headstones, he can tell a great deal about the lives they mark. Homewood has some real doozies, including an Egyptian pyramid made of white marble, and enough statues that a person never really feels alone.

Taylor's headstone was a plain marble slab, simple as the man it remembered. On it, above his name, a carving of his police badge and number told volumes about his life. Below his name, someone saw fit to put the words "one good cop."

Far from the throngs of sobbing mourners, there were only eleven of us at his funeral. Seven uniformed officers, the preacher, Maggie, Andi and myself. Of us, only Andi sniffled quiet tears of sorrow. Tears wouldn't express the loss I felt, so I stood there and stared into the open grave as the preacher scattered dirt and ash on top of his casket.

"Take him now, O Lord, into your glory, and give him a place at your table," said the preacher. "Amen."

The officers moved a safe distance from the rest of the mourners, raised rifles and, on command, each shot three reports into the air. Twenty-one guns. Taylor would've been proud.

The service concluded and most of the officers went back to their lives. Officer Menold lingered a moment while his partner spoke to Maggie and me.

"I know he was your friend," said Appel. "But he was our brother. Thanks for helping us catch his killer."

"Of course," I said. Maggie leaned forward and hugged him and kissed his cheek. For a moment, he looked like he didn't know what to do, but the moment passed and tears rolled down his cheeks. He broke her hold, wiped his eyes with the back of his hand, and headed off toward his partner. When they were gone, Maggie knelt beside the fresh grave.

"May the God and Goddess watch over you," she said as she sprinkled rosemary into the hole. "So long as you are remembered, you're never truly gone. We'll remember you always."

She put a white votive at the edge of his headstone and lit it, then bowed her head, stood, and moved away. Andi stepped up, tears in her eyes, and dropped a handful of rose petals onto the coffin. When they met, he duct-taped her mouth shut and threw her into the trunk of his car, and now she sobbed because he was gone. She kissed her fingers and pressed them to his headstone without a word, then turned away toward Maggie. Andi crutched along with Maggie's arm around her shoulders, and they moved a distance through a small grove of trees. I was glad for the privacy.

It wasn't until that moment, alone by the open grave, that it really hit me. Taylor was gone. Not just gone, but *gone*. He wouldn't come back as a ghost, his energy sucked dry and used up by Trevor. My friend, gone for good. My breath hitched in my chest and I poured out my sorrow into the open grave.

"It isn't over," I sniffed. "We got Trevor. He can't do it to anyone else, so I hope, wherever you are, you're at rest. We'll find the other one too. I promise. He won't get away."

I knew he couldn't hear me, but that wasn't the point. I didn't grieve for him. His torment was over, his troubles now a lifetime away. I grieved for myself, for Maggie and Andi, and for anyone else who knew him, that we had to go on living without him. For me, Taylor touched my life, left an indelible mark, and was taken away.

I stood there and sobbed for a few minutes before a warm arm moved over my shoulders and pulled me away. Maggie held me close while Andi took my other side. As we walked back to Maggie's car, birds sang in the trees and tweeted happy noises to the sun. To me, the world seemed a little less bright.

About the Author

Scott A. Johnson is the author of nine novels, three true ghost story guides, a chapbook and a short story collection. He currently lives somewhere near Austin, Texas, with his wife, daughter, four cats and a pug.

For more information, look to his website at
http://www.creepylittlebastard.com

OTHER BOOKS BY SCOTT A JOHNSON